The shock [of seeing him at her]
front door had rendered her speechless.

No one could know about that horrible day when she'd blurted out all her trauma to a complete stranger. No one could know they knew each other. The only thing Jenn could think to do was to jump up like a jack-in-the-box and introduce herself as if she'd never seen the man before. Thankfully, Cody had played along.

But the idea that he'd had a good laugh about her with his friends made her shrink in humiliation. Then fury took hold. How *dare* he? He insisted he hadn't shared details, but how could she trust him?

"Look, I told you—all I said was a crying woman came in and begged to use the bathroom. It was just office talk." Cody had the good grace to look guilty as he explained. "And I shared as many secrets with you as you did with me. So I'll tell you what—I'll keep your secrets if you'll keep mine. Do we have a deal or not?"

She didn't really have a choice but she still hesitated. Men were inherently untrustworthy, in her experience. But he was right—if he ruined her, she could ruin him right back. Guaranteed mutual destruction. Someone was pushing the door open when Jenn gave a quick nod and softly answered him.

"Deal."

Dear Reader,

This book is dedicated to my husband and was inspired by our first few months together. We were both coming off bad relationships, and neither of us expected, nor *wanted*, to get serious with anyone. We kept telling each other "I don't want a commitment" and "No, I don't, either!" over and over again. Meanwhile—I moved in with the guy after six weeks. It was just temporary. Friends...we never lived apart again.

And even living together, we kept telling each other "no commitment" before he finally stopped me as we passed in the hallway one day and told me he loved me. I'd already fallen, but I hadn't told him for fear of scaring him away. After all, we'd *promised*! We'll be married thirty years next June.

While Cody and Jenn have very different backstories, their relationship is a lot like mine and Himself's. No way do they want a relationship with anyone. Not *ever*. They keep reminding each other why relationships are for fools. And you guessed it—they fall hard, but they're the last ones to realize it. A surprise pregnancy might just be one commitment too much, though.

I want to thank my family and friends for being such loving cheerleaders through the years. And my fellow romance authors, for always supporting each other. Thank you to my agent, Jill Marsal, and my Harlequin editor, Gail Chasan. And thank you to my readers—you're why we do this!

Jo

THEIR WINTER SURPRISE

JO McNALLY

Harlequin

SPECIAL EDITION

If you purchased this book without a cover you should be aware that this book is stolen property. It was reported as "unsold and destroyed" to the publisher, and neither the author nor the publisher has received any payment for this "stripped book."

ISBN-13: 978-1-335-18021-6

Their Winter Surprise

Copyright © 2025 by Jo McNally

Recycling programs
for this product may
not exist in your area.

All rights reserved. No part of this book may be used or reproduced in any manner whatsoever without written permission.

Without limiting the exclusive rights of any author, contributor or the publisher of this publication, any unauthorized use of this publication to train generative artificial intelligence (AI) technologies is expressly prohibited. Harlequin also exercises their rights under Article 4(3) of the Digital Single Market Directive 2019/790 and expressly reserves this publication from the text and data mining exception.

This is a work of fiction. Names, characters, places and incidents are either the product of the author's imagination or are used fictitiously. Any resemblance to actual persons, living or dead, businesses, companies, events or locales is entirely coincidental.

For questions and comments about the quality of this book, please contact us at CustomerService@Harlequin.com.

TM and ® are trademarks of Harlequin Enterprises ULC.

Harlequin Enterprises ULC
22 Adelaide St. West, 41st Floor
Toronto, Ontario M5H 4E3, Canada
www.Harlequin.com

HarperCollins Publishers
Macken House, 39/40 Mayor Street Upper,
Dublin 1, D01 C9W8, Ireland
www.HarperCollins.com

Printed in Lithuania

Award-winning romance author **Jo McNally** lives in her beloved upstate New York with her very own romance hero husband. When she's not writing or reading romance novels, she loves to travel and explore new places and experiences. She's a big fan of leisurely lunches with her besties. Her favorite room at home is the sunroom, where she enjoys both morning coffee and evening cocktails with her husband while listening to an eclectic (and often Irish) playlist.

Visit the Author Profile page
at Harlequin.com for more titles.

This book is dedicated to the guy who routinely announces to random strangers in random places (from restaurants to golf courses) that they are "in the presence of an award-winning romance author" (that's me). He's my champion, my best friend, my Happily Ever After, and a darn good marketing manager...

To my husband, John, with all my love forever

Chapter One

Sometimes a woman just really needs to pee.

At the moment, Jennifer Bellamy was that woman. Jenn wasn't going to make it to Winsome Cove without finding a restroom, so she pulled off the Cape Cod Highway to look for a fast-food joint or even—shudder—a local gas station with one of those bathrooms that were only accessible with a key from the checkout clerk.

It was just her luck that she'd chosen one of the exits on Route 6 that just drops you in the middle of trees and houses and walking trails…but no businesses. At least not the kind with public bathrooms. She drove the twisting, narrow road, knowing that eventually she'd find a Dunkin. The famous donut shops were everywhere in Massachusetts, often several within a mile of each other. Sometimes two on the same corner, or so it seemed. But not on this stretch of road. *Of course*. She was hardly surprised. Absolutely nothing had gone right in her life for the past few months, so why should that change just because she'd left Iowa for Massachusetts? She shifted in her seat.

Wait…was that a restaurant? Nope. It may have been one at some point, but now it was a law office. Someone blew a car horn behind her. She hadn't even noticed she was slowing traffic, but there were several cars behind her. She accelerated and gave a little *sorry* wave. Moving to Winsome Cove was probably another major mistake. Just because her mother and siblings had settled into the cutesy Cape Cod town it didn't mean she belonged here. They'd all abandoned Des Moines one by one, but until this summer Jenn had figured she'd be an Iowan forever.

But hanging around Des Moines for one more minute was out of the question now. She couldn't take any more of the whispers or clandestine looks—some scandalized, some pitying. Both were excruciating for her, so she'd thrown her bags in the car and left town like a thief in the night.

She'd been driving for two days straight, and she still hadn't decided which family member to see first. Frankly, she didn't want to see *any* of them right now. Not that she didn't love them, but answering their questions…and telling them lies…made her feel sick. She couldn't let them know how foolish she'd been. What a disaster her life had turned out to be. She'd gone from being Miss Des Moines, then Teacher of the Year, to…

Tears welled up for the hundredth time in the past few days. It was amazing that she could still manufacture tears at all, but here they came, right on cue. She was never going to convince her family she was fine if she kept bursting into tears whenever she thought of her crushing downfall—drummed out of her job at Clinton Elementary right before the new school year started.

She grabbed the last of the tissues from the box sitting next to her on the passenger seat. Three tissues were never going to be able to stem the flood of tears she knew was on the way. The seat was piled high with the ones she'd already gone through. It was pretty disgusting. A car horn blew again behind her, making her flinch. Drivers in Massachusetts had zero patience. She flipped her middle finger at the guy behind the wheel of the BMW in her rearview mirror and he returned the gesture, laying on the horn again. Her tears began to spill over, making her blink.

She was in no shape to be driving in weekend traffic on Cape Cod. The summer tourist season may have technically ended a week ago with Labor Day, but autumn would be busy here for a few more months. And she still hadn't found a bathroom. She muttered a few swear words and turned down the first side street she saw, hoping BMW Guy wouldn't follow her in some road rage incident. That was all she needed. He gave one last, long blast on his horn as she turned, but he stayed on the main drag.

She just needed a damn minute. And a bathroom. But that would have to wait. Meltdowns took precedence. So did staying alive, and she could barely see through her tears. She pulled to the side of the quiet street and turned off the car.

Every bit of this was her own fault. She'd trusted the wrong man. Again. It was her very special talent. The tears increased. As long as she was having a meltdown, she may as well throw a good pity party into the mix. She rested her forehead on the steering wheel and just let herself cry. No one would notice or care.

A sharp knock on the hood of her car a few minutes later nearly made her heart stop. She gasped and sat back, her hand resting on her chest—just to check that her heart *was* still beating. A man stood in front of her car. He was probably mid-thirties, dark hair, dark eyes and a jawline chiseled from stone. Just what she needed. A man. Tall and good-looking or otherwise. If she never spoke to another man in her life, she'd be happy. Sure, this one was smiling, but didn't they *all* start like that?

"You can come inside now," he called out. "I assume you were waiting for the other clients to leave?" There was a company logo on his blue polo shirt, but she couldn't make out what it said. Why was he bothering her? Couldn't he see she needed a private moment? Men were so dumb. And annoying.

She blinked, trying to make sense of his words. Then she saw the For Sale sign in the yard of the house she'd randomly parked in front of. Beneath that sign was a smaller one reading Open House Today. *Perfect.* Leave it to her to park in front of a public open house for her private breakdown.

"We've been busy all day," he called out. "If you want to walk through by yourself, I suggest you do it now."

Walk through what? Oh, the open house. She might need a place to stay, but she sure as hell couldn't afford a house on Cape Cod. She shifted in her seat, her bladder reminding her that it was still unrelieved. Maybe the house had a usable bathroom? Was that allowed? She swiped her arm across her tear-soaked cheeks. Why couldn't this guy just leave her alone?

"Hey…is everything okay?" The man moved to the driver's door, his expression suddenly serious. The window was closed. The car was locked. She still tensed. He crouched down, staring hard at her. He must have noticed her tears. *Great.* Now he wanted to be her hero.

So typical—the infamous white knight syndrome. *Me Tarzan. You Jane.* She sniffed and took a deep breath.

"I'm fine," she lied. Her voice rose so he could hear her through the closed window. "I'm pretty sure I'm allowed to park on a public road without breaking any laws. So please leave me alone."

His eyebrows rose in surprise at her sharp dismissal. She was surprised, too—rudeness didn't come naturally to her. But she'd given up being "Midwest nice" three weeks ago, and she had no intention of going back. Miss Congeniality was no longer interested in being congenial. Especially to some *man.*

The corner of the stranger's mouth twitched. "You aren't breaking any laws that I know of, so you can stay in this car and cry as long as you like. You're *also* welcome to come inside. There are cookies." Jenn was getting used to hearing the New England accent. Her brother-in-law's accent was thick. Sam pronounced his Rs just like this guy, so that the words *car* and *are* sounded like *cah* and *ahh.* He made a point to look at the passenger seat and the pile of crumpled tissues. She felt her cheeks warm. "And there are tissues, too."

Her stomach growled as if it had heard and understood his mention of cookies. She hadn't eaten since that fast-food breakfast sandwich shortly after dawn somewhere in Pennsylvania. She glanced at the clock on her dashboard. It was late afternoon. The man gestured for her to roll down her window, but she didn't move. He visibly sighed. Did he really think this was a good time to try to sell her a house? Maybe he was just being nice. Trying to reassure her. Whatever. She still wasn't opening her window.

"I get it," he called through the window. "You're worried, and that's smart on your part." She rolled her eyes at his attempt to soften her with a compliment. "Look, everyone in my real estate office knows I'm here and none of them would go to jail for me if I committed a crime. I guarantee you that a minimum of three neighbors saw you pull up, and at least two are watching us talk right now. One of them has probably already written your license plate down. In other words, if I was going to harm you, I picked a really bad place to do it. Besides, I'd make a terrible ax murderer." He smiled, and she noticed again that this guy was seriously good-looking. He was pretty, all right. Too pretty to be trusted. She looked away, and he stood and patted the roof of the SUV. "You can come inside. Or don't. But you'll be missing out on some really fine cookies."

He stared for another moment—she could see him out of the corner of her eye—then he gave the slightest of shrugs and walked away.

Jenn could use a cookie or two. Or a dozen. She sniffed again, wiping at her nose and grimacing. She could use some tissues, too. And if she didn't find a bathroom in the next few minutes, she was going to have an embarrassing accident right here in the front seat.

Cody scolded himself all the way back to the house, and he wasn't kind about it. When he saw that woman's tearstained, devastated face, he'd felt an instant connection. He'd been there, where she seemed to be.

Rock bottom.

Her strawberry blond hair was disheveled. Her clothes looked slept in. Her gray-blue eyes were puffy, as if this wasn't the first time she'd cried recently. Despite her abrupt dismissal of him, he couldn't help caring about the woman. Malcolm had been telling Cody he was ready to sponsor someone in the program. Cody kept arguing that it was too soon—he'd only been sober himself for nine months. He didn't feel ready to be someone else's responsible guide to sobriety. There was something about this woman that could make him reconsider, though.

But he'd pushed too hard. Come on too strong. He'd been in his salesman mode, which was usually a good thing. It pushed him out of his own head and forced him to do things like make eye contact, smile and chat with total strangers as if he knew them. He could only do it for short spurts of time—and it was exhausting—but he was good at it. The problem was that the broken-looking woman wasn't there to buy anything. She'd looked frightened, and he'd probably come across as some smarmy dude trying to hit on her. No wonder she'd stayed locked in her car. He could have helped her. But he'd blown it.

The screen door squeaked when he opened it and walked into the kitchen of the Brennan house. The whole house was a little crooked and squeaky, but it *was* over a hundred years old. He went into the dining room and started picking up the brochures and vintage photographs that he'd put on display there for the open house. This had been a well-loved "Cape house" for three generations of Brennan family vacations—rarely lived in full-time, but kept as a summer and weekend gathering place and, in recent years, a vacation rental. Property prices were steadily climbing on Cape Cod, and the newest generation of Brennans, now scattered across the country, had decided to cash in and sell it.

He heard the kitchen door squeak again as someone came in. *Damn.* He'd been so distracted by that messy woman in her car that he'd walked right by the open house sign and forgot to pick it up. The open house technically ended in fifteen minutes. Maybe it was just a nosy neighbor checking out the interior of the place, which happened a lot with open houses. Maybe it was a tire-kicking tourist with no intention of buying, just day-dreaming about owning a house on the Cape someday. Or maybe it was someone looking to drop a cool million on the place. He straightened, sliding back into sales mode. He could sure use the commission.

He turned toward the kitchen, but his welcoming greeting froze on his lips. It wasn't a customer at all. It was the woman from the car. Her yellow cotton top was wrinkled, half tucked into her jeans, half hanging out. A large blue cardigan fell to her hips. She gave him a tentative smile from the opposite side of the dining table, nervously bouncing on her toes.

"Is there a bathroom I can use?"

Cody blinked. "A *bathroom*? No. Not one that's open to the public. This is someone's home."

Her eyes welled with tears. "Please… I'll be quick. I know it's not proper etiquette, but…please."

Was this a scam of some sort? He couldn't see how, unless she thought he was going to let her steal something, which would never happen on his watch. He could tell her to get lost, but she was practically crossing her legs as she bounced. She wasn't kidding. And this might give him another chance to try to help her if she really was spiraling.

"Down the hall on the left." She hurried past him before he finished. If she *was* an alcoholic like him, she might want a bathroom for another reason. "Hey, don't throw up in there."

"Oh my God, why would you…?" she glared at him over her shoulder, not slowing down. "Never mind!" She dashed into the bathroom, slamming the door.

Cody waited in the dining room, and he didn't have to wait long. She came back in just a few minutes, looking a lot less tense and bouncy. She must have quickly splashed some water on her face while she was there. Her hair was damp in a few places, and her lightly freckled cheeks had more color.

"Thank you," she said, standing again on the far side of the table. Was he really that scary? "I'm sure that's against real estate protocol, but I was desperate. You wouldn't believe the day…no, the *year* I've had."

"You'd be surprised what I'd believe." Cody smiled encouragingly, doing his best to appear empathetic. Her expression told him he'd failed. Cody thought about everything Malcolm had taught him about being a good sponsor. He didn't even know if she had a drinking problem that would *require* a sponsor. But she had troubles of some kind. Step one of being a good sponsor—establish a friendly, nonthreatening relationship to build trust. He tried to deepen his smile. She just rolled her eyes again.

"Don't waste your charm on me. I'm permanently immune." She checked her watch, and he noticed the way her gaze paused over the cookies on the platter in front of her. Denial and mistrust were common with alcoholics and others with dependencies. Where charm didn't work, food often did. That's why meetings usually had donuts. He pointed to the platter.

"Help yourself to the cookies—lemon-cranberry. They're from the coffee shop in town, and they're add—" he caught himself before mentioning addiction out loud like an idiot "—well, I'll bet you can't eat just one. You from around here?"

"No. I've visited the Cape a couple of times, but never for long. Until now." She sniffled. He forgot he'd promised her tissues. He grabbed a box and slid it across the table. She hesitated, then took a couple, dabbing at her nose and her eyes, which were threatening to spill over again.

"So I assume you're *not* here house-hunting," Cody said.

A soft laugh bubbled up, and her cheeks went rosier in color. She had porcelain skin, with tiny pale freckles. She looked around the old house, with the antique mahogany furniture and silk drapes. "Even if I were, this place would be *way* out of my price range." She grabbed a cookie, talking around the crumbs. "These are delicious—I really needed the sugar boost."

"When's the last time you ate?"

She was pale and slender, and he could have sworn he just saw her sway on her feet. But the question came out more as a demand than concern. Oops. His daughter, Ava, would say that was Corporal O'Neil coming out. Ava called him that whenever she thought he was being too bossy. The woman's chin rose in a slight act of defiance at his tone.

"Excuse me?" Her eyes flashed with anger, and he rushed to explain.

"I'm just saying there's half a turkey sub in the fridge

that I haven't touched. You look like you could use something more substantial than a cookie."

Her fury made her puff up like an animal ready to attack. "I'm not some homeless person looking for your scraps." She paused, a brief, shattered look passing behind her eyes—gone as fast as it had appeared. "Except… I guess I am. Homeless, that is. And jobless. And…" One giant tear slowly rolled down her cheek. "I really should go." A sob caught in her throat. Against his better judgment, Cody gave up on keeping his distance. He couldn't help it—he moved around the table to her side, but stopped short of touching her. A good mentor maintained boundaries.

"Look, I'm not trying to insult you. I offered food because I can see you're in some kind of crisis, and… I've been in your shoes."

She began to cry in earnest but also hiccuped a sharp laugh. "I can *promise* you that you've never been in my shoes." She blew her nose into a fistful of tissues. "My crisis is totally self-inflicted."

"Every addict feels that way." His thoughts had tumbled out of his mouth, but it was a stupid thing to say. Once again, he'd pushed too hard.

The woman looked up at him in surprise. "*Addict?* So you *do* think I'm some homeless junkie, trying to scam you out of cookies?" She straightened, bristling in anger behind her free-flowing tears. "I'm a schoolteacher. Or… I *was* a schoolteacher. Until…" Her voice trailed off. Her anger seemed to leave her, and her shoulders sagged. "I've had a lousy summer, but I haven't fallen so low that I've become an addict. Other than being addicted to attracting horrible men." She gestured in his direction. "Men like *you*."

His frustration with himself—and her comment about addicts—made him forget about staying in salesman mode. He jammed his fingers through his hair and stared up at the ceiling, counting to himself while he tried to maintain some level of composure. He failed, and his voice turned hard.

"Well, I *have* fallen that low. I'm a recovering alcoholic. So forgive me for thinking I might be able to help some stranger I found sobbing alone in her car. If that makes me one of your *horrible men*, then so be it." He was being defensive, and her eyes narrowed on him.

"How typical of a man to center himself in every situation. No offense to your addiction, but I don't need some guy thinking he needs to rescue me. All I did was sit in a vehicle that I own and have a good cry. I just needed a minute. I've been driving for two days and I thought I'd parked on a quiet street where I could regroup, where no one would bother me."

She thought he was *bothering* her?

"I didn't force you out of your car and into this house," he snapped. "You could have stayed out there and had your little pity party after I walked away." His temper was getting the best of him, and she seemed to have a short fuse, too. Not a good combination.

"I had to *pee!*" She shouted the words and seemed to startle herself. She was sputtering with anger. He knew that feeling all too well. Sometimes anger helped when panic was trying to take over. His therapist at the VA told him it was a coping mechanism, which was okay as long as it wasn't taken too far... As Cody tended to do. He took a breath to rein in his own annoyance, but she finished her thought before he succeeded. Her glare was unwavering. "I never would have come in here otherwise. You were a means to an end, and nothing more."

"Yeah? Well, you've also scarfed down three cookies, so it wasn't *just* that."

"Like I said—means to an end." She defiantly popped cookie number four into her mouth. "It's cute that you think you can relate, but you truly have no idea."

Oh yeah? "No one else on Cape Cod knows I'm an alcoholic or that I go to meetings every week."

Her eyebrows rose. "The secrecy is your choice. I just lost my job because of something someone else did."

So this was a contest now? *Game on.* "I lost my last job because I punched a coworker in the face. More than once."

"My stepmother got me evicted from my town house and my dad did nothing to stop her." She raised her chin. "Oh, and my stepmom is one year younger than me."

Ouch. That had to hurt. But he'd had family troubles, too.

"Moving to the Cape for this job took me an hour away from my daughter, who thought the move was her fault."

Her eyes softened for just a moment before she stepped back into the challenge.

"No one in my family knows why I lost my job, or the town house thing, or why I dumped my last—" she looked up to the ceiling and sighed "—and I *do* mean *last*—boyfriend."

Cody couldn't resist. "But the secrecy was your decision."

She huffed a short laugh, but didn't smile. "Fair enough. But still…"

"I'm a military veteran with PTSD," he blurted out. In a weird sense, this one-upmanship felt cleansing. His sponsor, Malcolm, and Cody's ex-wife, Lynn, were the only ones who knew all of these things.

He had her attention now. Her forehead furrowed. "Okay, you're dealing with a lot—"

"So when I say I've been where you've been—rock bottom—I mean it."

She rolled her eyes dramatically. Damn, she was good at that. "Dude, you can list all the hard times in the world and you won't match mine."

"I find that hard to believe—"

She threw both hands up in the air in frustration.

"Oh my God, will you stop trying to be the world's worst sufferer of all time? Unless you've had an ex share private naked pictures of you that cost you your reputation *and* your job *and* forced you to leave your hometown, you have *not* been in my shoes. Instead of competing with me, just be grateful that you're *not* me, okay?"

Chapter Two

Jenn couldn't believe she'd actually said that out loud. To a complete stranger.

Mr. Real Estate Agent stared at her in stunned silence. He finally cleared his throat.

"Okay, that's messed up."

"Exactly. And now I have to come up with some story to tell to the people I love most in my life."

"Why not tell them the truth?"

"You think I should tell my family that I posed for naked pictures like some bubbleheaded coed and texted them to my boyfriend so he could put them on blast? No, thanks. I'm already the family joke for being so bad at relationships. My marriage lasted all of fourteen months. And then *this* guy. And now my siblings are all in love with their perfect mates, getting married and having babies. Hell, even my *mom* has a boyfriend." She paused for a breath. Damn, it felt good to blurt all of this out to someone completely uninvested. A stranger she'd never see again in her life.

A man who was now staring at her as if he thought she might be falling apart again, like she had in the car. Oddly enough, she felt more in control now that she'd dumped all her angst on this random real estate guy who had a long list of his own problems to deal with. She reached out to pat his forearm.

"Don't worry, I'm not going to burst into tears on you again. In fact, I need to get going." She stared at where her hand was resting on his arm. She had no idea why it was still there and pulled it back while she gave him a reassuring smile. "This has been…fun. Or…not. It's been weird. Oh hell, I don't know *what* this has been, but I'm outta here."

This man had a boatload of baggage, and she was *still* somehow, just a little bit, attracted to him. Typical—messed-up men had always been her type. But she was done with that. Done with men. Forever. There was a beat of silence as the steam went out of both of them. He scrubbed his hands down his face.

"Weird describes it pretty well. I didn't mean to come across as creepy earlier. Or grumpy. Or any of the other dwarves."

The corner of her mouth twitched. "I don't remember a dwarf named Creepy. That would have made for a whole different fairy tale. I think *Nosey* would be more accurate than Creepy. I guess you could call me Weepy." She sniffled again and wiped her nose.

"I don't remember a Weepy, either. Speaking of names…?"

"Weepy will do."

No need for real names. Getting mad had snapped her out of her self-pity. That was interesting, since one of the things she *hated* to do was lose her temper. Today, though, she'd welcomed that wave of sharp anger. It reminded her that she didn't have to be a hot, crying mess every minute of every day. Time to suck it up and move on. All she had to do was come up with a plausible story for her family. Too bad she was such a bad liar.

"So you quit your teaching job. Just like that? Right before the school year started? I don't get it." Jenn's older sister, Lexi, set her coffee cup down and leaned across the dining table. "You're our little Miss Reliable. Our steady Jenny-Benny. The most practical of all of us. What the hell happened?"

They were sitting at her mother's small dining table, in her apartment above the office of the old motel Mom had inherited two years earlier. The two-bedroom apartment was compact, but colorful and airy, with a wall of windows facing the ocean. Beyond the large outside deck, the Atlantic was calm and blue in the sunshine. Her mother refilled the coffee mugs in front of Jenn, Lexi and their soon-to-be sister-in-law, Grace Bennett. Mom's hair was a darker pink than usual…at least what had been usual over the past couple of years. And it was longer, too, cut in a short bob instead of a spiky, fluorescent pink pixie. She'd explained to Jenn that she was toning down the color for Max and Grace's wedding.

For all of Jenn's life, and the length of her parents' marriage, her mother had been the epitome of country club chic. Tailored suits, sensible shoes and carefully coiffed auburn hair. But since the divorce and Mom's shocking move to this old motel, her style had changed completely. The pink hair was just the cherry on top of a curvy and strong body currently wrapped in a skintight black top, heavily torn skinny jeans and leopard skin boots with a kitten heel. At eleven o'clock in the morning.

"Leave your sister alone, Lexi. We're just happy to see

her, and if she says she's okay, then she's okay." Mom sat next to Jenn. "You *are* okay, right?"

"Yes, Mom. I'm fine." Jenn gave the women her most reassuring smile. "It's not uncommon for teachers to take a sabbatical year, and that's all I'm doing. My whole family has moved here to Cape Cod, so I figured I'd come see what the big deal is."

Lexi, ever the skeptic, sat back in her chair, staring hard at Jenn. "I've heard of sabbaticals for *college* instructors, but...you teach first grade."

"Which I imagine is an exhausting job," Grace added. She was going to marry Jenn's brother, Max, in December. "I tried running the elementary holiday pageant last year and couldn't do it—Max had to step in. I can't imagine teaching a class of young kids every day. Just keeping up with one first grader is a lot for me. Tyler wears me out some days."

Tyler was Max's six-year-old son. Jenn nodded. "It *is* a lot." And she'd loved every minute of it. "I just decided it was time to step back for a bit and think about... long-term plans."

"You *loved* teaching," Lexi said. "I don't buy it, Jenny."

Jenn set her mug down hard. "For God's sake, stop grilling me! You've moved around and changed jobs your whole damn life, so what's the big deal with me taking a year off, Alexa?"

Her sister's eyes narrowed. "You know I go by *Lexi*."

Once the home device with her sister's name became popular, she'd changed to Lexi to avoid the endless jokes. Jenn shrugged.

"And I told you yesterday that I prefer *Jenn* to *Jenny*. When *you* use the right name, so will I."

New start. New name.

"Okay, girls. Knock it off." Their mother gave them a stern look. Phyllis Bellamy may have changed in many ways, but she was still their mom and she knew how to quell a sisterly spat. "If Jenn needs a break from teaching, then it's our job to support her. And she's hardly the first Bellamy woman to reinvent herself, is she? Speaking of support—" her mother turned to Jenn "—is this a *paid* sabbatical or…?"

Jenn sighed. She could just tell them the truth—that she'd been forced out of her job for supposedly breaking the morals clause in her teaching contract—but it was all too raw. And humiliating. She shook her head.

"Very much *un*paid, Mom. I've got a little set aside, but I need to find a job pretty quickly. Need a new motel maid?"

Her mother laughed. "*I'm* the only full-time maid around here, and we're heading toward the off season, so I can't afford another one. Maybe Lexi needs a server at the restaurant?"

"Nothing personal…" Lexi smiled at Jenn, suspicion gone from her eyes. Despite their occasional spats, Lexi was a loving and protective big sister. She was also the head chef and part-owner of one of the most popular restaurants on Cape Cod. "But I really am fully staffed right now. Maybe Grace's office…?"

Grace ran her brother's dental office in town. She pushed a strand of honey-blond hair from her face and grimaced. "Sorry, no openings at the moment. But I'll keep my ears open for any jobs around. Would you consider substitute teaching at the elementary school here? Tyler's kindergarten teacher from last year is very pregnant, and I think she's out on leave starting around Christmas."

Jenn felt her heart pinch. She loved teaching little ones, but as soon as any school checked her work history, they'd hear all about her shameful downfall. The thought of never teaching again was scary, but she couldn't let herself think about it yet. She needed to find a way to survive and heal before she worried about what forever might look like.

"Hey, wait." Lexi snapped her fingers. "Devlin was at the restaurant yesterday—you've met him, he's Sam's cousin and was our best man." Jenn remembered Devlin. He was tall, like Sam, and had the same mop of dark, wavy hair. He'd seemed nice enough. Lexi was still talking. "Devlin said he wanted to hire someone to run his real estate office because he's out all the time showing houses. Business is really starting to boom for him."

Real estate... Intense dark eyes appeared in Jenn's memory. There's no way this could be the same office that Nosey from the open house worked at. There must be a hundred real estate offices on Cape Cod. And she needed a job.

"I thought he fished for lobsters?" She remembered Devlin's tanned face, worn from the wind and sea. He'd talked about the boat he kept at his cousin Sam's marina.

"You don't *fish* for lobsters." Lexi said with an exasperated sigh. "But yes, he has a lobster boat. He's leased it out to another lobsterman, though. It's a tough living, especially with just one boat, so he started selling houses.

He's done well enough to open his own office. It's on Wharf Street, next door to the restaurant."

"So it's a one-man office? What would I have to do?"

Lexi took a quick sip of coffee. "It was just Devlin at first, but now he has a female agent working for him part-time. Nancy Dale is a fifth generation Cape Cod native, just like Devlin and Sam. She's got a salty mouth, but a great heart, and she knows *everyone*. He might have another agent, but I haven't met them. The job won't be anything exotic—just answering phones and doing paperwork and stuff. Basically a glorified secretary."

Great. So much for that master's degree Jenn had. *Glorified secretary.* But it was a paying job. She blew out a long breath.

"If he's still looking, I'd be willing to talk about it."

"Maybe you could get a real estate license, honey." Her mom leaned toward her with a hopeful smile.

Jenn knew Mom wanted all three of her children to be settled. Happy. And self-sufficient. She'd welcomed Jenn into her spare room, but the apartment was small, and Mom had been living here alone for a couple years now. Phyllis Bellamy was used to having her home to herself. Or rather, to herself and her…man friend.

Jenn and her siblings were baffled by their mother's on-again, off-again relationship with Fred Knight, owner of the bar attached to Lexi's restaurant. They seemed to spend as much time arguing as they did being a couple, but it worked for both of them somehow. Fred was rough and surly, while Mom was bubbly and loved everyone. But she didn't take any nonsense from Fred. It was an odd matchup, but they weren't hurting anyone, so the Bellamy children had decided to let it run its course.

a signed listing contract in his leather bag for the million-dollar home. He was humming to himself when he came through the front door. Until he saw who was sitting behind the front desk, next to Nancy Dale.

He halted, blinking a few times in the hope that this was an illusion. It was the strawberry blonde from the open house. The one he'd gotten into a pity party battle with. The one he'd never thought he would see again. Ever. And she was sitting *behind* the front desk in his office. Like their first meeting, she was wearing a long cardigan over a knit top. Her hair was falling over one shoulder, the sunlight from the windows making it look like gold and copper spun together.

His mind sputtered, then began to whirl. Devlin had talked about hiring an admin person for the office. He may have even said something last week about finding someone. But surely not...*this* someone. Besides, she'd said she was a teacher. At least, she had *been* a teacher, before her jerk of a boyfriend had shared photos of her online.

Her wide-eyed expression told him he wasn't the only one who was shocked. Good. That meant she hadn't stalked him here on purpose or anything creepy like that. But how...?

Nancy, normally a shrewd cookie, was thankfully oblivious to the sudden tension in the room. "Oh, hi, Cody! This is our new office person, Jenny Bellamy. Jenny, this is our other full-time agent, Cody O'Neil."

Bellamy? So she was part of the Bellamy family, who he'd learned were fairly recent arrivals to Winsome Cove but had already made an impact. He'd met Phyllis Bellamy, the energetic owner of the Sassy Mermaid Motor

Fred was Sam's uncle and Devlin's father, and they both vouched for his honor, if not his personality.

Lexi looked up from her phone, which had just pinged with an incoming text. "Sam says Devlin hasn't hired anyone yet, so the job's still open. Want me to give him your number?"

"Sure. Hopefully it will pay enough for me to afford rent somewhere."

Her mother sat up abruptly. "You don't need to worry about that. The guest room is yours as long as you want it, sweetheart."

Jenn and Lexi looked at each other across the table, having a quick, silent conversation. Lexi had lived in the guest room for several months when she first came to Winsome Cove. The lowering of her eyebrows and a barely visible shake of her head told Jenn that she didn't want to stay here any longer than necessary. Jenn turned to her mother with a smile.

"Mom, I love staying here with you, but I need my own place if I can swing it. I'm used to having my own home—" the one her stepmother had kicked her out of unceremoniously "—and I have my own routines and stuff. Besides, the other night I felt like a third wheel when Fred came over for dinner. I had the distinct impression you two wanted to be alone."

Her mother's cheeks went one shade darker pink—interesting. Mom wasn't much of a blusher. She smoothed the hem of her shirt and brushed something off her capris, her lips pressed together, but curved into a mischievous smile.

"I won't lie to you, honey. Fred and I usually have some snuggle time after dinner. We like to watch the sunset and…well…you know." She met Jenn's gaze. "But we don't want to make you uncomfortable. You're my daughter, and you are always welcome here."

Jenn huffed a soft laugh. "But only for so long, Mom. What's the old saying? Guests and fish start stinking after a few days, right? I don't want to get stinky."

Grace had been watching silently, smiling at all the family dynamics. She was more introverted than the Bellamy clan, but she insisted she loved observing the spirited back-and-forth between everyone. She set down her coffee mug. "You know, I might have a solution for both of you." Mom, Lexi and Jenn turned to her, and she gave a little shrug. "My brother was talking about moving into my old place, but he's decided he'd rather keep paying the ridiculous HOA fees for his waterfront condo. The house is only partially furnished right now, because Max and I have been trying to decide what to do with it. I hate seeing it sit there empty. If you moved in, it would give us time to make up our minds."

"Oh, great." Lexi laughed. "You'd be moving out of Mom's place and moving right next door to our overprotective brother." She paused, reconsidering. "But…you'd have a whole house instead of a spare bedroom, and it's a nice house, too."

"It *is* a nice house," Grace said. "My brother and I grew up there. And it's not necessarily a bad thing to know your neighbors."

Jenn had seen the house on her visits. It was a cute Cape-style house in a historic neighborhood, freshly painted white, with green shutters. It had a wide front porch, and the whole property was as neat and tidy as

Grace was, with a picket-fenced backyard where roses and hydrangeas grew.

She'd heard the story several times of how Grace and Max had met over that picket fence, arguing about local property covenants. Grace had been appalled to learn Max was going to build a forge in his carriage house to create the swords and sculptures he made his living on. But, like in any good love story, they'd bonded over Max's son, Tyler, and eventually fallen in love. The whole freaking world was falling in love successfully...except for Jenn.

"Jenn? If you're interested, I'll let your brother know so he doesn't sell off any more furniture. I took some, and my brother grabbed a couple of old family pieces, but there's enough to make it livable until your furniture arrives."

A house would be great, but it felt almost too good to be true. Was it possible she'd just landed a job *and* a house over coffee?

"I don't want to get ahead of myself. Let me talk to Devlin and see what this job entails, and how much it pays. I need to know my budget before I make a move." That cushion she'd mentioned was *very* small.

Grace nodded. "I get it. But you know we'll give you a generous family discount on the rent. It's better for us to have the house occupied than just sitting there. You'd honestly be doing us a favor."

Just sitting there.

Funny—that was exactly how Jenn felt. She was just sitting here, letting everyone worry about her and offer their kindness when they didn't even know why she was here in the first place. Her cheeks warmed. She needed to get busy with this Rebuild My Life project. She'd been in Winsome Cove for almost two weeks, and she couldn't let herself wallow any longer.

Chapter Three

"Dad, those pillows look perfect! Don't you think? Let me just shape them…" Ava gave a karate chop to each of the brightly colored pillows that now covered his brown leather sectional. The neon colors were quite a change to Cody's drab apartment. The pink pillow was furry. The green one had sequins.

His eleven-year-old daughter had deemed his place "super boring" when she arrived Friday night. It wasn't the first time she'd shared her opinion of his home, but this time, she did it with her hands on her hips and an eyebrow arched high. The adult pose on his little girl made him smile. This was his favorite Ava age. But then again, every age of Ava before this had been his favorite, too.

Baby Ava had been a dark-haired, dark-eyed angel of a baby. Happy most of the time, and very vocal when she wasn't. Toddler Ava had been a terror—the minute she *could* run, she *did*. Endlessly, from place to place, climbing anything she could get a toehold on. She was three when he'd walked into the dining room and found her climbing the open stairs to the second floor…on the *outside* of the railing, clinging to the spindles six feet off the floor. And wearing a proud grin.

Kindergarten Ava had been a revelation. She absorbed information with the same enthusiasm she'd had climbing those stairs. She had opinions and enjoyed friendly debating at the dinner table over things like whether SpongeBob could be real and if cats were better pets than dogs. By the time she was six, she'd convinced him that a cat was best and she needed one right away. That was when Binksy entered their lives. That was also the year she skipped first grade because she was bored. And the first time he and his now ex-wife, Lynn, had heard the term *gifted*.

Ava wasn't a genius who'd be in college at fourteen or anything, but she was more intelligent than most kids, and too impatient to sit through lessons that she already knew. They bumped her up to second grade and enrolled her in a program for gifted children. Luckily, she hadn't started kindergarten until after her fifth birthday, so she wasn't too much younger than the other second graders. It was fun to see her blossom and mature over the next few years. Maybe because she was an only child, maybe because she was learning with older kids, or a combination of the two. Despite all the problems at home.

By the time she turned nine, he and Lynn had split, and his drinking had gotten much, much worse. Booze became the center of his life, even ahead of Ava, and she'd known it. That was the problem with having a smart kid.

"Do you like it, Dad?" Ava's smile had faded.

He realized he hadn't answered her question. That was another challenge of having a gifted child—it was very difficult to get away with lying. He pretended to scratch his chin as if deep in thought as he took in the pillows, a new painting of a shockingly pink carousel horse on the wall and a tall green vase on the kitchen table filled with silk sunflowers that matched the new kitchen towels.

"It's great, honey. But I think maybe the carousel horse might look better in *your* room than out here. Would that be okay?"

Her face lit up. Clearly she'd been hoping for exactly that. "Oh, could we? It really is so pretty." She held up her hand abruptly. "But…you still need some artwork on the wall. Maybe Shelly could help us?"

Shelly Berinson owned an interior design business at the top of Wharf Street—SeaShelly Designs. With Ava's current fascination with all things HGTV, she'd been thrilled to meet a *real* designer, and Ava stopped by the shop to say hi on nearly every visit. Shelly was kind enough to allow Ava, who would pretend to design a room for an imaginary client, to flip through books of wallpaper, fabric and paint colors.

As much as he'd chafed at the idea of moving from the Boston suburbs out to Winsome Cove, he was coming to appreciate the sense of community here. He'd scoffed at small-town life for so long that it took him a while to lose his cynicism, but the locals here were genuinely kind under their Yankee crustiness.

His apartment above the real estate office wasn't meant to be a long-term living situation, although he'd been grateful when his employer, Devlin Knight, had offered it to him at a reasonable rate. Devlin and his father, Fred, owned several old buildings on Wharf Street, including the Salty Knight Pub at the end of the dead-end street, the adjoining restaurant, 200 Wharf, this building and a still-empty storefront next door.

The upside was that the apartment was large, with high ceilings and original woodwork. And his commute to work was easy—down the back staircase to the office. The bedrooms both overlooked the harbor, where sailboats bobbed at their moorings. There were a lot of original wood floors and trim. The downside was that it was... old. The kitchen and bathrooms were especially dated.

Devlin had plans to gut most of it and remodel it into a vacation rental, but he wasn't in any hurry. He called it a "someday" project. But because he was going to tear it up, he'd given Cody carte blanche to paint walls and hang stuff. While Cody had never really cared much about wall colors, Ava was thrilled to have a pink bedroom, which would now feature a very large and colorful carousel horse painting over her bed. It was the decorating that had helped Ava warm up to coming to Winsome Cove two weekends a month.

"I'm sure Shelly can find a painting for the living room that you and I will both enjoy," Cody said. Hopefully something that wouldn't cost him a month's pay. The pillows and painting came from one of those discount home stores, but Shelly's usual clientele had much deeper pockets than Cody did. But that was a problem for two weeks from now, when Ava returned. "Come on, kiddo. We need to get you back to Mom's. Tomorrow's a school day."

Cody drove out to Truro the next morning to do an appraisal. One thing about being a real estate agent on the Cape was that your territory tended to cover *all* of the Cape—from Bourne to Provincetown. But it was worth the drive, because he came back to the office with

Lodge. She was president of the local business association and on the library board. Devlin's cousin, Sam, had married one of Phyllis's daughters, Lexi, who ran the popular restaurant next door. He'd heard there was a Bellamy son who'd moved to town, too. Devlin had mentioned there was a wedding coming up. Cody was going to have to tread lightly here. She suddenly jumped to her feet and thrust her hand out toward him.

"Nice to meet you, Cody. And please, call me Jenn." Her eyes briefly narrowed in warning, letting him know she expected him to play along. Pretend they were strangers. He was more than happy to oblige.

"Uh…hi, Jenn. Um…any relation to the other Bellamys in town?"

Jenn nodded with a tense smile. "I told Nancy that my family seems to be trying to take over the place. My mom, Phyllis, owns a motel here. My sister runs a restaurant, and my brother moved here last year, too." She paused, still staring at him. Damn, her steely blue eyes were intense. Almost hypnotizing. He glanced away to break the hold she had on him, clearing his throat way too loudly.

"Well, welcome to my…uh…this office. I'm sure we'll use you… I mean, I'm sure we can use your help." He was flailing verbally, if not physically. "Excuse me, but I have a listing to prepare."

"Oh!" Nancy exclaimed. "You got the Truro house? You're in beast mode, Cody!"

Nancy was a tough old bird, but she knew the Cape Cod real estate scene inside and out. She'd been selling houses out here for four decades. She'd taken him under her wing when he'd arrived last year and introduced him to a lot of the locals. In small towns, like the ones connected like a chain the length of Cape Cod, business was conducted with people someone knew or knew of. She'd helped him break a lot of ice out here.

Well into her seventies, Nancy was mostly retired. But she had enough return clients and referrals from her years in the business that she'd kept her license active. Her hair was brassy blond, clearly out of a bottle, and she wore it teased and sprayed into a golden halo of firmly affixed curls that wouldn't move in gale-force winds. She always wore lots of gold jewelry and proudly displayed her expensive Birkin bag on her desk. The woman probably made, and spent, more money in her "retirement" every year than Cody did. But she hated doing office duty, and she'd pressured Devlin into hiring someone to cover the clerical work and phones. Which was just…great.

"I'd tell you to hand it over—" Nancy playfully reached out a hand, then pulled it back "—but it's Jenny's first day. I want her to learn the phones and the basics of the office before we dive into entering contracts and creating listings. So you're on your own."

"I get it. I'll leave you two ladies alone." He practically ran to his desk in the back corner of the small storefront office, with a desk in each corner and reception desk front and center. He pulled out the listing contract and stared at it, but he wasn't seeing the potential five-figure commission. He wasn't seeing anything but Jenn Bellamy's face, wide-eyed and stunned, when he'd walked in. He was going to see that face every workday now. Which meant he was going to be spending a lot more time on the road, checking out listings or…something. Anything to avoid being with the woman who knew all of his secrets. Or at least, *most* of them. Would she keep that knowledge to herself? He had no idea what kind of person she was. For all he knew, she was just waiting for a chance to give Nancy all the juicy gossip on him. Then again, she'd made it clear she wanted to pretend they were strangers.

He swore out his frustration under his breath and started entering the listing information into the computer. The sooner he got it on the market, the sooner he'd collect that commission. He did his best to concentrate on the task, and he was almost done when he heard Nancy mention his name. He looked up to find both women laughing. Nancy was telling Jenn about the time Cody had walked into a bankruptcy listing they'd received from a bank, only to find the former homeowner still living there. With her fifteen cats wandering around the cluttered house, and the ammonia smell taking his breath away. The woman had chased him back out the door by throwing cat feces at him. Yeah, real estate could be interesting.

"We see some characters in this business, Jenny." Nancy seemed stuck on using the name Jenn obviously didn't like. "Oh, Cody—tell her about the crazy lady at your open house a couple weeks ago!"

Cody felt all the oxygen leave his lungs and it refused to return.

No, no, no. Don't go there, Nancy—

"The one who was crying about needing a bathroom?" Nancy prodded.

If there *had* been any air left in his chest, Jenn's deadly glare vaporized it. He'd never seen blue eyes go black the way hers just did. Her chin worked back and forth as if she was imagining devouring his beating heart. This was bad. *Deflect! Deflect!*

"It wasn't *that* bad, Nancy," he said, desperate to change the subject. "Remember the story you told me about the poker lounge you found in the basement of that cop's house in Falmouth? It was behind a hidden door, right? The one that looked like a speakeasy, and had a stripper pole?"

Nancy waved off the comment. "That was weird, not funny. Some random woman showing up sobbing at an open house is funny." She turned to Jenn, oblivious to the rage burning in her eyes. "You never know what's going to happen at an open house. When Cody came back and told Devlin and me about this lady, we couldn't stop laughing. She ran in, used the bathroom—which is a huge no-no—grabbed a fistful of free cookies and left. Can you imagine?"

"No." Jenn's voice was cold as ice, and just as pointed. "No, I can't imagine it. And you say Cody couldn't wait to tell you all about this random woman?"

Son of a...

Nancy turned to answer an incoming phone call, and Cody did his best in facial expressions and silent gestures like holding his hands up in innocence, shaking his head and mouthing "no" a few times to let Jenn know it hadn't happened the way she thought. Yeah, she'd created a unique situation, and yes, he'd shared some of the story with his coworkers. But he hadn't made fun of her or anything like that. He didn't think... Her face had paled at first, but now her cheeks were mottled with red spots of rage and embarrassment. He could handle the first, but the second made him squirm.

Nancy hung up the phone and stood. "Our lunch order is ready. I'm going to walk up to Sal's on Main Street and grab our sandwiches." She pointed a finger at Cody. "Be nice to the new girl while I'm gone."

He braced himself for the storm that was coming, but silence, heavy and kinda scary, settled over the office when Nancy left. He looked everywhere but at Jenn. How did she get here? How were they ever going to be able to work together?

"Look, I never expected to see you again…" He felt he had to explain himself, but the spoken words felt inadequate. "And I didn't say anything about our conversation that day. My boss asked how the open house went, and I shared a story about someone wanting to use the house as a public restroom. You're one of the more interesting things I've ever had happen at an open house, Jenn." She opened her mouth to speak, but snapped it shut again when he held up one hand and continued. "I didn't tell them *everything*. Even thinking I'd never see you again, I did *not* share our conversation."

"But you *did* share that a 'sobbing woman' came in to use the bathroom and ate your damn cookies, didn't you? And then you had a good laugh over the 'crazy lady.'"

"I didn't call you that. Not once. Nancy thought the story was more funny than I did, and she started calling you cra—" He thought better of finishing that sentence. "I shared it as something…unusual. I felt bad for you. You know I did—I offered to help you, remember?"

"You mean when you thought I was an addict, like you?" she snapped. "That was a great help, Cody. Did a lot for my self-esteem. Give the man a cookie." She sneered at him. "Oh, that's right, I ate the poor widdle boy's cookies, didn't I?"

Yikes. She was really hot about this.

"Look, I get that you're angry, and I don't blame you. But they'll never know it was you. And again, I did *not* share anything about what we said to each other. How the hell did you end up with *this* job anyway? Out of all the businesses on the Cape?"

"Trust me, I'm not any happier than you are. Like I said, my sister is married to your boss's cousin, and she knew he was looking to hire someone. He offered the job, and since I enjoy little luxuries like food and a roof over my head, I took it."

He scrubbed his hands down his face, staring up at the ceiling. "And I don't suppose you'd consider taking a different job?"

She folded her arms stiffly. "I don't suppose *you'd* consider quitting?" She didn't wait for an answer. "This might come as a shock to you, but places aren't exactly begging for employees out here now that the summer season is winding down."

That was true enough. Most places on Cape Cod stayed open at least through fall, but after that a lot of them would close down until late spring. Jenn's posture changed, as if her indignation was running out of steam. Her eyes went from cold and angry to vulnerable. He couldn't believe he preferred angry to this look. She leaned forward in her chair, and her crossed arms seemed to be more of a self-embrace now, like she was holding herself together.

"Are you sure you didn't say anything more about me? If my family hears..." The edge was gone from her voice. She was nervous, and he knew why. She'd lost her teaching job because her asshat ex had shared compromising pictures of her.

"I swear I did not." He shook his head emphatically. "I never even knew your name until now. There's no way anyone could put *you* into that story, unless you told someone you stopped at an open house."

"Of course I didn't," she scoffed. "And now that we're here in this office together...you won't say anything, right?"

"Is that why you pretended not to know me when I walked in?"

"It would be pretty awkward to have to explain how we'd met, even though we didn't exchange names." She made a face. "But we *did* exchange our deepest, darkest secrets with each other, which no one can know." She tugged at the front of her cardigan, her voice soft and pleading. "Promise me you won't tell..."

"You're not the only one with something to lose, you know. I shared things with you that no one in Winsome Cove knows." He let out a long breath, slowly realizing how truly bad this could be. "You know things about me that could get me fired *and* cost me my apartment, because my boss is also my landlord. I live upstairs." They needed a plan. A truce of some kind. "Spilling *your* secrets would motivate you to spill *mine*, and vice versa. We both have leverage against the other one, so the best thing to do is agree to forget that day and just...be random coworkers who know *nothing* about each other. Deal?"

His life would be a hell of a lot easier if Jennifer Bellamy had never walked into this office, but here she was, and they were going to have to deal with it.

Chapter Four

Jenn wound her fingers together in her lap as she tried to get her brain to function. The shock of seeing Cody walk through the front door had been enough to render her speechless. Nancy had jolted her back to reality by introducing him, and she'd only had one thought. *No one* could know about that horrible day when she'd blurted out all her trauma to a complete stranger. No one could know they knew each other. The only thing she could think to do had been to jump up like a jack-in-the-box and introduce herself as if she'd never seen the man before. Thankfully, Cody had played along.

But the idea that he'd had a good laugh about her with his friends made her shrink in humiliation. Then fury took hold. How *dare* he? He insisted he hadn't shared details, but how could she trust him?

"Are you *sure* you didn't share any more details with your buddies?"

He raised one eyebrow high in disbelief. "Nancy is hardly my buddy. But I promise. I didn't describe your looks or your car or anything that could identify you. I definitely didn't share our conversation. And I think you and I carried off pretending not to know each other pretty well when I walked in just now. Nancy won't be suspicious of anything. That was a good call, by the way. I wasn't sure how to react, but you did the right thing."

Despite herself, she started to relax at the sound of his steady voice and calm demeanor. She was a horrible judge of character, but…he seemed sincere.

"It's still embarrassing that you told them anything at all, but I guess I'll have to take your word on it."

He sat back in his chair with a heavy sigh.

"I told you—I only said that a crying woman came in and begged to use the bathroom. That's it." He had the good grace to look guilty as he explained. "It was just… office talk. Open houses almost always have something weird happen. They asked the next day how it went, and it was just…a story to share. It was—"

"You made it sound like I stole those cookies." That stung Jenn more than him talking about her crying. "The cookies *you* told me about before I ever came inside… which you *invited* me to do! Did you tell them *that*?"

"Of course not!" His voice had a frustrated edge, but he took a breath and dialed it back. "Look, Nancy will be back any minute with lunch. I'll keep your secrets if you'll keep mine. Do we have a deal or not?"

She didn't really have a choice, but she still hesitated. Men were inherently untrustworthy in her experience. But he was right—if he ruined her, she could ruin him right back. Guaranteed mutual destruction. Nancy was pushing the door open when Jenn gave a quick nod and softly answered him.

"Deal."

The next couple of weeks flew by for Jenn. She'd decided to accept Grace's offer to rent her semi-furnished house. She'd hesitated at first because she wasn't convinced living next door to her protective big brother, Max, would be any better than living in Mom's apartment.

But one night of her mother having Fred Knight stay over for some *very* vocal and energetic lovemaking in the bedroom next door was enough to motivate her to pack her bags. At least there were the two driveways—hers and his—between Max's house and the rental. She shouldn't have to worry about hearing him and Grace getting frisky all the way over there.

Grace's family home was lovely. It was cozy inside, with a modern kitchen and a nice sunroom across the back, overlooking a tidy backyard and Max's carriage house next door. The house was very much like her future sister-in-law, Grace. Organized. Classic. Welcoming. Some rooms were empty, or partially so, but there was a sofa and overstuffed chair in the living room, along with a couple of small tables and a flat-screen TV. The formal dining room was empty, but there was a kitchen table next to a big window facing Max's house—with curtains she could pull for privacy. The primary bedroom was empty—Grace had taken her bedroom furniture over to Max's to replace the old set he had acquired with the house. But one of the guest rooms was still fully furnished, which worked fine for Jenn.

She spent her rare free time with her family, and she was starting to forget about all the things they didn't know about her. They were busy planning the events leading up to Max and Grace's December wedding, and next up was the bridal shower in ten days. Jenn was girding herself to face the onslaught of lovey-dovey romance everywhere. She was happy for Max and Grace. They were complete opposites—the tatted-up swordmaker and the quiet piano teacher—but Grace made Max happier than Jenn had ever seen him. Jenn loved them both and she was *happy* for them…even if she had to keep reminding herself of that.

She was trying to be happy for everyone falling in love. Just because *she'd* given up completely and forever on some fairy-tale love story happening for her, that didn't mean she wanted her loved ones to be miserable. Big sister Lexi had had a bad ex once—she'd almost ended up in jail because of him—but Lexi had recovered and met Sam Knight, who loved her completely. They were so sweet together, especially now that little baby Amanda had come along.

It was sickening. And adorable. *Damn it.*

Jenn didn't just have one bad ex, though. She had a string of them—starting with an ex-husband right out of college who'd tried to extort her at the divorce, and ending with Will, who'd shared naked photos of her as revenge after she'd dumped him. Proving she was right when she'd called him a creep.

She'd be happy if she never saw another wedding, or another cootchie-coo couple for that matter, ever again. But everyone in her family, even her mother, just kept falling in love in Winsome Cove. And with a wedding coming up, it would be raining hearts and cupids for the next few months. Which was just…g*reat.*

At least she could escape all of that at work. The real estate office was busy enough to keep her mind occupied without taxing her brain too much. This wasn't going to be a lifelong career for her—she hoped—but she was enjoying learning the ins and outs of the business. The phone rang steadily, between clients, buyers, other agents, home inspectors, attorneys and banks. She was responsible for examining and filing contracts and offers to purchase. She followed up on any properties in the process of being sold, confirming dates and arranging surveys, inspections, utility transfers, and so on.

Her favorite thing to do was entering the listings into the shared online real estate database. Devlin, Cody and Nancy supplied the photos of any listings they acquired, and the data required, like square footage, HOA fees, and extras like swimming pools or beach access. Jenn would enter all the data into the listing system, and then she'd work on writing a creative description for the property. Not creative in the sense of not telling the truth exactly, but finding a way to tell the truth in a way that always sounded appealing.

Nancy was a real character, but she didn't always write the most colorful property descriptions. It was Devlin who'd taught Jenn a lot of the real estate lingo. A house wasn't small, it was *cozy*. A place that had been partially gutted wasn't a mess, it was a *blank slate*. Did the house have weird features, like needing to walk through the bathroom to get to a bedroom? Well, that was a *unique floorplan*. Was it old, as many Cape houses were, and not updated? That was a home with *vintage charm*. Isolated homes were *peaceful*, and ones near busy town centers were *conveniently located*.

For some reason, the play on words appealed to Jenn. She had to run any listing past Devlin, Nancy or Cody before uploading it, of course, and they'd let her know if she forgot anything, or if she got a little too clever with her wording.

She and Cody had managed to act as casual coworkers in the office. It wasn't all that difficult, because despite knowing each other's darkest secrets, they really were strangers. The only things they had in common were a similar sarcastic sense of humor, mutual disdain for anything slightly romantic, and the power to destroy each other.

"So you blurted out all of your personal issues to a stranger, and now she works in your office?"

"I only gave her the highlights, but…yeah."

His sponsor, or, as Malcolm Adwari preferred to be called, *sobriety coach*, took a sip of his coffee, looking skeptical. They were sitting at the window in Jerry's Java coffee shop in Winsome Cove for their weekly conversation, following the weekly Wednesday noontime meeting of a twelve-step program for alcoholics and addicts. It had been a routine for almost ten months now—as long as Cody had been sober.

"And this woman," Malcolm continued, trying to puzzle it out, "was clearly in an emotional crisis of some sort when you first met…so much so that you thought you might want to be her sobriety coach? What do you think made you decide it was safe to blurt everything out to her? And why am I just hearing about it now?"

Those were two very fair questions. Malcolm had insisted on full and honest disclosures between them when he agreed to be Cody's sponsor. And Cody hadn't mentioned his first encounter with Jenn Bellamy a few weeks ago.

"As for why I didn't mention it earlier…" He paused, then sighed. "Look, it was just a weird blip that I thought I'd never have to think about again." Although he hadn't stopped thinking about it. About her. "And nothing about her made me feel safe. She…she *annoyed* me. Got under my skin. Before I knew it, we were trying to out-trauma each other."

Malcolm had set his cup down now, his dark eyes concerned. His black beard was stippled with gray. Cody braced himself for the lecture that was about to come. Malcolm took his responsibility seriously, which was a good thing—he was the first person who'd been able to get Cody to stay sober for more than a few weeks at a time. But despite that success, Malcolm was always looking for, and trying to repair, any weaknesses he saw.

"Cody, *weird blips* are dangerous for anyone in the program. You know that. Those are the moments that can knock you off-track. I see big red flags whenever someone tells me another person got under their skin, or that something highly unusual wasn't important enough to share. Those moments are when cracks in your sobriety can open up. What was it about her that goaded you into that verbal competition?"

"I don't know," Cody muttered. He knew that wouldn't satisfy Malcolm, a successful immigration attorney. The man was relentless when he wanted to make a point.

"Bull." Malcolm scoffed. "You *know*, you just don't want to tell me. Or admit it to yourself. A strange woman is sobbing in her car, which is packed with luggage, and she doesn't accept your offer of help. How did that make you feel?"

"What are you, a therapist now?" Cody felt his temper rising at being pushed. "How did it make me *feel*? Really?"

Malcolm just stared calmly, knowing Cody hadn't answered the question. He thought about how he'd felt when Jenn had basically said *get lost*, while she was still locked in her car.

"I felt like I'd failed."

"Why?"

"Because I was trying to be a nice guy and she didn't want that. She wouldn't even roll her window down, and she tried to tell me she was fine, which was clearly a lie."

"And that made you mad." Malcolm's brows rose.

"Yes, a little. Rejection is never fun, and it was a rejection."

Malcolm's mouth twitched. "A woman, lost, alone and sad, parked on a quiet street for a moment to collect herself. You wanted to be her white knight, but she didn't want a white knight act from some strange guy who knocked on her car window. Don't you think that was her setting boundaries—a good and safe thing— more than rejecting you personally?"

Cody scowled at his coffee, not bothering to give the obvious answer. Why did Malcolm have to be right all the damn time?

"Think about it," Malcolm said. "Didn't you learn in those anger management classes that not everything is about you?"

"Okay, okay. I get it." He sat back with a huff of frustration. "I made that first encounter about me, not her."

"And then you did it again when she came inside the house." It wasn't a question.

Cody hesitated, unwilling to admit defeat. "I really

was trying to help her. You're the one who keeps saying I'm ready to be someone's sponsor."

Malcolm laughed at that. "Come on, man. That doesn't mean you go looking around for some random stranger to rescue and force them to accept your so-called help whether they want it or not. How would that have gone over if I'd tried it with *you* when we met?"

"Not well," he agreed.

He and Malcolm had first met at a Wednesday meeting last November. The attorney was eighteen years sober and still coming to regular meetings. He often led them. At first, Cody had resented the reality that sobriety was going to be a long haul. It wasn't something he could just take care of and go back to living his life. A month later, Malcolm had invited him for coffee, and a friendship formed. *That* was when Malcolm had mentioned the possibility of being Cody's sponsor, but only if they both agreed it would be a good fit. Malcolm didn't mention it again, but their coffee meetings became more regular, and Cody had asked him to be his sobriety coach in January.

He returned Malcolm's sardonic grin. "You're telling me I tried too hard, and then took it personally when she told me to go pound salt."

"You meant well, Cody, but you were overeager. Turns out the woman didn't even have a substance abuse problem. She has *other* problems, but they're not ones you're qualified to address. And now the two of you know things about each other that you really shouldn't. How's that going at work?"

He told Malcolm that it was actually going surprisingly well in the office. Jenn had picked up the day-to-day tasks of her job quickly. She was organized and smart. And she was funny, in her own sarcastic way. Cody used sarcasm, too, and they'd been trading light-hearted zingers with each other. But they were just co-workers. No sparks, thank goodness, and no animosity or awkwardness.

Cody shared that, just yesterday, a young couple look-ing to buy their first home—with lots of financial help from their parents—had been sitting at the conference table in the back room by the stairs. The door had been open, with Jenn in Cody's line of sight. No one else was in the office. Every time the newlyweds said something mushy, like they were looking for a "forever home" to live out their "dream" of a happily-ever-after, Jenn would roll her eyes dramatically. At one point, she'd put her fin-ger in her mouth and pretended to gag.

Cody couldn't react, of course, because his clients were sitting in front of him and he needed this commis-sion. But the woman wasn't easy to ignore, and he even-tually had to cough sharply to cover the laugh that almost escaped. The new bride had been gushing about wanting a house near the beach, preferably new construction, with room for the family they were soon going to start. Her husband, on the other hand, wanted something on a golf course, and preferably an older, and therefore cheaper, starter home. He understood, more than his bride did, that even their parents' wallets had limits. Behind them, Jenn had gestured with her two fists bumping each other like charging bulls, then exploding. It was her accurate interpretation of how well this young marriage was going to go once they started trying to reach an agreement on a house. He'd managed to sign them as clients, but he knew they'd be a challenge.

Malcolm looked thoughtful. "So…the woman who was furious with you is now a woman who makes you laugh? I don't need to give you the *no relationships* lecture, do I? You're not quite a year into sobriety, and—"

Cody laughed so loudly that other customers turned their way. "*Relationship?* Did you forget who you're talking to? I don't *do* relationships, and that has nothing to do with my sobriety. They just don't work for me. Just because a coworker made me laugh doesn't mean I'm going to fall in love with her."

Chapter Five

Jenn sat on the steps of her front porch and tightened the laces on her running shoes. It was early on Sunday morning, and the weather was cloudy and cool. She was ready for it, wearing warm leggings and a hooded sweatshirt over a snug running shirt that was supposed to wick moisture away so she wouldn't get chilled. Her hair was pulled through the back of a blue *Field of Dreams* ball cap, forming a ponytail.

She'd taken a couple of quick runs on the beach while she was staying with her mom, but the move and the new job had kept her too busy lately. At least that was the excuse she'd been using. But she hadn't been sleeping well, and that was always a telltale sign that she wasn't getting enough exercise.

Without being physically tired, her brain would go into overdrive the minute she lay down in bed. It was like watching a slideshow of every mistake she'd ever made, and that wasn't a good thing. Because there'd been so many. She couldn't keep thinking about the past if she really wanted to make a fresh start here in Winsome Cove. Even if this was just a temporary hiatus from her real life back in Iowa. She couldn't imagine how she could make going home ever work, though. It wasn't like anyone would soon forget seeing those pictures of her.

No more dwelling in the past, Jenn.

She stood and did some stretches before starting off down Revere Street toward town at an easy pace. She'd driven around the other day and mapped out a few routes. Today she was going to try the five-mile loop—through Winsome Cove center, then winding through residential streets to get back here.

Some of the homes on Revere street dated to the late 1700s, and some, like the one she was renting from Grace, were from the 1920s. All the houses were lovingly maintained, in accordance with the covenants for the district. Any changes to the character of the houses had to be approved by the historical association, which Grace was president of.

In fact, that was how Grace and Max had first met— not only as neighbors, but as adversaries when she'd explained what he could and could not do with the house he'd just bought. There were tall trees lining the street, and the hydrangeas that seemed to be *everywhere* on the Cape were still blooming at the end of September. Jenn paused at the end of the street and looked back, jogging in place as she waited for a car to pass so she could cross over. If she had been interested in ever marrying and starting a family, Revere Street was the type of place that would be perfect for that. But that wasn't going to happen. Not for her.

She crossed the street and lengthened her strides. It felt good to move again. Almost like her old self, before… well…everything. She shook her head sharply as she ran. *Do. Not. Dwell.* Eventually, the rhythm of her shoes hit-

ting the sidewalk cleared her mind and she got into the
zone. No thoughts. Just movement and breathing. Within
two miles, she was entering the business center of Winsome Cove, still quiet this early on a Sunday morning.

She could understand why her family liked it here.
The businesses were painted bright colors, with images
of lobsters, crabs and clams everywhere. Main Street was
what Mom called the town's tourist hub. Lexi called it a
tourist *trap*. It was where all the retail shops were, filled
with T-shirts, hats, sunglasses and all sorts of knick-
knacks—from mugs to key chains to stuffed lobsters for
the kids. The biggest store was Admiral-Tees, owned by
Mom's friend, Genevieve, and her wife, Amy, the mayor
of Winsome Cove. She'd met both ladies at a women's
picnic her mother hosted at the Sassy Mermaid to welcome Jenn to town.

Jenn could see herself making friends here and staying. But was that what was best for her? She brushed a
wayward strand of hair from her face and looked across
Main Street at Sal's Seafood House—Nancy's favorite
lunch stop for all things fried. Devlin was the one who'd
handed Jenn an actual menu and pointed out an impres-
sive list of salads for the days she didn't want to choose
from beer-battered everything.

"Good morning, Weepy."

A familiar voice spoke behind her, and she stumbled
slightly before stopping and turning to face Cody O'Neil.
She'd been so lost in her own footsteps and thoughts
that she hadn't heard him approaching up Wharf Street,
which she'd just passed. Despite the cool weather, he
was in shorts and a well-worn gray sweatshirt that had
the word *Boston* emblazoned on it in faded red. The only

thing not faded or worn were his neon green running shoes. Her eyebrows rose at those—they were not at all what she'd expect him to buy.

"Uh…good morning," she replied, taking in his mussed mop of dark hair. He looked like he'd just rolled out of bed. "I…uh…didn't know you ran, Creepy." If he wanted to use their nicknames from their first meeting, she would, too.

"I haven't seen you out here before, either. New at it, or…?"

"Not new to running, but I've been a bit distracted lately…" This felt awkward, making small talk with him on the sidewalk in a still-sleeping town. But it would also be awkward to just turn and jog away from the man. "You're a morning person, too?"

"I never was before," Cody said, making a quick face. "But I'm starting to appreciate the peacefulness of running in the early morning." He gestured at the empty sidewalk in front of them. "Mind if I join you, or would you rather run alone?"

He knew his runner's etiquette, at least. Never fall in with someone without their permission. She hadn't seen him away from his real estate job—at the open house or in the office—since they'd met. It might be crazy, but she was too curious to decline his offer.

"Feel free to join," she said. "Although I have to warn you, I'm not out here to run a marathon in record time or anything. If you need to go on ahead of me, just do it."

"It's fine. I'm not training for a race, either."

They fell into step with each other. His stride was longer, of course, but he adjusted his pace so they were in sync. They ran the last few blocks in town, then he turned down a side road. She slowed, not sure how many miles she had in her.

Cody smiled at her over his shoulder. "It's only a mile longer than taking the main road, and it's more scenic."

She followed, recognizing the street name now. "This is where my sister and her family live. Sam owns the marina. And my mom's motel is at the other end of it—the Sassy Mermaid Motor Lodge."

He nodded. "I've met Sam. And your sister runs the restaurant next to the office, right? The food's good there. Whenever I'm feeling flush with cash, I pick up a take-out meal from there."

"No one to dine with in public?"

"Team Single, remember? And sitting at a table alone just feels…pathetic."

She gave a little laugh. "Team Single—I like it." They ran a few more strides. "And I know what you mean. Eating alone in public isn't my favorite thing, either."

"Maybe we could have dinner together some time, just so we don't lose our restaurant manners."

She slowed. "Are you asking me on a *date*?"

"Uh, no." He gave her a look that suggested she was mildly insane. "I'm asking you to sit at the same table as me and eat a meal. Two single people, staying single, but eating together so we don't look like weirdos."

"People might talk." She said the words playfully, but this was a very small town.

Cody chuckled. "Oh, people would *definitely* talk, but that's their problem, not ours. But if you don't want to eat with me, that's fine. It was just a suggestion."

"It just feels…too much. Sorry." They ran past the marina, and she hoped her sister wasn't looking out any windows to see her jogging with Cody. The questions would be endless.

"Too soon after your ex screwed you over?"

Cody's question came out of the blue, and her stride faltered again. She'd almost forgotten that he knew so much of her story.

"Something like that, yeah."

Neither of them spoke until they went by the Sassy Mermaid. Her mother's motel was straight out of the 1950s, with orange, turquoise and brown doors on the rooms. Mom had embraced the vintage feel and redecorated all the rooms in mid-century modern style, down to the drapes with giant daisies on them, and wildly patterned wallpaper in the bathrooms.

"Your mom's quite the character," Cody said.

"That's putting it mildly." Jenn shook her head. "She wasn't always, you know. When we were kids, she was just an ordinary suburban mom. Her wardrobe was navy blue and shades of brown, and so was the interior of our colonial house. Her hair was nowhere near being hot pink, and she wouldn't have been caught dead wearing anything in leopard print."

Cody snorted. "I think she was wearing leopard print pants the first time I met her. What made her change?"

Jenn thought for a moment. "I think she had this version of herself bottled up all those years she was with my dad. She wanted to create a home he'd be proud of, and one that was loving and secure for the three of us kids." She was glad when they moved past the motel, as she didn't need her mother seeing them together, either. "My dad was a serial cheater, by the way. Always has been. One day he came home and told her he'd actually fallen for one of the young chickies he ran around with, and he wanted a divorce. It sparked something inside of Mom. I think she finally admitted to herself how unhappy she'd been. Then she inherited this wacky motel on Cape Cod from an uncle she barely remembered, and here she is—thriving in Winsome Cove."

"Did I hear she was dating old Fred Knight at the bar?"

Jenn rolled her eyes. "No one really knows what's happening there. They're the epitome of on-again, off-again relationships. Fred was her plus-one at my sister's wedding, and he's coming to Max's wedding, too, if Fred and Mom don't kill each other by then. She was spittin' nails mad over something he said last week, so murder is a real possibility." Her right calf started to cramp, and she slowed to a walk and stretched it. "Sorry, it's been a while since I ran any distance at all, and my body's telling me about it."

"We can head back toward town on the main road." He stopped next to her. "Will you be able to walk it?"

"Sure." She hoped that was true. "Don't you have your daughter this weekend?" She remembered him mentioning that he'd be picking her up after he left the office on Friday.

His mouth thinned as he pressed his lips together. "That was the plan, but I took her back home last night. Turns out my ex forgot to tell me that Ava wanted to go to a friend's birthday party later today. The girl's mom is best friends with Lynn, so me taking Ava to the party wasn't going to work."

"So Lynn is your ex and Ava is…how old?"

"Eleven going on thirty."

Jenn smiled. "Oh, she's heading into her *tween* years. Not a child, but not quite a teenager, either. And those hormones…"

Cody had relaxed when the subject changed to his daughter, but now his forehead furrowed.

"The thought of all that—tweens, teens, hormones— scares me to death."

Jenn turned to face him, walking backward and grinning.

"A big, bad guy like you is *afraid*, Creepy? I don't believe it. What's scary about it?"

There was something about Jenn's smile that pinched Cody right in the center of his chest. They'd had some fun in the office the past week or two, but her smiles with him had always been a little guarded. Her laughter had been quick to fade, as if she didn't want to act overly friendly with him at work. But they weren't at work now, and no one else was around to worry about keeping up an act for.

He'd been surprised when he saw her jogging up Main Street, and even more surprised when she agreed they could run together. It had been nice to hear her talking about her family, but when she switched the subject to *his* family, it didn't feel so nice. She already knew the highlights of his situation, but even with no one nearby, he was hesitant to share too much, especially when it came to Ava. He'd gotten so used to not sharing his personal life since moving here that it had become second nature to deflect.

And yet…he'd just blurted out one of his greatest fears to Jenn. She had a way of getting him to open up without hesitation, and he wasn't sure that was a good thing. Time to change the subject.

"I'm not wild about being a Creepy dwarf."

She was still feeling sassy, walking backward and looking straight at him. "Well, I don't like being Weepy, either, but here we are… Whoa!"

He saw the ridge in the sidewalk just before her heel hit it. Her momentum sent her flying backward, mouth open in surprise, but he managed to catch her forearm and pull her upright. She ended up standing right in front of him, chest to chest. This close, he could see that her freckles, like tiny specks of cinnamon on her porcelain skin, were transparent. When her cheeks went pink, so did her freckles. It was…wonderful. He wondered if they tasted like cinnamon, too…

What the…?

He coughed, releasing her and taking a step backward. "Sorry to grab you like that—"

"You just kept me from landing ass-first on the sidewalk. Thank you!"

There was something fascinating about how she could look so…sweet, like a schoolmarm, with her reddish blond hair and freckles, and yet have such a quick, sharp tongue when she wanted to.

"What are you grinning at?" Jenn asked.

"You just surprise me sometimes," he answered, hoping she wouldn't probe any deeper.

"Yeah, well… I surprise *myself* these days, to be honest. Reinventing yourself isn't that easy when you don't know what you're reinventing yourself *into*." They started walking again, passing Wharf Street. "Hey, wait—you didn't answer my question. What scares you about Ava going through puberty?"

He winced at the word, and she grabbed his arm and stopped him. Again. Only this time, she waved a finger in his face.

"Don't do that," she said firmly. "Don't make faces about girl stuff. Especially around your daughter. Don't make her feel any more awkward than she already will when changes start coming. Has she started her period yet?"

He wanted to cover his ears. He wanted to be having *any* conversation other than this one, but Jenn was right. He couldn't stick his head in the sand and pretend his daughter wasn't growing up.

"I... I don't think so. She hasn't mentioned it, and neither has her mother."

"Well, you need to find out, Cody. And stop being scared. Kids are smart. They smell fear. Educate yourself and be someone she can talk to about these things."

They walked in silence for a few minutes. She was right, of course. He needed to educate himself. He'd been an only child, so he knew absolutely nothing about *girl stuff.* He'd have to do some research and teach himself what to expect. Or...he could just ask an expert.

Like the woman walking next to him, who didn't hesitate to put a finger in his face when he was wrong. But that seemed a step too far. They'd both managed to establish a *friendly coworker* relationship. It had started as an act for Nancy and Devlin's sakes, but she was genuinely funny and clever. Jenn had a way of making him feel lighter and more open when he was with her.

But that was dangerous. He needed to remember she knew secrets that could ruin things for him here. He needed to keep his distance.

Chapter Six

"Are you ready for the big, mushy girls' party this weekend?"

Jenn stared at her brother, Max, over the hood of her car and sighed. Living next door to him meant that some mornings they came outside at the same time. It wasn't as bad as her mother getting lucky in the room next door, but…it wasn't great. She'd known this could happen, of course, and neither he nor Grace had been intrusive in any way. She quickly smoothed her expression into a smile.

"Good morning! I can't wait for the shower—it'll be a blast!"

Damn, it was getting way too easy to lie to her family. The truth was that she was dreading Grace's "Christmas Tea Party" bridal shower this weekend. Max shook his head.

"I love the woman, but I'm sure glad Grace changed her mind about making it a couples thing. I'd feel like a bull in a china shop with all that frilly stuff she has planned for you—it's going to be a full-on Christmas cupid assault. In October." He brushed his hands together as if to wash himself of the whole thing, then pretended to hold up a mug of beer in a toast. "Me and the guys will be up in Boston at an Irish bar, thank you very much."

He had no idea how much Jenn wished she could join the men. But she was a bridesmaid and had no choice but to attend the shower on Sunday afternoon. It was being held at the local country club, where Grace's dentist brother, Aiden, was a member.

Their December wedding was *all* about Christmas. It was an extra-special holiday for them, so everything, even the shower, was Christmas-themed.

"Would it really be so terrible if I skip this thing on Sunday?" Jenn tossed her bag onto the front desk at Wharf Street Realty.

Nancy laughed as she lifted an enormous mug of coffee for a sip. The mug was blue, with a giant orange crab on it holding its *own* mug of coffee. "Girl, get a grip. You're going to a bridal shower, not an execution." Nancy's thick New England accent made the word *shower* sound like *show-ah*. Jenn had even heard the accent sneaking into her own family's conversations. Nancy waved her hand in the air. "Wear a pretty dress, drink some champagne, play the silly shower games, and be a good little bridesmaid. It's a couple of hours out of your life."

"You're right. I know. It's just…" Jenn sighed as she sat at her desk. "I *love* Grace, and she makes my brother so damn happy it makes me want to cry. Max has never smiled as much as he does these days, and that's because of Grace. And Tyler, of course. But…"

Max had discovered he was a father just a little over a year ago—the father of a five-year-old whose mother had just died in a car accident. Max used to make his living traveling from one Renaissance fair to another. He made swords and knives and metal sculptures. But a mutually-agreed-upon casual fling in Ohio had resulted in a pregnancy that Max never knew about. The mom had decided to raise Tyler on her own, but she'd put Max's name on the birth certificate. To say the news was a shock was putting it mildly, but Max had stepped up and settled down next door to Grace Bennett in Winsome Cove to raise his boy. Together they'd figured out a way to become a family. He still did metalwork for a living, but now he did it in the forge behind his house.

"But…?" Nancy coaxed. She'd finished her coffee, and immediately popped two sticks of gum into her mouth. She said the gum was to keep her from smoking, which she'd stopped doing thirty years ago.

"But I'm just so sick of romance being shoved in my face!" Jenn knew she sounded awful, but she needed to vent. "Everywhere I look it's hearts and cupids and couples cooing at each other like my whole family is in some sort of lovey-dovey *cult*. They weren't like this back in Iowa, that's for sure. My dad was a womanizer and my mother put up with it for years before she finally dumped him. So how are we suddenly the family of love?"

"Oh, wow…" Nancy's eyebrows rose dramatically. "I can see how terrible that must be, to see everyone you love being happy."

"Yes, I know I'm a terrible person. It's selfish to think of myself instead of them. But…" She took a deep breath and was shocked to realize it was shaky with sudden emotion. "I had a bad breakup, Nancy, and it happened right before I came here, so I'm just not in the mood."

Nancy nodded, suddenly serious. She walked over to where Jenn was sitting and perched on the corner of the desk. "After my Kenny died, I used to get mad whenever I saw other couples doing…couple stuff. It felt like salt being rubbed into an open wound. Even random strangers walking down the sidewalk together, laughing and holding hands, made me so sad, and then instantly angry. Why couldn't *I* have that? Did they have any idea how lucky they were?" She leaned toward Jenn. "What you're feeling is normal. But good God, you're young and smart and beautiful. You'll have another chance at love, I promise."

"That's just it, though. I don't want another chance. I'm *done*. I'm the odd one out in the Bellamy family, and that's okay. Love is not in the cards for me—I intend to be single *forever*."

"That's a pretty firm statement, honey." Phyllis Bellamy took Jenn's hand and squeezed it. "Forever is a very long time."

They were sitting at their table at Grace's shower, and Jenn had just explained to her mother the same thing she'd said to Nancy the day before. She'd skipped over the part of being sick of romance, of course, but felt she had to clarify things after a friend of her mom's had stopped by, giving Jenn and her mom a pointed look, and asking "Who's walking down the aisle next?"

Mom's relationship with Fred seemed to be on shakier ground lately, but she had a feeling that was a pattern with them. Mom was still an absolute romantic, especially now that her two oldest children had found love in

Winsome Cove. Jenn didn't want Mom to turn her cupid eyes toward *her*. Better to be honest and let everyone know it was not going to happen for her. And she was *okay* with that. Really.

"Mom's right, Jenn." Lexi was across the table, and looked concerned. "I had a bad breakup, too. I was done with men, but look at me now—a married mommy! Don't give up—"

"It's not about giving up," Jenn insisted. "*Giving up* implies I'm deciding not to chase after something I want. I don't *want* that." She gestured toward Lexi. "I'm happy for *you*. But this is more than a bad breakup or two. I don't feel like I'm cut out for being with someone, and that's *okay*. I'm *fine*. There are millions of happy single women in the world, and I'm one of them."

Her mother and sister both stared doubtfully at her, not saying a word. It was awkward being so serious in a room brimming with holiday sparkle. The function room at the country club was draped with holiday garlands and Christmas lights for the shower. The tablecloths were a mix of red and green linens, with Christmas tree centerpieces.

It was Grace's best friend and matron of honor, Maya, who broke the silence. "Look, I don't know any of your life stories or anything, and I'm a *very* happily married woman, but I do know that married life isn't for everyone. My big sister has never married, and she's happy as a clam. Has a great job, loves to travel, loves being auntie to her nieces and nephews, and she hooks up with a good man occasionally—just long enough to scratch that itch." Maya winked playfully, and everyone laughed. Jenn hadn't quite figured out what she was going to do about *that itch*. She liked sex, but unless it was in some random guy's back seat—very much *not* her thing—sex usually came with some sort of commitment.

Maya continued. "But my sis often says the world is annoyingly designed for pairs. She has to pay a big premium when she travels to have a room to herself. Some restaurants treat her weird when she dines alone. And people are *constantly* trying to set her up with someone. Especially at weddings. She skips them whenever she can—not because she's against marriage, but because it feels like pressure to her."

Jenn nodded emphatically in agreement, surprising her mother.

"Honey, is that why you've been so twitchy about the wedding events? You think we're pressuring you? So you don't like the hearts and kisses stuff."

Lexi started to laugh before Jenn could respond. "If that's the case, you're totally screwed with this wedding. Not only are you a bridesmaid, but Grace is going all-out on the frilly stuff." She glanced guiltily at Maya. "Which is lovely, of course."

Maya barked out a loud laugh. "I get you, girl. It's a lot. I know it's a Christmas wedding, but even *I* didn't realize how over-the-top Grace was going to go. Thank God she's not being a bridezilla about anything, but I never pictured my practical girl being this sparkly."

Jenn welcomed the chance to laugh, and to talk about *anything* other than her singlehood. She reached out and flicked a branch of the miniature white Christmas tree centerpiece with her finger. Each table had one, adorned with tiny crystal ornaments and red velvet ribbons, with tiny gold satin tree skirts. The tree toppers were little gold cupids. The Christmassy porcelain teacups were mementos the guests could take home, and each saucer had Max and Grace's names and their December wedding date etched in gold. Jenn sighed. "Grace has definitely embraced the sparkliest of holiday spirits."

Her mom agreed. "I thought Iowa was all about the cutesy theme weddings, but I have *never* been to a holiday tea party bridal shower. And she said you bridesmaids are carrying furry white hand muffs instead of flowers at the wedding?"

Lexi nodded. "We're trying to talk her out of white ones. All we'd be missing would be the ice skates, and I'm half-afraid she'll pop that on us as a last-minute surprise."

"Hey, ladies!" Grace, the bride-to-be, walked up to the table, and didn't seem to notice the flurry of coughing and throat-clearing at her arrival. "Sorry I was gone so long, but I felt I should visit each table and chat, you know? Isn't this holiday tea party theme fun?"

"It's the cutest!"

"Really unique, Grace!"

"Very clever!"

"*So* unique!"

Grace paused, her eyes narrowing just a bit. Jenn had learned Grace was caring and kind under her sometimes brittle exterior. She was also very smart.

"You hate it," Grace said flatly.

"No!" Lexi jumped up and gave Grace a hug. "No, of course not! We love *you* and this really is—"

"If you say *unique* again, I swear…" Grace held up her hand. "I mean, I *wanted* it to be something special. We've already put two households together, so we don't need much, and a kitchen and bath shower with a tea party seemed like a good fit."

"It's a perfect fit, Grace." Jenn put her hands on her chest, not willing to allow Grace to feel bad for another minute. "Blame it on me. I was being a humbug about all things romance before you walked over, and…well…" She nodded toward the miniature cupid atop their centerpiece tree.

"Ohhh." Grace's expression softened. "I know it's not my usual thing, but Tyler suggested we have an over-the-top Christmas wedding, and…well… I know it seems silly. In fact, *silly* is the point. One thing Max and I learned last year was that Christmas can be goofy and childlike and still be full of love, so we told Tyler we'd do it. But it must seem overwhelming. I'm sorry—"

"No, don't you dare apologize! We're gonna be sisters, and if *you're* happy, I'm happy. Besides, everyone here talked me out of my little pity party and I'm fine now."

"That's good," Maya said, standing. "Because it is time for the games to begin!" She clapped her hands to get everyone's attention as another woman—Jenn thought she was the Winsome Cove mayor, but she might have been the mayor's wife—handed out printed forms to all the tables.

"Ladies," Maya's voice rose, "we are starting with *He Said, She Said*, and we're playing this one as teams. Each table has to decide whether it was Max or Grace who said each line on here. You've got five minutes to decide, and the winning table will receive some special gifts— fancy teas to take home with your teacups. And…" She paused for dramatic effect. "*All* tables will be receiving bottles of a little somethin' somethin' to *add* to your tea while you're here. The sober part of this event is *over*!"

Cheers and laughter rose up around the room. Their table was exempt from this game, since they were mostly family and the bride was sitting right there. But the next games were open to all, some as table teams and some as individuals.

Guess How Many Condoms in the Jar.

Pin the Veil on the (picture of) the Bride.

Match the Quotes to the Right Romantic Movie.

Jenn gave it her all, determined to be a good sport for Grace. Also because her mother kept giving her the *concerned mama* side-eye. She even contributed to the big Date Night Jar, where everyone was encouraged to give suggestions for places to go or things to do on date nights for the couple-to-be. Since she wasn't all that familiar with Winsome Cove, she didn't suggest a place. But she *did* suggest something to do. At home. In the privacy of their bedroom. Lexi peeked at what she wrote and gave her a wink, speaking softly enough to keep it between them.

"Excellent choice. Especially for someone who is determined to never be with a man again."

"I never said I was going to be celibate." She winked right back but felt a weight in her chest.

She was going to have to figure out how to navigate that, especially being the new girl in town. A man's touch was still something she wanted. She just didn't want the *man* once it was over.

Chapter Seven

Cody plopped down on his sofa with a heavy sigh, pushing a pile of Ava's bright pillows out of the way with one hand while clutching a can of soda with the other. The pillow collection had grown to at least a dozen over the past few weeks. And they'd finally agreed on a long, narrow painting above the sofa—it was a splashy, modern take on an ocean sunset, with a sailboat leaning into a turn. Ava insisted the intense colors were just right with the pillows, and he couldn't argue with that. At least it didn't have fur or sequins. It was one hell of a lot better than the giant carousel horse, which now hung in her bedroom.

He leaned his head back and closed his eyes. He'd done two different open houses that Sunday—one in Winsome Cove in the morning for Devlin and one in Hyannis in the afternoon for an agent he knew from another office. He tried to stay busy on the weekends when he didn't have Ava, just to avoid sitting around the empty apartment. He missed his daughter's chaotic energy when she wasn't there.

Luckily, it wasn't hard to stay busy on the weekends in real estate. When he wasn't actively showing homes to clients, he was volunteering to sit at open houses for friends, or driving around to view properties he wanted to learn more about. Anything other than sitting in this apartment in silence. Silence and boredom weren't good for his sobriety.

Selling homes on the Cape was a different world from selling houses up in Boston. A lot of the properties were second homes or investment properties for rentals. And they were all very expensive. He'd shown a house just last week that was barely eight hundred square feet and was listed for a half million dollars. His buyer didn't believe him when he said it would probably sell for over asking price, but sure enough, it was already under contract.

He'd picked up a new listing to sell that week, which was very good news. An elderly couple had owned the farmhouse in Falmouth for decades, but they couldn't keep it up any longer. Their son and his family lived in California and didn't want it. It needed updating, but nothing major, mostly paint and floors. Cody smiled to himself, eyes still closed. Maybe he should recommend Ava's decorating expertise to whoever bought it.

Things were still fragile, but getting better between him and Ava, thank God. He knew that was partly because she was having so much fun filling his apartment with pillows. It felt like she wanted to trust him but just couldn't do it yet. The idea broke his heart a little.

He didn't think her mother, Lynn, had badmouthed him to their daughter intentionally, but Ava was sensitive enough to pick up on her mother's doubts about Cody. Lynn didn't wish him ill, or at least, he *hoped* she didn't. But his actions when they were married had hurt her and Ava. His drinking. His anger. His PTSD. He knew Lynn was hopeful, but unconvinced, about his current sobriety. Patience wasn't his finest trait, but he was working on it. Malcolm had told him it was going to take more time with some people than others to re-earn trust, and the people closest to addicts tended to be the ones who were hurt the most and took the longest to truly forgive…if ever.

He took a sip of his cola. Fretting about what he couldn't control wasn't healthy. He had to accept it and focus on doing better. It was all part of the process, and he'd prove himself somehow.

Cody sat up abruptly when he heard the door to the office open downstairs. It was almost six o'clock on a Sunday, and Devlin had said he was going to be in Boston with his cousin Sam, and Sam's future brother-in-law, Max Bellamy. They were avoiding the big bridal shower by heading to an Irish bar and watching the New England football team play on television. Devlin had invited Cody to join them, but an afternoon and evening in a rowdy bar was a bad idea for him. He'd have to explain why he wasn't drinking alcohol like the rest of the boys, and it felt like too much effort. It was another reason why he'd booked two open houses today. *Sorry, too busy.*

He could hear drawers being opened and closed downstairs. Maybe Nancy was dropping off a contract? He was sure he'd locked the front door, but just in case, he went to investigate. It would be terrible to sit there assuming it was Nancy and then discover they'd been burglarized. And there had been a couple of break-ins in town recently. He moved down the stairs quietly, opening the door just enough to see into the office.

It wasn't Nancy. And it wasn't a burglar. It was worse than that. It was Jenn Bellamy. It was hard enough to stop thinking about her, and here she was showing up on a Sunday night. She was muttering to herself while shuffling through some folders on the reception desk. She found what she was looking for, and he smiled when he heard her self-satisfied "Aha!"

She looked different. Instead of her usual practical slacks and long cardigans—she told Nancy once that it was her schoolteacher uniform—she was in a pale green dress that swirled around her calves when she moved. A matching jacket was tossed on the desk. Her reddish-blond hair was in Hollywood waves, falling loose past her shoulders. A few strands were pulled back from the sides into a barrette with tiny silk roses on it.

They'd spent a lot of their working hours snarking on other people and having a good laugh together. He'd learned that, despite her Iowa schoolmarm image, she had a sharp wit and a sharper tongue. But this look softened everything about her. Even her sensible flat shoes were gone, replaced with bone-colored pumps with a short, skinny heel. She spotted him peering through the door and turned with a startled squeal.

"Oh my God!" One hand rested on her chest. "Are you *trying* to scare me to death, Cody? What are you doing lurking back there in the shadows like a psycho murderer? Maybe I *should* call you Creepy."

He winced, stepping into the office. "Sorry, Weepy. I didn't mean to look like I was spying on you. I heard a noise down here and I know Devlin's not back until later, so I came to check it out. Aren't you supposed to be at a shower or something?"

"I escaped." She took a sharp breath, then waved her hand back and forth as if she was erasing her words.

"Forget I said that. It was a lovely shower, but I scooted out as soon as I saw a few other ladies heading home. On the way back, I remembered that I told Nancy I'd rewrite a couple of property descriptions for her, so I thought I'd get a head start tonight at home."

Cody wasn't surprised that Nancy had asked Jenn for help. Nancy was great at sales but tended to stick to the blunt facts with her listing descriptions. *Three-bedroom, two-bath home on a quiet street in Mashpee. Come check it out.* Where Jenn's descriptions were almost poetic. *Picture yourself hosting cookouts by the pool at this recently remodeled ranch in Mashpee with three large bedrooms and two bathrooms. The open floor plan is perfect for entertaining...*

Jenn had a way with words, whether she was using them as weapons or as marketing copy. He couldn't help noticing she had a way with wearing a dress, too. She was comfortable in it, but it changed how she carried herself just a little. Or maybe it was because they were alone together in an office getting darker by the minute. Neither of them had turned on any lights, and the shades were pulled on the front windows, only allowing outside light along the narrow transom windows at the top, where no one could see in.

Cody leaned his shoulder against the doorframe and smiled. "You escaped, huh? The shower wasn't your idea of a good time?"

"It's all just a little too lovey-dovey for me."

"Isn't *lovey-dovey* the whole point of a wedding shower, or a wedding, for that matter?"

She gave him a pointed look. "You, of all people,

know why I'm not crazy about that stuff. It's the last thing I want in my life and the last thing I want to see."

He remembered the story of her ex sharing embarrassing photos of her, costing her a job she'd loved. "Yes, I know. And *you* know I feel the same way. I'm done with all of that, too. It's not worth the effort for me to become someone else's dream version of me."

"Exactly!" Jenn said, flipping her hair over her shoulder. "People *change* when they fall in love, as if a requirement of their relationship is giving up who they really are. You should have met my sister before she met Sam and had Amanda. Lexi was the queen of snark and cynicism. Now she's all soft and gooey and she feels like a stranger to me." Jenn slapped the folders in her hand down against the desktop with a smack. "And now my brother—the surly nomad swordmaker who never had any roots—is not only a *dad*, but he's getting married to the nicest, classiest, most settled-down woman ever. He's marrying a woman who just had a Christmas *tea party* for a shower. Who *are* these people?"

She sat hard on the edge of the desk, her face pink with emotion. "Even my *mom* is part of a couple now." She was almost talking to herself, her voice low as she scowled at the floor. "My stupid *dad* got married. That'll never last, but still…everyone is part of a couple. And me? I'm the female version of 'Just Ken.' I'm Just Jenn. Me. Alone. I mean, I'm better off that way, because I clearly missed the coupling gene the rest of my family got. I don't *want* to be a couple, but sometimes…" Her words trailed off. She seemed to have forgotten Cody was even there and startled when he pushed off the wall and walked toward her.

"But sometimes…?" he asked. He stopped a few feet away, but close enough to see something he recognized in her shimmering gray-blue eyes. Loneliness. It was the downside of avoiding relationships.

She buried her face in her hands. "And here I go having another whiny meltdown in front of you. I want you to know that I'm not always a complete basket case." She glanced up at him through her fingers. "I used to have an actual grown-up life, until my rotten taste in men screwed me over one last time." She dropped her hands to her lap. "I *want* to be alone. But all this wedding stuff is just getting worse the closer we get to the date." She sighed. "If only society was evolved enough to allow a woman to be single without constantly trying to fix her up in a relationship. To allow a woman to have a freakin' one-night stand if she wants, with*out* all the baggage of *oh, are you dating now? Is it serious? Do you think he's the one?*" She'd worked herself back up into a fury again. "Why can't I just *be*, without everyone wanting me to be *with*?"

"Do you *want* a one-night stand?" The words sounded rough in his own ears, as if they'd worked their way out of his mouth of their own accord, without his permission. And hearing them aloud made his pulse go hot.

"Out of everything I just said, *that's* what you heard?" He shrugged, not denying that it was the most interesting part…to him. Jenn pushed herself farther back to sit on the desk, on top of her jacket, her feet swinging below her, making the hem of her dress move like a soft bell. "But yes, I want to be *able* to have a one-night stand without any of the baggage. Does that make sense?"

Surprisingly, it *did* make sense to him. "Yeah, it would

be nice to have a physical outlet with someone without things getting weird. And no offense, but women tend to get serious *fast* once you sleep together. Blowing up my phone, showing up to 'surprise' me somewhere—" he made air quotes around *surprise* with his fingers "—wanting to meet my daughter. It doesn't matter how firmly I say there's not a chance in hell of us getting serious, or how emphatically they agree, I can see them taking it as a challenge. And the ones who *are* totally fine with just sex are not..."

"Right? It's a paradox. The guys who want one-and-done tend to be the type who expect me to climb in the back seat of their car in some parking lot, and...ew."

He chuckled. "And the women who want a one-night stand think they can convince me to give them a relationship once I sleep with them."

They stared at each other for a long moment in silence. He'd moved closer as they'd talked, and Jenn finally started to laugh.

"Wow, are we a jaded pair or what? People should be grateful they can't get either of us into a relationship. We're terrible people!"

He started to agree, then thought better of it. "Not terrible. We're...honest."

"Cody, I'm mad at my family because they're *happy*. That makes me a terrible person."

"No." His voice was firm. He was close enough now to reach out and take her hands in his. "You and I have been through it, and we're smart enough not to want to go through it again. That doesn't make us terrible. But it can make us tough for other people to understand. We're...we're defying all of their expectations."

She lifted her chin, chewing her lower lip. "So you're saying we're somehow more evolved than they are?"

"Something like that, yeah." She hadn't pulled her hands away. They were soft and warm, and he didn't want to release them. "Look, I know for a *fact* that I am not relationship material. I'm not any good at it, and I don't want it. Ever. If that means I become some sexless old hermit, then fine." He chuckled. "Well…not fine, but…"

Jenn's smile was wistful, and she was staring off into space over his shoulder as she spoke.

"I don't know if I'd say I'm bad at relationships, but I'm *terrible* at choosing men. My sister says I'm a tool magnet, and she doesn't even *know* how accurate that is. The men I date are universally *bad* people. If that's fate's way of telling me that I am destined to be alone, I accept that." She gave him a pointed look. "But I haven't quite accepted the idea of being a sexless hermit."

All this talk about wanting sex and climbing into back seats and not wanting to be hermits made his pulse go hot. A beautiful, smart woman had just announced to him that she was looking for commitment-free sex. And that just happened to be Cody's specialty.

They stared at each other for what seemed like forever. He didn't remember moving, but somehow he was standing between her open legs. He lifted his hand toward her face, then hesitated. Her lips parted and she ran her tongue across them nervously. She was *killing* him. The question of will they or won't they was hanging in the shimmering air between them. Every second that passed added to the torture.

She was struggling, too. He could see the battle behind

her eyes. He wasn't going to rush anything. Wouldn't try to convince her. This had to be mutual.

Just when he thought it was over, her gaze changed. It went soft, and her eyes grew dark and round. She was in this with him. But despite all her talk, he needed to be sure.

"Any kind of relationship between us would be a disaster. But…" His fingertips brushed her cheek, and she leaned into him until her face was cupped in his hand. His heart wasn't racing. Instead, it was beating slow, but so strong that he could feel it like a drumbeat in his chest. "…what if we *don't* have a relationship? Are the two of us evolved enough to have sex and not get all lovey-dovey about it?"

"You're asking if we can be friends *and* lovers, but without the love part?" She patted the desk next to the jacket she was sitting on. "Maybe have a quick shag on top of this desk right now and *not* have any baggage afterward?"

Yes, please!

He rested his hands on her waist, his fingers slowly tugging her skirt up. He had no idea how they'd reached this point, but he had no intention of stopping. Not as long as Jenn was as enthusiastic as he was. Judging from the way she'd scooted forward on the desk, and the way her hands were tugging on his belt buckle, she was *very* enthusiastic.

Jenn could feel the heat radiating from Cody, pulling her in. She could feel her own arousal rising inside of her. She wanted him. There'd been a spark of sexual attraction between them from the moment they'd met, without any of that pesky emotional attraction. Here in this moment, he made her feel desired.

Will had taken that away from her. He'd turned physical intimacy into something cheap. He'd weaponized it against her. If she and Cody could do this, and do it right, it might help her heal. She leaned back, looking up into his eyes. He froze, waiting for her to speak.

"He took something from me," she said. Cody frowned in confusion as she continued. "He took away my ability to trust my heart, but he also made me look at sex as something—" she glanced away "—as something that was transactional. Able to be used against me. He took my sexual agency away from me, Cody, and I want it back."

He paused, then brushed his knuckles softly down her cheek. "I can help with that. The physical part. No hearts involved." He moved against her, his chest brushing hers. His face was just above hers. His lips…right there.

She started to turn her face up toward his. She wanted to kiss those lips. But she pulled back again, shaking her head sharply. "This is crazy. We're crazy to do this. I barely know you." Her body was absolutely humming with desire. And fear. Cody looked deep into her eyes for a moment, then stepped back, taking his heat with him. He held both hands up.

"It only works if we're on the same page, Jenn. You say you don't know me, but you know more about me than anyone else in Winsome Cove does, other than my sobriety sponsor."

Too fast. This was happening too fast. She was exhausted from putting on a happy face at the shower, and Cody was someone who understood. But this was crazy…

wasn't it? Or did it actually make perfect sense? She'd been missing a man's touch, and here was a man ready to make love to her on a desktop—which was totally *hot*. If he could be believed, he didn't want anything more from her than that. And as long as she was willing, was it really wrong? She'd just told him she'd lost her sexual agency, and now she had a chance to reclaim it.

She must have taken too long to think it through, because Cody took another step back. She grabbed his shirt to stop him, then tugged him closer. The corner of his mouth lifted in amusement.

"Are we doing this, or...?"

She tugged again, and he was hard against her. And... *hard* against her. Something low inside her went soft and warm. But she still had to be practical. "This can't turn into anything resembling a relationship."

"Jenn, you have nothing to worry about. Believe me when I say I want a relationship even less than you do. But... I want *this*."

His hands were back on her waist now, gently tugging her skirt up above her thighs. She started pulling his rugby shirt up out of his jeans. Her fingers brushed on his skin and she nearly gasped from the spark she felt. And she didn't want to waste any more time fretting about the rules.

"No hearts. No feelings. Just bodies." She started to unbutton his jeans. He started doing the same to her dress, slowly and gently. His fingers brushed her breasts as he worked, sending a shiver from her toes to her scalp.

"Just bodies," he echoed.

Chapter Eight

Cody murmured the words under his breath, then forgot what they were even talking about as he pushed Jenn's dress off her shoulders, revealing a yellow bra trimmed in lace. *Sweet mother of God.* Jenn's breasts were plump and full. Inviting. She'd been right to say this was crazy, yet here they were, undressing each other in the semi-dark office. He sure hoped she'd be able to keep her promise to keep emotions out of this, because he wanted her, and he wanted her right-the-hell now. Right here. She undid his zipper and pushed at his jeans.

"No kissing," she said, still concentrating on getting his jeans past his hips.

He was cupping her breasts in his hands through her bra.

"Yeah, sure." He mumbled his response, distracted as he reached behind her to unfasten her bra. Her breasts barely shifted when he slipped the bra away from her. Round. Full. Perfect.

"I'm serious, Cody." Her tone forced him to look up. "No kissing. No snuggling. Nothing that might feel like relationship territory. Let's avoid any chance of confusion."

Cody quickly glanced back down at her chest. Not

kissing her mouth would be torture, but worth it if it meant getting the rest of her. But not kissing *those* would be criminal. "How about…no kissing on the lips?" He understood her concerns. Kissing on the mouth was intimate. "I mean…if it's gonna be just sex, then we should at least make sure it's pleasurable sex."

She considered, then nodded. She'd managed to push his jeans, along with his briefs, down over his hips, freeing him. "No kissing on the lips," she said, glancing down at his rock-solid erection. "And definitely pleasure."

Her jackass of an ex had taken something away from her, and Cody wanted to give it back. He wanted her to enjoy this. He hesitated. They were in the office. She was on a desk. Wouldn't a woman want something… softer? And safer?

"We don't have to do this here. My bed's right up the stairs, and so are my condoms."

Jenn shook her head. "I'm on the pill. And this is where I want to be."

"Are you sure…?"

"We're doing this here, Cody."

He hesitated again, unsure what Jenn really needed, despite what she said she wanted.

Meanwhile, she was shimmying her way out of her panties while sitting, sliding them off and kicking them away with her toes. And suddenly he no longer had the desire to sort this out in his mind. Her shoes had come off somewhere along the way. The top of her dress was unbuttoned and open to her waist. Her skirt was hiked up to her hips. His thumbs brushed her breasts. She slid forward until they touched—her warmth was as soft as he was hard. His mind went blank of any thoughts other than being inside her.

"Now, Cody," she said in a voice so whiskey-deep that it wound through him, around him, moving him closer. Her hand slid down his back to cup his buttock, and she put her mouth next to his ear. "Here. Now."

And that was it. He slid into her with a groan of white-hot pleasure. Jenn wrapped her legs around his hips and held him there, and neither of them moved. They were both so completely in the moment, their breaths deep and in sync. He wasn't sure who began moving first, but they were in sync there, too. Slow and easy. He leaned her back on the desk and held her dark gaze. His hands went from her breasts to her hips, and he held her in place as they picked up the pace. She let out a moan and her head dropped back. They were…incredible…together.

Her legs tightened around him and he lifted her upright again, wanting to have her body against his when they came. Jenn's arms locked around his neck, and he thought he felt her lips brush his shoulder. Then her teeth against his skin. Everything went red behind his closed eyes, then burst into a flash of white when they both reached release at the same time. He yelled something, but he wasn't sure what. Did he cry her name out loud, or was it just a bellow of incomprehensible sound? Jenn was only slightly more composed. She was making sounds, but buried them against his neck as they rocked their way down from the peak of release.

He stroked her back slowly with one hand while holding her close with the other. There was a shimmer of sweat making her skin even softer, like silk beneath his fingers. He was lost in the pleasure of touching her. Holding her while still buried inside of her. And not wanting to move. Ever.

This was different. *Everything* felt different. And he couldn't wrap his head around why. He'd had sober sex before, so it wasn't that. He'd had plenty of boozy sex, too, but nothing like this. He'd even had desktop sex before, although never in his own workplace. *Sorry, Devlin.*

Jenn's body began to soften against him, as if drained of strength. He knew the feeling. He rested his cheek on top of her head. Was this that *snuggling* thing she'd warned against? He closed his eyes. He didn't care. He wasn't letting go. Not yet.

Jenn's brain and her body were having two totally different conversations at the moment. Her brain was telling her she'd just made a terrible mistake—having sex with a coworker was a horrible idea. Having sex with *Cody O'Neil* was a nightmare. He knew all of her vulnerabilities. And she'd shared even more tonight when she blurted out that bit about Will taking something from her. What was it about this man that made her share every personal thought that crossed her mind? She should push him away, get her clothes back together and get the hell out of here as quickly as possible. They would never speak of this again. Even when she had to come to work and sit at this very same desk.

You are a foolish, desperate woman!

But Jenn's body was responding very differently. Her body *had* been desperate, but it wasn't anymore. Now it was satisfied. Like…*really* satisfied. Almost defiantly so, as if making love to Cody could purge all the frustrations she ever had about everyone else in the world hooking up as couples. And it had worked. If she had been capable of glowing from satisfaction, she was sure her body would now be glowing brightly enough to light the room. And all *without* the entanglement of a relationship. That…that…*whatever* it was they'd just done, had been exactly what her body needed. Hard. Fast. Forbidden. Commitment-free. And very, very good.

Gurrl…you need to do that again.

No. She straightened in Cody's embrace, lifting her head. She didn't want to pull away, but they'd agreed to no cuddling. Neither of them spoke. They just stared in silence. He looked nervous, afraid to do something wrong. Her mouth twitched. She probably looked the same.

"I'm not sure that was a good idea," she said softly.

"Maybe not," he answered. "But it *was* very good."

She started to giggle. She hadn't giggled in a long time. "I can't argue that. It was… Well, it was what I needed. Thank you."

His face twisted. "Sex isn't transactional, remember?" He smoothed her hair back from her face. Why did his touch still feel like fire on her skin? He lightly tapped her chin to get her attention. "I didn't do it *for* you. You didn't do it for me. No thank-yous required. This is where we find out if we can keep our deal—no relationship baggage."

"I can keep the deal if you can," she said emphatically. Maybe *too* emphatically.

He stepped back with a chuckle, gently pulling her skirt down over her legs. She made a mental note to be sure to find her panties before leaving. Having Devlin or

Nancy discover those in the morning would be mortifying. Cody pulled up his jeans and winked at her.

"That sounds like a challenge. Are we putting money on who can hold out the longest?"

"No." She fastened her bra and began buttoning her dress. "Because that means we're expecting one of us to get mushy about this, and that is not going to happen." She wouldn't let it happen.

Cody tugged his shirt over his head. "Fair enough. I think we're in agreement that any of that romance nonsense would spoil things."

His head came back into view as he pulled the shirt down. His dark hair was tousled and on end. Had *she* done that? She had a vague memory of clutching his hair when they'd both hit their climax. She reached up and ran her fingers through it, in an attempt to settle it. Good lord, he was one handsome man. Too bad she'd met him after swearing off all men, because the heartache might almost be worth it with a guy like this. He knew his way around a woman's body, and he'd set hers absolutely aflame.

He went very still, staring at her. She realized she was still stroking his hair—almost tenderly. *Oops.* She jerked her hand away and mumbled an apology. The fact was, she *had* sworn off men, and that was a good thing. Because she had an idea that losing *this* particular man—if they'd ever had a chance at a relationship—would really hurt.

Chapter Nine

Cody cleared his throat sharply at her sudden move and stepped out of reach. He wasn't sure what that little moment was when her fingers moved through his hair, but it felt...dangerous. They were both dressed now, and if anyone had walked in, they would never guess that Cody and Jenn had just made love on top of the reception desk. He couldn't stop a snort of laughter.

"Making love to you—to *anyone*—in this office was never on my bingo card." He looked around in amazement. The only light came from the streetlights outside, shining through the transoms above the window shades. The glow bathed the room in soft, muted shadows. No one walking by would have any idea they were there. "It's a good thing Devlin hasn't put up those security cameras yet."

Jenn looked around to the corners of the office, eyes wide with panic. "*Cameras?* Oh my God..."

"Relax. They're still in boxes over there behind his desk. Dev's a bit of a procrastinator." She'd gone pale, and he kicked himself. She was thinking about her ex and the trouble he'd caused with photographs. He should never have mentioned it. "Jenn, I promise—there are no cameras in here. The shades are all down. No one saw anything and no one will ever know about this other than you and I." He glanced at the front door. "You did lock that when you came in, right?"

Her eyes went even wider. "Um…no. I was planning to just grab the file and go right back out."

Cody laughed again. "Now, *that* would have been interesting. It's a good thing Devlin's up in Boston tonight."

Her cheeks went pink, but she joined him in laughter. "I didn't even think about it after you came down into the office. Can you imagine?" Her laughter faded. "That was so careless—"

He cupped her face in his hands and waited until they locked eyes. "Nothing happened. No cameras. No one walked in. Tonight was just between us." He released her and quickly moved to lock the door. "There's no sense tempting fate." On his way back, he noticed a pair of pale yellow panties dangling from the arm of Nancy's chair. He snatched them up and handed them back to Jenn, resisting the odd urge to stuff them into his own pocket. A memento of their wild and sexy little adventure. "But next time, let's use my bed upstairs, just to be safe."

He hadn't meant to speak his thoughts out loud, but there they were—out of his mouth and causing that bemused expression on Jenn's face. Yes, of course he wanted to do that again. She'd felt amazing in his arms, and their bodies were terrific together. Continuing this might be more dangerous than either of them was ready for, though. He thought of Malcolm's caution about getting into a relationship. But this wasn't that. It would never be that.

"Who said anything about a next time?" Jenn asked, one eyebrow arched high.

"Are you saying you wouldn't like to do that again?"

Her mouth opened to answer, then snapped shut as she considered the question. "It was fun, Cody. And yes, very satisfying. I'm just not sure if doing it again would be wise. After all, we agreed to no relationship stuff."

"I'm not asking to be your boyfriend, Jenn. But if one of us gets the itch and the other is willing…why not? It's just a sex thing, not a dating thing."

"Friends with benefits?" She was at least thinking about it, and that was a good thing.

"I think the new term is *situationship*. If the situation's right and we're both in the mood, we do it. If not, we don't. Meanwhile, we do our jobs and live our lives with no one else being the wiser."

"But you want me to come up to your apartment…"

"I didn't ask you to move in. Just to maybe enjoy each other for an hour or two, on a bed, without the risk of someone walking in on us. Eventually, Devlin *will* put those cameras up. This desk was fun and very, very sexy, but there's nothing wrong with being more comfortable."

"What about your daughter?"

"During the school year I only have Ava every other weekend, and a few holidays." He and Ava were just starting to rebuild their relationship, and bringing a new woman into the mix would *not* be helpful. "She wouldn't know anything."

Her lips pursed together as she thought about it. *Please say yes…*

"Planning feels too official, if you know what I mean. But I'm not going to say no to the possibility. Why not?"

Honestly, he could think of several reasons why not,

but he sure as hell wasn't going to mention them now. She was leaving the door open, and that was good enough.

His brave words about them being able to simply do their jobs and live their lives were much harder to act on in the real world. In the harsh light of Monday morning, walking past that reception desk without immediately picturing Jenn on it proved impossible. He could see her leaning back, sitting on her jacket, her hair splayed out on top of the folders. He picked up a property folder from his desk. Was this the folder that had been hidden under her? If he tried, would he be able to smell her perfume on the papers?

Get a grip, man.

He put the folder back in the organizer on his desk and tried to focus on anything but the image of him and Jenn making love right here in the office. The office where his boss, Devlin, was frowning at a large wall map of Cape Cod. He stuck a magnet with a tiny green flag on it somewhere in the vicinity of nearby Chatham. The green flags represented active listings of theirs. Yellow flags were properties under contract, and red were recent sales. The blue flags indicated rental properties they were managing. It was a fairly new side of the business, and a bit of a hassle, but Devlin liked the steady income it provided in between home sales.

"Is that the new commercial listing in Chatham?" he asked.

"Yes. There's an apartment above the former candle store, like we have here." Devlin closed the box of multicolored magnets and walked back to his desk. "The owner is a friend of mine, but the candle business was his wife's thing. They split up a few months ago, and she's moving to Maine. They agreed to sell the building and she'll get the profits, while he gets to keep their house. I think they'd have done better long-term to keep the downtown shop and lease it out for steady income they could split, but they want a clean break from each other."

"Kids?"

"No," Devlin answered. "It's just as well since things didn't work out, right?"

"It keeps things simpler, for sure."

One thing he was thankful for in his divorce was that Lynn was a Boston girl, born and bred. He couldn't imagine a situation where she'd ever decide to move and take Ava out of the Boston area. Devlin gave him a funny look.

"Was your divorce complicated?"

Cody hesitated. He liked Devlin a lot, but he'd kept his private life private since moving to Winsome Cove. The less he talked about it, the less chance there was of accidentally revealing the fist fight that cost him his last job, or his drinking problems, or the PTSD from his military service that had led to the drinking and the fighting. And to his divorce. He cleared his throat, still unsure how much to share.

"There's no such thing as a 'clean break' when there are kids involved," he finally said. "You can't just go your separate ways, you know? You're forever connected— birthdays, graduations, weddings... God forbid." He stared at the framed photo of Ava on his desk. She was giggling on the beach last summer, wearing giant red sunglasses she'd declared had *drip*. He assumed that was a good thing. She was growing up way too fast. "One thing we agreed on is that Ava is our number one priority, no matter what." He sighed, staring straight ahead but not seeing anything. "I didn't want the divorce, but I screwed up, and I *kept* screwing up." Kept *drinking,* to be accurate *"*Lynn rightfully got sick of it. But we're working at being better co-parents."

Devlin studied him for a moment, then smiled slowly. "Wow, that was the equivalent of an entire speech for you. You don't usually string that many sentences together at once, unless you're schmoozing a client." He chuckled. "Do I need to be worried?"

Damn. The Jenn-effect was spilling over into Cody's life even when she wasn't around. He was sharing information everywhere. As if he'd summoned her with just his thoughts, she walked in the door just then.

She smiled at Devlin, but the smile changed almost imperceptibly when her gaze hit his. There was a tightness at the corners of her mouth, as if she wanted to look disappointed to see him, but didn't dare in front of Devlin. She regrouped quickly as the door closed behind her.

"Happy Monday, guys! Nice to see the sun shining out there, isn't it?"

She set her tote bag on the front desk. The one where, just last night, she'd sat while he…

Her porcelain skin went even more pale, making her tiny freckles stand out across her cheeks. She was staring at the desktop, having the same memories he was having. He couldn't tell how she felt about those memories, though, not even when the color rushed back to her face. Embarrassed? Or aroused?

Devlin frowned and started to stand. "Is there a spider on your desk or something?"

Jenn flinched. "What? No, no. I thought I saw something but it was…just a shadow." *A shadow of a memory?* She sat down and fired up her computer. "What's on the agenda for today, fellas?"

Devlin sat back down and started scrolling on his tablet. "I left the folder for the new commercial property on your desk, and the photos are in the shared file," Devlin answered. "I'd like that one in the listing system this morning. Also, Nancy got an offer accepted yesterday on that house in Mashpee, so we'll need to get that contract processed and reach out to the attorneys and the bank, and get an inspection scheduled." He glanced over at Cody. "You got anything Jenn might need?"

It was a good thing that Devlin had his back to Jenn, because her face flushed red. Cody bit the inside of his cheek to keep from laughing. "I've got nothing for her this morning, but…maybe later." Jenn's eyes went wide, then narrowed dangerously at him. He held up a property file. "I'm doing a second showing at that place on the beach at one o'clock, and I think my buyers are ready to make an offer if there are no surprises."

"That would make for a sweet start to the week," Devlin replied, checking his watch. "I've got to run down to the condos in Woods Hole. The homeowners had their quarterly meeting on Saturday and the president wants to go over some concerns with me."

"Better you than me," Cody muttered, loud enough for Devlin to hear.

"I know the homeowners groups can be a pain," he said, heading for the door with a leather business bag in hand, "but it's a good, steady income stream. And this didn't sound like anything major—just some concerns about noise levels in the units that are being used as vacation rentals. I've looked into putting decibel monitors in the units like you suggested, and I think that might help a lot." He snapped his fingers and turned in the doorway. "Speaking of monitors, don't let me forget to put those security cameras up in here this week. There was another break-in up on Main Street last week, and having a security system should help deter any mischief."

"I agree," Cody said with the straightest face he could manage. "Cameras will definitely discourage mischief in the office."

Jenn glared at Cody until Devlin had securely closed the front door and walked away. She wanted to smack that smug look off his face. Or kiss it off…

Stop it!

They'd agreed to no kissing. And she should have flatly insisted on no *anything* after yesterday. One and done. Lots of fun—her body was still humming from it—but such a bad idea.

"There won't be any *mischief*—" she formed air quotes with her fingers "—to worry about, Cody. Especially if you keep up with all your cutesy little innuendos."

"No one knows they're innuendos except you and me. I doubt anyone in Winsome Cove would ever guess that you and I had sex on that very desk last night."

He walked over to where she was sitting, and she made a point to wheel her chair back away from him. There was that smug grin again. How could he possibly know what his touch had done to her last night? Had hers done the same to him? She licked her lips, and saw his caramel eyes darken to chocolate. Oh… Maybe she *had* had an effect on him. Was that a good thing? Probably not. But she couldn't help smiling just a little in satisfaction.

"We agreed last night that we'd come back to work just like normal," she reminded him, her voice low, even though they were alone. "And this—" gesturing at the small amount of space between them "—does not feel normal. Get back to your desk and do your job. I don't want to feel uncomfortable being in the office with you."

His smile faded, and he took a step back. "I don't want that, either." He ran his fingers through his hair, pushing it back. Just as *she* had done last night. He dropped his hand. "I was trying to keep things light, but it came across as juvenile. This is new territory for me, too. I've never had a relationship with anyone I worked with… directly."

"I told you it was a bad idea." She shook her head. Of course, she'd been just as eager for the release as he'd been. "And it's *not* a relationship."

"Okay," he answered, taking a seat back at his desk. He kept his voice at a near whisper. "I've never had *sex* with anyone I worked with directly. And I *still* say there was nothing *bad* about what happened yesterday."

Her curiosity was piqued. "Why do you keep clarifying it wasn't anyone you worked with *directly*?"

He stared at his desk and she could have sworn his cheeks went a bit red. "It's just…well, I haven't been a monk since my divorce, and I… I hooked up with another real estate agent, but she wasn't from my office. We saw each other a few times, but it's been awhile."

At first, she didn't recognize the sharp, hot emotion

sprinting through her veins. Like anger, but not quite. Why on earth should she care who he "hooked up" with? Or that it didn't sound like it was over? He only said it had been a while, not that it had ended. Then she realized what she was feeling.

Jealousy.

Which made absolutely no sense at all. They were two adults just getting a little sexual release with absolutely no emotions involved. *Especially* an emotion as ridiculous as jealousy. She pushed the reaction aside and sat up straight.

"Look, we both agreed this was just a…what did you call it? A *situationship*? I'm determined to never get involved with a man again, and you feel the same way about dating anyone, am I right?" He nodded and she continued. "If either one of us even begins to act like we're a *thing*, the other has to nip that in the bud immediately, okay?"

"You mean we need to keep each other honest?" He considered it. "That makes sense. In fact, we should watch out for each other with *other* people, too. You and I aren't a thing, but don't let me even *think* about getting serious with anyone *else*, either. And I'll do the same for you."

She wasn't sure she understood. "Are you saying we should be monogamous? We aren't even…" As much as she didn't like the idea of Cody being with someone else, committing to monogamy felt way too much like a relationship.

"I'm not talking about being monogamous with anyone. I don't even think monogamy is sustainable. But if you see me take some girl out more than once or twice, pull me aside and remind me that it's against the rules."

She shifted in her seat, fighting the irrational jealousy that tried to flare up again. But that feeling only proved Cody was right—they needed to help each other remember their commitment to *no* commitments.

"So we'd act as support buddies to each other? *Stay Single* coaches? What was it you said the other day? Team Single?"

"Exactly!" Cody leaned forward and rested one arm on his desk. "In the sobriety program, I have a sponsor, and he keeps me on track. Takes my calls anytime, always there to give me honest advice and encouragement. In fact, he's adamant that I avoid relationships completely while I'm still in my first year, because it could disrupt my progress. You'd be doing me a favor, Jenn."

She couldn't help a short laugh. "Are you suggesting we hold regular meetings?" Cody's eyes raked over her, and she felt the heat on every inch of skin his gaze touched. "I didn't mean *that* kind of meeting."

Cody sat back with a smile. "I already have meetings to attend each week, so I don't need another." She admired the work he was putting into staying sober. It couldn't be easy to do that, and also to hide it from everyone he knew. He turned serious. "The only way this works is total honesty, with no hurt feelings getting involved. If you see something, I want you to say something right away, whether I want to hear it or not. And I'll do the same."

"Okay," she agreed. Then she almost laughed again. "It's ironic that you and I are agreeing to this bluntly honest buddy system, considering the only thing we have in common is knowing each other's secrets." She paused. "And wanting to remain single forever."

His expression softened. "And having great sex together."

Ah yes, there was that.

And it was something she wouldn't mind doing again.

Which was still a very bad idea.

Chapter Ten

Cody was twenty minutes early for his agreed-upon pickup time for Ava. He parked at the curb in front of the two-story colonial he and Lynn had planned to live in forever. Together. Located in the Boston suburb of Dedham, the big old house was on a quiet street with spacious lots and mature trees. He'd managed to get it for a great price as a direct deal from an estate attorney who'd said the family was anxious for a quick, clean sale. The interior had been a near-museum-quality homage to the worst of early 1980s style, but Cody had done a lot of the heavy remodeling work himself. Lynn had been great with the paint and wallpaper work. Together, they'd made it a home.

And now he didn't even feel comfortable pulling in the driveway to get their daughter.

For a while after the split, Lynn wouldn't let him take Ava at all. It had ticked him off at the time, but looking back, he was grateful. He wasn't proud, but there had been too many times when he'd driven after drinking. After all, for a couple of years he'd been drinking nearly nonstop. If he'd ever had an accident with Ava in the car, he would never have forgiven himself. The thought of it was enough to make his stomach turn.

It took another year or so for the divorce to be finalized, and he was in a twelve-step program by then. But relapses are part of the early sobriety process, and every setback he had made Lynn that much more distrustful. Even now, with ten straight months sober, he only saw his daughter every other weekend. This past summer, Lynn had gained enough confidence in his sobriety that she'd allowed Ava to stay longer on the Cape with him a few times until school started. They were beginning to actually co-parent, instead of battling each other. It was good to be able to finally see his ex-wife's face without always seeing hurt and mistrust in her eyes.

To his surprise, the front door opened, and it was Lynn in the doorway, not Ava. She was waving to him to come inside. That didn't happen very often. Worried that something might be wrong with their daughter, he hurried out of the car and across the lawn.

"Come on in," Lynn said with a small but genuine smile. "Ava's still packing. I swear this fashionista era of hers is going to drive me out of my mind. Everything has to be a *statement* piece or she won't wear it. I mean, she's eleven."

He stepped inside, his tension easing at her relaxed chatter. "She's been redecorating my apartment."

Lynn's smile deepened. "Oh, I've heard all about it." She put her hand on his forearm. It surprised him—he hadn't felt her touch in a long time. He sensed caring, but the heat her fingers used to ignite was no longer there. The marriage was well and truly over. But hopefully a friendship could be built on the ashes. She pulled her hand back. "She told me about all the pillows you let her pick out, and something about a horse painting you didn't like?"

"I didn't *dislike* it, but a giant pink carousel horse was a bit much over my leather sofa. It looks nice in her room, though, which I suspect she planned all along."

Lynn laughed, tucking her dark bob behind her ears. "You're probably right. Our little girl is quickly becoming a clever preteen." Jenn had said the same thing. How scared should he be about this preteen stuff? Lynn's expression sobered. "I wanted to talk to you before Ava says anything." She glanced at the staircase, but Ava's music was still blaring in her room upstairs. "I'm... I'm seeing someone, Cody. And Ava met him last weekend."

The news landed the same as her touch had—as if he *should* feel something, but didn't. In another life, he'd have been devastated if Lynn fell for another man. But their marriage was done, and he was the one who'd broken it. If a new relationship made Lynn happy, then he was happy, too. Well...maybe not *happy*, exactly. But not upset. It seemed the normal progress of things. He realized she was staring at him, waiting for some kind of response.

"Is it serious?"

"It could be. I wouldn't let him meet Ava if there wasn't a chance it might become...something longer-term. We're taking things slow."

"Does he have kids?" Cody was finally thinking about how this might affect Ava. The divorce had been hard on her, and she was just beginning to get used to the shared custody routine, not to mention forgiving him for moving out to the Cape. A "new dad" and stepsiblings would be another huge adjustment for her.

"No. Brian's wife fought cervical cancer for years, and eventually died from it." She paused, as if trying to decide how much information to share. "He's a scientific engineer at the big robotic company in Waltham. A real brainiac, and a bit of a geek, but he's funny and...kind."

It was hard not to take the words as a personal condemnation, even though he knew Lynn didn't mean them that way. Cody was a soldier and a salesman—no one had ever accused him of being a brainiac. Or all that funny. Which was fine, but hearing Lynn mention kindness stung. She hadn't seen a lot of that from him in the final years of their marriage.

"You deserve someone kind, Lynnie."

Her eyes widened in surprise, then went soft, along with her voice. "I didn't mean..." She hesitated.

"I know," Cody said. "Don't apologize for moving on. I want you to be happy. How did Ava take to him?" He didn't mind the idea of Lynn moving on, but bringing some stranger into his daughter's life was another matter.

"She'll probably tell *you* more about that than she told me, but she seemed okay. She was a bit quiet with him at first, but we went hiking at Blue Hills and he was telling her all about the different plants and bugs they saw. You know how our girl loves to soak up information." She paused again. "He wants to take us to a football game next weekend. That's why I wanted to give you the heads-up. Ava will always be *our* girl, but new people are going to come into her life. I want you and me to keep each other informed, so there are no blindsides."

That was fair, except... "Just keeping it real, Lynn— *this* is a blindside. You didn't tell me about this guy until *after* he and Ava met. And you already have plans for next week together. I didn't even know you were dating."

Lynn's mouth stayed open for a moment before snapping shut. "My dating life is none of your business. I've been casually dating for over a year now. Brian's far from my first. I'm assuming *you* haven't been a saint since the divorce?"

Cody rubbed the back of his neck in frustration. He hadn't wanted this conversation to turn into an argument. "Serious dating is a no-no in the program, at least for the first year or so. But yes, I've seen a few women." *And made love to one incredible woman on an office desk a week ago.* "I'm not saying you need to update me on your dating life. But you introduced a man to our daughter. It would have been nice to know that ahead of time."

Lynn turned away with a heavy sigh, then called up the stairs. "Ava! Hurry up—your dad's here." She turned back to Cody. "You're probably right, but I don't like the idea of including my ex-husband in my love life."

"Not in your love life, just your co-parenting one." He took a breath and relaxed his shoulders. He did not want to fight with Lynn, because it was bound to devolve into tossing personal insults. They both deserved better than that. "I'm sorry. I didn't mean to make it sound like you need my approval. And I do appreciate you telling me about Brian. This is a new phase of divorce for us, I guess. Strangers joining our circle of three."

"There was a time when that idea was inconceivable. It was us three against the world." Lynn smiled softly, and Cody returned it. They had just crossed some very thin relationship ice, but the ice had held.

"I'm sorry I messed us up, Lynn."

She shook her head sharply. "We can't change it now. I'm glad to see you're getting closer to defeating those demons of yours. How many months?"

"Ten. It's easier this time—maybe because I've had enough relapses for it to finally stick, and maybe because I had that extra motivation." Like staying out of jail. The coworker he'd punched declined to press charges as long as Cody quit his job at the real estate office they shared, but it could have easily gone the other way.

"Congrat—"

"Daddy!" Ava's shout interrupted Lynn. "I didn't know you were inside." She stopped on the stairs, her backpack falling to her feet. She looked between Cody and Lynn. "Is something wrong? Are you still taking me this weekend?"

And there came another wave of guilt. Being in this house was making them hit harder. The pain he'd caused Lynn. And the pain his little girl had felt from the fierce battles her parents had here, and his drinking, and his random anger. The canceled custody weekends, sometimes canceled by him because he was on a bender, or canceled by Lynn out of spite or worry. He forced a reassuring smile onto his face, making a mental note to talk through all these feelings with Malcolm.

"Everything's great, baby girl!" She ran into his arms and he lifted her up for a tight hug. "Mommy and I were just catching up with each other. And I forgot to tell her that you and I are going whale watching this weekend!"

Ava let out a squeal. "Really? On your boss's lobster boat? Out on the ocean? Yay!"

He knew he'd made a mistake as soon as he saw Lynn's face. He'd just lectured her about blindsides, then sprung this on her. He mouthed *sorry* as he set Ava on her feet and rushed to explain all the safeguards.

"It's actually my boss's cousin, so it's not the lobster boat. Sam has a big cabin cruiser, with a sofa and a kitchen and everything." He looked at Lynn, speaking quickly and quietly. "Sam does charter work with the scientists at Woods Hole and he's taking a couple of them out tomorrow. He asked yesterday if I wanted to join him with Ava, and I said yes. It's very safe, and she'll have a life jacket on the whole time."

Lynn's mouth twisted, then she rolled her eyes before shaking a finger at him. "You and I are *even* on surprises."

A blindside for a blindside. He could handle that.

"Oh my God!" Ava exclaimed. "What am I going to *wear* to look like a scientist?"

Lynn and Cody groaned together as Ava bolted back upstairs to add more options to her backpack.

Jenn had agreed to work Nancy's usual Saturday morning shift at the office. The phones tended to be busy on the weekends and today was no exception. After a week, she was finally managing to be able to sit at her desk without constantly thinking about what had happened there a week ago. It only happened two or three times an hour now.

She and Cody had been great together—their bodies had melded perfectly. But she'd decided it was best if that didn't happen again. Not just on her desk, but *anywhere*. If she and Cody were going to be Team Single, it would be best not to complicate things with sex.

Even really, really good sex.

Damn, she was doing it again—thinking about Cody in carnal ways instead of coworker ways. She got up to get a bottle of water from the office mini fridge and heard the door open behind her. It was her boss, Devlin Knight, and his…*friend?*…Carm Toscanio from the fish market two doors up Wharf Street from the office— Joseppi's Seafood.

"Hey, Jenn," Devlin said. "Thanks for covering the office today. I just stopped to grab the folder for that Chatham commercial property. I might have a buyer for it—Carm's cousin wants a retail spot on the Cape. We're going to meet him there later and grab dinner after."

Winsome Cove was just as gossipy as any other small town, and Jenn had heard that Devlin and Carm might be an item, but no one was really sure. Nancy insisted they must be dating because they were together so much, but Lexi was just as adamant that the two were just good friends, and had been since grade school. Carm's family had owned the fish market for three generations, and, after a few slower years, business was picking up again now that Wharf Street was getting more foot traffic.

Wharf Street was undergoing a transformation. Originally, the waterfront street was the heart of Winsome Cove. But then someone, back in the 1940s, had decided to run the new main road along the top of the small ridge above Wharf Street, and *that* turned into the business hub. As more and more stores and restaurants opened up there, one side of the now dead-ended Wharf Street became parking lots for the shops above. The other side of the street had struggled to survive, from the historic Salty Knight Pub at the bottom of the street, up to Sea-

Shelly Designs at the top of the street, where it connected to Main Street.

Jenn's sister, Lexi, had taken over a closed-up restaurant connected to the pub. 200 Wharf had become a destination restaurant for seafood and modern Italian cuisine under Lexi's guidance as its head chef. Forgotten little Wharf Street was now attracting well-heeled diners. Devlin had opened this office in one of the buildings his family owned. He was trying to lease out two other storefronts between here and the fish market, and the Knight family had been sprucing up all the buildings with paint, benches and planters of flowers.

"How have the phones been today?" Devlin asked, sifting through the call book. "Looks like the Mashpee house is getting some traffic."

"Yes," Jenn answered. "It's being shown at least four times today. I told all the agents to play nice if they got there and another agent was showing the property. I think you'll see multiple offers on that one by Monday."

"Is that the cute bright blue place near the water with those giant hydrangea bushes along the fence line?" Carm asked.

"Yes," Jenn smiled. "Max and Grace drove me by there the other day and it is a perfect little gem of a house."

"You're living in Grace's old house, right?" she asked. "I heard they were thinking of selling it?"

Jenn shook her head. "They can't make up their minds about it. It's the house Grace grew up in. She hates the thought of strangers moving in when she lives right next door. But I'm grateful to be able to rent it for now."

"That was good timing, for sure. Your sister said this move was kind of last-minute for you."

Jenn's jaw tightened at the thought of Lexi discussing her with people Jenn didn't really know. Carm seemed to be waiting for a response, even though she hadn't actually asked a question. Jenn sensed it was more friendly curiosity than maliciousness, but if she hadn't shared the truth with her family, she certainly wasn't going to share it with a virtual stranger. She gave her a thin smile.

"It was a bit sudden, but with my brother's wedding coming up in a few months, moving here gives me a chance to help with the planning."

Carm gave a sharp laugh. "Grace doesn't strike me as a woman who needs help planning *anything*. That woman likes to be in charge, and luckily, she's very good at running things." She hesitated, her cheeks shading pink. "Of course, I'm sure she's thrilled to have you here in a support role. And I *know* your mom is thrilled you're here. She's been telling everyone how excited she is to have her family together in Winsome Cove."

"Hey, *I'm* thrilled, too!" Devlin came out of his office with a few folders in hand. "She's been a huge help in freeing us all up to actually go sell things instead of answering phone calls all day." He patted Jenn's shoulder on the way by her desk. "And don't sell her planning skills short. Jenn's already reorganizing things here, and she offered to redesign our company website. Cody's even been singing her praises, and Cody doesn't go out of his way to say nice things about *anyone*."

Carm frowned. "Yeah, he is kind of sullen, isn't he? Not the kind of guy I would think of as a salesman, but you keep saying he's good at it."

"Oh, Cody can be very charming when he wants to be," Jenn said, feeling she had to defend him for some reason. "His clients appreciate his no-nonsense style, and he knows the business inside and out. Devlin's very lucky to have him."

A curious silence fell over the office. Devlin and Carm both wore the same bemused smiles. Had she overdone her praise? Maybe, but it was true. Cody *was* good at his job. And these two had no idea how hard he had to work at it. They didn't know about his sobriety struggles. Or that he'd been fired from his last job for punching a guy.

Devlin's smile deepened. "You're right. I *am* lucky Cody came on board. His style is different from mine, but there's nothing wrong with that. In fact, we complement each other in a lot of ways."

Carm laughed, putting her arm through his. "Are you saying he completes you, Dev?"

He laughed, too. "Not exactly, but he is good at what he does. He's been in this business longer than I have, and I trust his opinions. But what I value most is his honesty."

Jenn's heart stuttered. Cody said Devlin didn't know about his drinking, or about the guy he'd punched in Boston. What would happen if Devlin ever found out the truth? Would Cody lose his job? She couldn't let that happen.

She'd guard his secrets closely.

She hoped she could trust him to do the same with hers.

Chapter Eleven

"How's my Team Single partner doing this Monday morning?" Cody came down from his apartment to find Jenn already at work at her desk, alone in the office. Her hair was pulled back into a low ponytail, and she was wearing her usual black slacks and a yellow cotton top, covered with a long, rust-colored cardigan sweater. The colors of a piece of candy corn. Sweet and tempting.

Damn it. He had to stop thinking of her that way.

"Well, I'm still single, so pretty good, I guess." She was concentrating on her computer screen, typing away as she talked. She clicked Send on something and sat back, looking up at him with a smile. "I should have stopped for coffee, though. We have three offers on that Mashpee house, with a couple more on the way. I told the real estate agents they had until noon today to submit any new offers. Did you show that house to anyone?"

"I had a friend show it to one of my clients for me on Saturday, but they want to be farther out on the Cape than that." It would have been nice to see that commission in his checking account. But he did have some money coming from a family who'd made an offer on the house where he'd met Jenn in September. He'd have to split it with the listing agent, but the couple had met Cody at the open house and ended up making their offer through him.

"That's right—you had your daughter over the weekend." Jenn smiled. "I wondered why I didn't see you out running. You don't work at all when she's here?"

The idea that she'd A—looked for him, and B—missed him made something catch and go warm inside his chest.

"Nope. That was the deal I made with Devlin. If there was some emergency, of course I'd handle it, but I don't see Ava enough as it is, so I don't want to disrupt my time with her. This weekend was one she'll remember—we went out on the ocean with Sam and some scientists from Woods Hole, and she got to see a real live whale."

The researchers were doing audits on the shark and seal populations as the seasons changed, so the whale had been a delightful surprise mid-trip. Luckily, Ava had been looking in the right direction and got to see the humpback breach. Sam's cruiser, the *KatyDid*, was forty-some feet long and had all the comforts of home, including a sofa inside the heated cabin for Ava to nap on during the ride back to the marina.

"Wow—a whale! She must have been thrilled. Is she into animals and sea life?" Jenn turned in her chair to face his desk after he sat down.

"She's more into fashion and design and watches all kinds of videos online. She wants to be an interior decorator when she grows up. She's been practicing in my apartment."

Jenn had gone silent, her forehead furrowing.

"What's wrong?"

"Just… I don't mean to tell you how to parent or anything, but…be careful about what she sees online, Cody. There's a lot of stuff out there that…" she paused "…that kids shouldn't see."

Once again, he'd forgotten about Jenn's experience with her ex. Were there compromising photos of her still floating around out there? He'd never look, of course, but the possibility must torture her.

"I get it. Her mom and I do our best to limit her screen time and control what she sees. She has a cell phone, but we have parental controls on it, and she's not allowed to take it to school or into her room. She has to put it on the kitchen charger before she goes to bed. She can't post anything without our permission, and we check her activity." He gave a quick shrug, admitting the hard truth. "It's tough to control everything, and kids are clever. But we're doing our best."

"It sounds like it. That's good." Jenn turned back to her computer. "You and your ex are getting along well?"

Cody thought he caught more than just casual curiosity in the question. "Are you asking as my stay-single buddy? Because there is no way in hell Lynn and I are ever getting back together. I burned that bridge thoroughly a long time ago. But we work together when it comes to Ava, and that's getting easier for us over time."

Their conversation had gone well when he'd picked up Ava on Friday. It wasn't as stilted as their usual talks. They'd been open with each other, and less defensive. Something had shifted between them.

"That's good…" Jenn turned back toward him, making a face. "I don't mean to sound like you need my approval. Sorry. I'm sure you're a great dad, just from the way you talk about Ava, and prioritize her in your life. How is your apartment surviving her design efforts?"

"It's more pink and ruffly than I'd choose for myself, but she lives there sometimes, too, so..." He paused, pondering an idea that popped into his head. Probably a bad one. But it wouldn't leave. "Why don't you come up and see for yourself? The office doesn't open for another half hour or so and I can make you a big mug of coffee."

Her mouth opened and closed a few times. "I'm not sure that's a great idea. Your place for coffee sounds a little...date-like." She wasn't wrong, but he was sharply disappointed for some reason.

"Well, we *did* agree that my bed would be a lot more comfortable, and private, than the reception desk if we did—" he nodded toward her desk "—*that* again."

She blinked, nervously glancing at the front door. Her cheeks went pink under her freckles.

"I don't think I technically agreed to anything, especially doing 'that'—" she made air quotes with her fingers "—again."

"We definitely talked about the possibility," he reminded her.

"And you think that's a good idea?"

Of course not.

Also...yes.

Jenn turned back to her computer, glancing at him over her shoulder when he didn't answer.

"I think I'll pass," she said, "on the coffee *and* getting together again for...that. We both have a lot on our plates, and we don't need the complication."

That was fair and logical reasoning on her part. So why did he feel like going somewhere to sulk about it?

* * *

Cody told Malcolm about Jenn after the support meeting on Wednesday. They were at the coffee shop, as usual. Malcolm knew Cody was hiding something and he wanted to know what was going on. Cody had made a compact with the man to always tell the truth, and the *whole* truth. And Malcolm had promised to be a steel vault—he wanted to know everything but would share *nothing*. And Cody believed him.

He skipped over the graphic details of that Sunday night in the office, but Malcolm got the picture. Unplanned but consensual sex with a hot coworker. And wanting more.

"And you've been running together?"

That wasn't what Cody expected as a first question, but he nodded. "Not anything organized, but we bump into each other running now and then." Malcolm stared, not saying a word. Finally, Cody couldn't let the silence go on. "It's not a big deal. We're…friends, I guess. Friendly."

"I'd say so," Malcolm scoffed.

"But we're in total agreement that nothing serious is going to happen. We are both hard core anti-relationship people. We even call ourselves Team Single."

Malcolm set down the scone he'd been eating. He set it down *very* slowly, and Cody knew he was in trouble.

"You…you call yourselves Team Single," Malcolm said. "Are you a rock band now? Going on tour? Starting a podcast? You tell me you're not going to get serious, but you've given yourselves a *name*? Damn it, Cody, you're coming up on twelve months sober. Are you *trying* to sabotage that?"

"Of course not! You said to avoid serious relationships. And this *isn't* one. It was just that one time. It's not a big deal, but I wanted to let you know about it. Full disclosure and all that."

They drank their coffee in silence for a few minutes before Malcolm spoke. "If it really was *just one time*, that's one thing. Being in the program doesn't require celibacy. But I get the feeling you'd like it to be more than one time, and now we're treading into relationship territory. And relationships bring…feelings. Emotions. Highs and lows. Relationships are a risk, especially new ones." His voice was soft and serious as he spoke, and Cody listened, because this was the voice that meant Malcolm was sharing something important. "Don't get me wrong—I've got nothing against relationships in general. I've been happily married for thirty-five years. And I don't have anything against having a roll in the sack, either, under normal conditions." Malcolm shook his head. "But you, my friend, are not in normal circumstances, and you know it."

Cody sat back and stared out the window overlooking Main Street. People were hustling up and down the sidewalks. It wasn't as busy as summertime, but it was a bright sunny day and nearly everyone was smiling. Except him. He rolled Malcolm's words around in his head. He couldn't argue with any of them.

"It's true, I'd like to be with Jenn again. But we set very firm rules about *not* getting serious, even if we had a Round Two—" he held up a hand to keep Malcolm from interrupting "—but that doesn't matter because *she* agrees with you. She's made it very clear that it's not going to happen again. I invited her up to my place and she said no. She said neither one of us needs any more complications in our lives."

"Did she, now?" Malcolm licked scone crumbs from his fingers one by one. "Sounds like a smart woman."

"She is."

Malcolm shook his head.

"Careful, Cody—smart women are the dangerous ones."

Jenn was surprised to see Cody jogging up Wharf Street on Friday night. She didn't often run in the evenings, but lately she'd been having more and more trouble sleeping at night. Sitting in an office wasn't helping. She was used to being on her feet, chasing after first graders all day. And she needed to get some sleep tonight, because tomorrow was Dress Fitting Day.

Off to Boston with Mom, Grace, Lexi and Maya to try on their dresses for the wedding. And while this would be much smaller in scale than the bridal shower, they were going to have a ladies' lunch after shopping. A full day with women she adored, but also a full day of wedding talk.

She and Cody had run together a few mornings since that first time, but it was never planned. If they saw each other, they'd run the same route for a bit before splitting up again. Conversations were usually limited, and generally about work or some local gossip.

Cody saw her and slowed to wait at the Main Street intersection, his eyebrows high in surprise. "I know why *I* don't have anything to do on a Friday night, but I didn't expect to see you out here. It's not quite as convenient at night."

It would be next to impossible with summer crowds, but in October there was at least room to move, even downtown. There would only be a few *excuse me* and *pardon me* comments to make to get by the before- and after-dinner groups.

"Once we're out of the town center, it'll be easier." She gave him a sideways glance. "You can join but be forewarned—I'm doing the short loop and I'm not in a chitchatty mood tonight."

"And you're saying that because I'm usually such a talker?" It was a fair point. "Bad day?"

"Not really, just a typical Friday. I'm tired, that's all."

He laughed. "So you decided a run would make you *less* tired?"

She couldn't help smiling. "I know it sounds silly, but I'm hoping it will make me more sleepy. I've been fighting insomnia all week."

Cody slowed a bit. "Are you okay?"

"I'm fine, but eventually the lack of sleep is going to catch up with me. And tomorrow's a busy day." She looked his way again. "It's Dress Fitting Day."

"Uh-oh. For the wedding?" She nodded and he made a funny face. "I heard you tell Nancy the wedding is holiday-themed. You're not dressing like a Christmas elf or anything, are you, Weepy?"

People tended to think of Cody as uptight and serious, so it was odd how easily he made her laugh.

"I wouldn't put it past Grace, but no, I think the dresses are normal, although they *are* red and green. Mine's a very dark green, though—I've seen the swatch. But we *are* carrying furry hand muffs instead of flowers. My sister says we'll look like Currier and Ives ice skaters."

"She told the bride that?"

She laughed harder. "No! We adore Grace, by the way. She and Max are just having some fun with the wedding for Max's son, Tyler. There was a big thing last year at the school holiday pageant, and Max made a speech to Grace in front of the whole town while dressed as a nutcracker." Cody's mouth started to open, but she stopped him. "Don't ask, I wasn't there. Apparently there was a lot of smooching and tears and cheering and bingo-bango, everyone was happy. You know—romancy stuff."

"Ugh. Romancy is the worst."

"Exactly. Team Single all the way." She gave him a fist bump, but he didn't do the sparkly part after. Not surprising, but a slight disappointment anyway. They ran at an easy pace without saying much more. By the time they were coming back into town again, it was getting dark.

"Maybe I should make sure you get back okay," Cody said, looking at the cars driving by with their headlights on.

"Please. It's not that far and the streetlights are on. I'll text you when I get th—"

And she was airborne. Her toe had caught on the same uneven paver that she'd stumbled on the first time they ran together. Only this time, she was running, not walking, and her momentum sent her flying. She put her hands out and managed not to literally faceplant on the sidewalk. Her wrist and knee broke the fall…painfully.

"Jenn!" Cody knelt and grabbed her shoulders as she sat up. "Jesus, are you okay?"

She rubbed her right wrist and grimaced. "Yeah, but I'm such a klutz."

"You're bleeding." He was looking at her knee. She was wearing light gray leggings, and there was a growing patch of red on her right knee. *Perfect*. She'd look just lovely at the dress fitting tomorrow with a gash on her knee. "Can you stand?"

"Of course I can." She let him pull her up by her good hand and took a test step. "Ow."

"Can you make it to my apartment?" Cody slid his arm around her waist for support, and for a quick, hot moment she felt all better. Until she put weight on her bleeding knee and hissed in pain.

"Why would I want to go to your apartment? Are you seriously hitting on me right now?"

"I'm not *all* dog, Jenn. Wharf Street and the apartment are right here. I have a first aid kit and I can get you bandaged up and drive you home."

He was right—the apartment was a heck of a lot closer than her place. The thought of limping all the way there—or bleeding all over Cody's car if he drove her now—wasn't appealing.

"Fine. A quick stop to clean this up, and then I'll go home."

Chapter Twelve

It was weird having Jenn in his apartment. To be fair, it was weird having *anyone* there. It wasn't like he'd done much entertaining. Devlin had been there, of course. Malcolm had stopped by a few times. But ninety-five percent of the time, it was just Cody or him and Ava. He put a pod in the coffee maker and turned to watch Jenn as she walked around with one pant leg higher than the other.

She'd sat on a counter stool when they first got there, and rolled up one leg of her leggings so they could take care of her knee. Cody had cleaned up her scrapes with soap and alcohol wipes, then bandaged the cut and put a soft wrap and an ice pack on her slightly swollen wrist. She'd watched, bemused, and he had to remind her that he *was* a dad, and had cleaned up a few of Ava's scrapes before. He didn't mention that he'd also had field medic training in the army.

Jenn was taking in the array of neon-colored pillows on the sectional with a soft smile. Her eyebrows rose at the abstract sailboat painting on the wall, and she tipped her head to the side as she studied it.

"That's…intense. But I like it." She glanced at him. "Your choice, or Ava's?"

"I'd call it a compromise. Her original choice for that

spot is in her room now." He nodded his head toward the open bedroom door, and Jenn turned the light on and laughed.

"The pink carousel horse? It's pretty, but I would definitely say the boat is a better choice for the living room." She took in Ava's room and turned to him with a smile. "This room is a little girl's dream. It's great that you let her make her own choices in her space. She actually has pretty good taste, even if it's heavy on the pink." She looked at the closed door nearby. "Did she decorate your room, too?"

He chuckled, setting the full mug of coffee on the counter and starting another for himself. He knew she drank hers black, just like him. "She's been hinting at it, but so far I've resisted. My tastes are much more, um… utilitarian than hers."

Jenn put her hand on the doorknob. "I'm trying to guess—is it messy or is it as organized in there as the living room is?"

"Definitely organized, not that there's much stuff to worry about. It's a bachelor pad."

He thought she was teasing, but she opened the door to his room.

"Whoa, it's dark in here." She hit the wall switch. "Oh, it's because you have light-blocking shades. You weren't kidding about being utilitarian. A bed and a dresser… that don't match."

"And a night table and a closet." He walked over and handed her a coffee, realizing he'd left his back on the counter.

She thanked him and took a sip, then shook her head. "That's not a night table, it's a folding TV table. All you're missing to complete the college dorm look is a few posters and some bookshelves made of plastic milk crates."

He'd never thought about it that way, but she was right.

"It's a place for sleeping, Jenn. A room with a bed. And that *is* a night table, because it's a table next to my bed that holds a lamp and a clock. I said my tastes were utilitarian."

She gave a snort. "This is definitely that. And not one bit more. As your single buddy, I am reassured that this room will *not* easily lead to romance." She patted him on his chest with her bandaged hand while taking another drink of coffee. She'd left the ice pack on the counter. Jenn glanced up at him through her long eyelashes and suddenly the apartment felt very warm.

He covered her hand with his, holding it against him. She didn't pull away. The combination of her being in his bedroom and talking about his bed and romance and touching him… He cleared his throat roughly.

"This room *could* lead to something."

Her lips parted in surprise, and all he could think was that he deeply regretted agreeing not to kiss that mouth. She turned her head, breaking the exchange that had held them. But she was looking at his bed now, which was not helping at all. He wanted to see her on that bed. And the way she was staring, he had a feeling she was picturing the same thing. Then she pulled her hand free and stepped back.

"It's probably time to drive me home."

"Hey, you're the one who wanted to see my bedroom."

"Not for *that*."

He clasped his hands on his chest and laughed. "Try not to sound quite so disgusted at the thought."

She hesitated, then smiled. "Sorry. But you and I are Team Single, remember?"

"True, but we're not Team Virgin. What better way to avoid being tempted by a relationship with anyone else than to take care of our...*physical* needs with each other? No strings attached, of course. Just like we agreed." Yes, he really wanted her that badly. He'd justify it whatever way he could think of.

He ushered her out of his bedroom and closed the door to eliminate the distraction. She stayed close, looking at the door thoughtfully. Was it possible she was thinking about it?

"I'm sorry if I'm acting overeager," he said, trying to not sound eager at all. "But we *did* say we were good together. If we're sticking to full honesty, yes, I'd very much like to do it again. But it's just to...scratch that itch, you know?"

"You want me to help you save yourself from temptation?" There was a teasing slant to her grin. "Is there a woman who's tempting you, Cody?"

Only you, Jenn.

She let out a soft breath, putting her hand on his chest again. Creating that same jolt of heat and desire. His hopes rose, then crashed when she looked at him with a sad smile. "Giving in to an impulse once is one thing, but to do it again? That's a pattern, and patterns lead to expectations, and expectations...well, that's how relationships start." Jenn's hand dropped, and he missed her touch immediately. Deeply.

Neither of them moved. Without saying a word or

moving a muscle, something shifted in Jenn. He sensed it more than saw it. Her face softened. Her eyes went from gray-blue to cobalt. And still she didn't move, probably trying to talk herself out of whatever she was thinking. Or maybe talk herself into it.

He reached out and brushed his fingers across her cheek. Her chest expanded sharply, and she looked into his eyes, searching for…something. Something she could hold on to. Someone she could trust. Cody felt a flare of anger at the man or men who put that fear in her. His fingers traced down her jawline and he lifted her chin.

"If I open that bedroom door again, we're going in. And we're going to make love on that bed. And it's going to be a *lot* slower than the first time. I'm going to taste every inch of you, and then I'm going to lay back and let you do the same to me. And when we are both exhausted and satisfied, I'll drive you home and we'll see each other in the office on Monday and we'll be the same two people. No googly eyes for each other." Her mouth, that beautiful mouth, twitched into a smile. "No expectations of a repeat, unless we both want one. No relationship. Just friends. We'll stick to all the Team Single rules we made that night, except one."

Her brow lowered suspiciously.

"Which one?"

"This one."

He dropped his head to kiss her, but stopped just as his lips brushed hers. He wouldn't do it without her permission.

"I want to kiss you, Jennifer Bellamy. It was torture for me the last time *not* to kiss you, and I don't want tonight to involve any torture. Just pleasure." He was whispering now, talking against her mouth. "I want to kiss you."

After a heartbeat of a pause, she whispered back.

"Well, what are you waiting for?"

The moment Cody's mouth took hers, all logical thought left Jenn's mind. She didn't care that she was bandaged and sore. She didn't care that she was gripping a half-filled mug of coffee. She didn't care that this was probably the worst. Idea. Ever.

All she knew was that Cody O'Neil was kissing her, and the man was a *very* good kisser. He'd been tender at first, learning his way around, nibbling at her playfully until her knees almost buckled. When her lips parted, he turned his head and went in, with strength and purpose.

His tongue swept into a dance with hers, and she felt like she was drowning in this kiss. As if sensing her surrender, his arms tightened around her. Wordlessly, he took the coffee mug from her hand, set it on a nearby bookcase, and opened his bedroom door. All without breaking the kiss. She put her hands on his chest and shoved him into the room, flinching when her wrist protested. Cody lifted his head, then took her sore hand gently into his, lifting it up and kissing her fingertips, one by one.

"Be careful. Remember, tonight is only about pleasure, not pain. You should have ice on that."

Her laughter bubbled up at the sudden practical comment in the midst of a sensual moment.

"I think that would be a little tricky while we're doing this."

She raised her sore hand and ran her fingers through

his thick, dark hair. He let out a growl and kissed her again. It was more urgent this time, and she returned it eagerly. One of his hands cupped her buttocks and pulled her against him, where she could feel him hard and quivering. They'd talked about *slow*, but that could wait. Right now she wanted him hard and fast. And she wanted him immediately. She tugged at his sweatshirt, then made a face, thinking of them both running together.

"We're sweaty."

He was nuzzling the base of her neck now, alternating between kisses and nibbles.

"I don't care. I like the taste of salt on your skin." He ran his tongue up her neck to prove his point. She tightened her fingers in his hair and held him in place so she could kiss him. He did taste *very* good.

So that was settled. In a blur of kissing and touching and laughter, their clothes came off and Cody gently pushed her onto the bed. She playfully started to crabwalk away from the edge, but he grabbed her ankles and pulled her forward, dropping to his knees next to the bed, and then his mouth was... *Oh, my*. His mouth—that very talented mouth—was exactly where she wanted it. She propped herself up on her elbows and watched. He didn't raise his head until she cried out his name and fell back, seeing fireworks inside the lids of her closed eyes.

He crawled up on the bed, determination on his face. Without a word, he scooped her along with him so they were fully on top of the mattress. And then he was inside of her, and she let out a long, low moan of pleasure. They moved together, rocking slow and deep at first. Eyes locked. Lips locked. She was ready before he was, but she held on to it, savoring every movement.

The pace picked up until they were both clinging tightly to each other and grunting in ecstasy. Jenn couldn't hold on any longer, giving him the briefest of warnings by shouting his name. He came with her, pushing so hard her head was up against the headboard, finally letting out a long, low groan before his head fell to her shoulder.

They stayed like that, both breathing heavily and not speaking, for a few minutes. She ran her fingers down his back and his skin twitched under her touch. It was funny to think she'd been worried about being sweaty, because they were both drenched in sweat now, and it had nothing to do with running. She didn't want to break the moment, but Cody was like deadweight on her, and her knee was starting to ache. She shifted her body, and he mumbled something against her skin. She couldn't sort out actual words, but she got the feeling he wanted her to stay still.

"Cody, you're crushing me. My knee…"

He rolled off to her side, keeping one arm tight around her waist.

"Sorry. I got… I got a little lost there for a minute. I think we broke something in my brain, because I'm still not thinking straight." He grinned. "Was it just me, or was that…fantastic?"

"Not just you. My body is still humming."

He pretended to pluck at invisible strings on her stomach. "Can I play a tune on you?"

She liked playful Cody. He looked at her with a goofy smile, continuing to "play" her like an instrument. His smile was open, his eyes trusting, his body relaxed. She realized she didn't often see those things all at once in him. He usually held at least something under guard. He made a funny face as his fingers traced up and down her body, and something did a little flip inside her chest. He was a good man. A good friend. A very good lover. And for now, he was the man who wanted a strictly physical relationship with her.

No…what did he call it? A *situationship*. When they wanted to, they could have some fun together, and then just walk away. It was a good deal for both of them. And harmless, because they were in agreement that no emotions would be involved here, other than physical desire and physical pleasure.

He sat up slowly, shaking his head with a quick laugh. "Woman, you have sapped all the strength from me. But I need to get up for a minute. I'll be right back."

She was surprised when he returned with her ice pack and handed it to her. She sat up against the headboard, and he sat at her side, sliding his arm around her. She rested her head on his shoulder and he put the ice over the wrap on her wrist.

"Does it feel okay?"

She sighed with a smile. "It feels amazing."

His chest vibrating with soft laughter. "Your sprained wrist feels amazing? How's the knee?"

"That feels amazing, too. Sex is a great painkiller. Who knew?"

Chapter Thirteen

Cody agreed, and he did his best to ignore that pesky voice in his head—that sounded a lot like Malcolm—telling him he wasn't supposed to use sex as a pain-killer, any more than he was supposed to use booze as a painkiller. But that wasn't what tonight was. He hadn't been looking to escape anything. It wasn't like he'd set out to find her and make love to her. It was unplanned. Spontaneous. Terrific. Two adults agreeing to have commitment-free sex on a Friday night. In his bed. Nothing wrong with that.

Jenn's body melted against him, and her breathing changed. She was asleep. He smiled and kissed her hair. He knew exactly how she felt—he was exhausted, too.

They both dozed for a while, sinking down into the bed but staying wrapped up in each other. After an hour or so, they woke and Cody made turkey club sandwiches for a quick dinner. They'd chatted about nothing important—the weather, the new season of a popular drama that was streaming, music…everyday stuff like that. Surprisingly enough, they had similar tastes in television and movies. In music…not so much. He preferred rock and blues, while she liked pop and ballads.

After the break, they'd showered together—*that* was

fun—and returned to bed, where he'd fulfilled his promise to taste every inch of the woman. They napped again,
then she'd woken him while tasting every inch of *him*,
and nearly made his brain explode with pleasure. Cody
might be in his prime, but three times in one evening
was…a lot. Despite the no-cuddling rule, they'd wrapped
themselves around each other again and fallen asleep for
another nap before he'd have to drive her home.

His eyes snapped wide awake when he felt a hand slap
hard against his chest. Before he could get his bearings,
someone started yelling at him.

"Get *up*! We've got to *go*!"

"Holy…" Cody woke up enough to see that Jenn was
sitting up in his bed, naked, her hair falling over her
shoulders, wide-eyed in a panic over…something. Memories of the evening came flooding back, and he smiled,
even as she smacked him again. "Ouch! Is the apartment
on fire or something?"

"Cody, we slept all night—the sun is coming up."

His room was always dark, so it was hard to tell. He
rolled over and pulled the shade away from the window
while yawning. It sure looked dark out to him, but there
was a faint glow on the horizon. He looked at his phone
on the night table and it was almost six. He stretched and
propped himself up, taking a minute to appreciate Jenn's
naked, angry glory.

"The sun is *not* up," he said, "but it's close. What's the
big deal? God knows, we needed some rest after the evening we had, and you said you haven't been sleeping well,
so…now you have. Let's catch a couple more hours—"

Jenn hit him again, and this time she closed her fist.

"What's the big deal? What's the big *deal*? I'm going to the dress fitting today!"

"Okay, fine." he sat up, reluctant to face the day, but she was giving him no choice. He wasn't sure why she was so upset over a dress fitting that surely wasn't happening at dawn. "I'll make us some eggs for breakfast and take you home."

Her mouth dropped open, and he didn't get the sense that it was with joy. "Are you insane? I'm going with my future sister-in-law. Who lives right next door to me. Lives with my *brother*. They both think I'm home sleeping. Alone. What are they going to think if they see me being dropped off by you this morning? They'll know we slept together, and…oh, God…" She covered her face with her hands. "I'd never hear the end of it."

"Hey…" Cody pulled her hands from her face and wiped away her panicked tears. "Slow down. First, we didn't do anything wrong last night, so screw 'em if they don't like it." Her mouth opened, but he talked over her. "And if you don't *want* them to know, we'll figure out a way to make that happen. You and I are very good secret keepers, remember?" He rested his forehead on hers, waiting as her breathing slowed to normal. "Get dressed, and I'll take you to a spot around the block from your place. You can walk, or even jog, from there, so even if they see you, they'll think you took a morning run."

She thought about it, and then nodded, taking a deep breath. "Okay. Okay. That…that could work." She lifted her head. "And I know we didn't do anything wrong last night. Something stupid? Maybe. But I don't regret it."

They both dressed quickly. Jenn borrowed a pair of his sweats so she didn't have to pull on her bloody leggings. Her wrist was bruised, but not very swollen, and her knee looked fine. She sat in his SUV in silence all the way. Even though he hadn't been to her house, he knew where it was as soon as she gave him the address. As a real estate agent, he was familiar with most streets in Winsome Cove. As planned, he parked around the corner, leaving her about a block away, and completely out of sight of neighboring houses.

She unbuckled her seat belt and looked over at him. "It really was a great night, you know. But…"

He took her hand. He'd been thinking about this moment on the way here, and he knew she'd start getting practical and having her doubts. "No expectations," he started. "No strings. No emotions. No labels. We're not dating. We're not boyfriend and girlfriend. We'll be here physically for each other until one of us decides they want to move on. Those are the rules for Team Single, right?"

Her mouth curved into a smile. "I'll add one more rule."

"And that would be…?"

"Next time, one of us sets an alarm so we don't oversleep."

He returned her smile. "We'll need to if we keep wearing each other out like we did last night."

He tugged on her hand until she was close enough to kiss, then they whispered goodbyes. Daylight was coming fast, and she needed to go. He watched her start to jog, reconsider it with her sore knee, then start walking away. He put the vehicle in Drive and pulled away, his smile growing as he drove. Out of everything that had been said this morning, only two words mattered to him.

There was going to be a *next time*.

* * *

"Girl, what is wrong with you? You've been in a fog all day." Lexi's arms were folded on her chest as she stared at Jenn. They were finishing up dinner at 200 Wharf—Lexi, Mom, Grace and Jenn—after spending the day in Boston being fitted for their dresses. Maya had gone to the fitting, but had to skip dinner after getting a call that her youngest, Zander, had a stomach bug.

The fitting hadn't been *quite* as bad as Jenn had feared. The mood was festive and more focused on female friendships and less on romance. Even the dresses were better than she'd expected. She should have known not to worry—Grace had excellent taste. As much as she wanted to have fun with the Christmas theme when she could, Grace made it clear that the wedding itself would *not* be silly in any way. The dresses she chose for Lexi and Jenn were dark green with a soft train falling from the single shoulder strap. Maya's dress was the same style, but in a deep wine red. The gowns themselves were form-fitting sheaths that clung to their curves without being uncomfortable.

They didn't scream *Christmas!* the way she'd feared they would. And the hand muffs they'd be carrying were small and actually very pretty. Lexi had convinced Grace to go with a natural fur color, so they didn't stand out too much from the dark dresses. Fresh sprigs of holly with a spray of white roses would be pinned to them for the wedding.

"She's right, Jenn," her mother said. "You've been quiet today. Is your wrist bothering you that much? You should be more careful running."

"No, it's fine." She looked down at the slightly swollen wrist, which was beginning to turn muted shades of blue and green from bruising. "I'm just tired. Work's been busy."

And I had sex last night. All night. With Cody O'Neil.

"Really?" Lexi responded. "That's interesting, because when Devlin was in here the other night, he said the holidays are usually slow in real estate. He was looking forward to what he called the *December-January lull.* But now you're saying it's busy. Interesting." It was Lexi's passive-aggressive way of suggesting she didn't believe Jenn. Her big sister was getting almost as good at reading her as their mother was.

"It's not all *that* interesting." Jenn took a sip of her wine. "Devlin may not get as many listings this time of year, but that doesn't mean *my* job at the office gets any easier. The phone is ringing off the hook with calls about the rental properties we're managing. They'll be full for Thanksgiving and Christmas, and all those people need to be catered to."

Lexi stared hard, running her tongue over her teeth, deep in thought. Searching for a crack in Jenn's story and not finding one.

"I suppose that makes sense," she said at last. "But maybe you need to look for something to help you sleep better."

Oh, she'd found something, all right. She'd found some*one.* She'd slept like a baby last night. But she sure wasn't going to talk about that.

"I'm *fine.* This is Grace's day. The dresses were all beautiful, and I especially loved *Grace's* dress." She looked across the table to her soon-to-be sister-in-law. "You will be a stunning bride." The champagne-colored bride's dress had a heavily-beaded fitted short jacket that could be removed at the reception. The strapless dress underneath had the same beads and crystals tumbling down more loosely over the mermaid skirt. "Max is going to lose his mind when he sees you coming down the aisle."

Grace blushed and thanked her. "I hope we're not burying you in too much mushy stuff again."

"Oh, don't listen to Lexi," Jenn insisted. "I had a great time today. My sister's just trying to start something, and she's mad because she's not getting a rise out of me."

Lexi stuck her tongue out, and Jenn threw her cloth napkin at her sister, who swatted it away. Just like when they were kids, when things started being thrown—fists or objects—their mother stepped in. Mom snatched a napkin from Lexi's hand, giving them both a *seriously?* look.

"Okay, girls. We're here to celebrate Grace, not fight."

"Sorry, Mom," Lexi said. "I just feel like Jenny's been acting different ever since she got here. Don't you?"

"Since she got here to the restaurant today?" Mom asked. "Or since she got here in Winsome Cove a month ago?"

"Definitely tonight, but honestly, she's been different since she arrived—"

Jenn threw her hands up and interrupted. "*She* is sitting right here, and *she* doesn't like being referred to in the third person. And I *am* different. I told you that. I'm sorry if Jenn 2.0 just isn't as cool to you as Jenny 1.0."

Lexi blinked. "I never said that."

"You may as well have."

"All right, that's enough. Seriously." Their mother set

down her wineglass and gave them both a stern glare. "What is going on with you two? You used to be tight as…well, as sisters."

Jenn scoffed. "Maybe when we were teenagers, Mom. Then Lexi left for college and work and Max took off on the road and then it was just me left in Iowa with you. Being the good girl."

Lexi waved a hand in dismissal. "Oh, boo-hoo. You *chose* to stay in Des Moines, and you loved it. Don't play victim, Jenn."

"Sure I chose it, but I didn't know I'd be the last Bellamy standing. You and Mom came here to Cape Cod on your grand adventure and found brand-new lives. It was me who took care of everything for you in Des Moines. Sold the house. Got your cars and furniture transported to you. I did the same for Max. You were all living your best lives here on the beach while I was back in Iowa. Alone." She stopped for a breath, realizing she was talking faster and louder with every word. She didn't know how far she was going to go, but damn, it felt good to get this out. It was like lancing a festering boil, relieving all that pent-up, poisonous pressure. "I was the one left to deal with Dad and Bambi."

Her mother stifled a sudden laugh. "Her name is Caylee."

Lexi immediately interjected. "Caylee with a C."

Mom ignored her. "And Jenn, you weren't exactly the little boy in *Home Alone*, forgotten by his family. I invited you to join Lexi and me when we came to check out the Sassy Mermaid." She took Jenn's hand in hers. "But Iowa was your home, and you never gave any indication you didn't want to stay there your whole life.

You were settled." She hesitated. "At least, I *thought* you were settled."

She had been. Until she wasn't. Until Will shared those pictures with the entire school board. She'd loved her job. Loved her students. Loved her town house overlooking the Des Moines River. The one Caylee threw her out of.

Lexi frowned. "What *did* change, Jenn? And what do you mean you had to *deal* with Dad and Bimbette?"

"It's Caylee," their mother said sternly.

Lexi winked. "With a C…"

Grace giggled, then quickly straightened her face, trying to be serious. Mom had firmly insisted they were all going to treat their father's new wife—and possible future mother to their half sibling—with civility. Actual affection might be too much to ask.

"Oh, you know how Dad is," Jenn replied. "Always needs to be the center of everyone's attention. I was the last family he had left in Iowa, so he thought I should be at his beck and call all the time. Come help at the dealership. Come help at his stupid new house. Be nice to his little gold-dig…well, you know. He actually thought I was going to treat that girl as my stepmother. He wanted me at their house for Sunday dinner every week, as if we were one big, happy family. By the way, Caylee with a C can't cook her way out of a paper bag, and she treated me like I was trespassing whenever I was there. She's more insecure than Dad is."

Phyllis Bellamy stared out the window for a long moment, her eyebrows drawn tightly together. Jenn braced herself for the usual *treat them respectfully* speech. He'd cheated on her regularly, but Mom had been determined not to speak ill of him to his children.

"Your father always was a fool." She sat back in her chair, looking over at Grace to explain. "Their father was handsome and funny and made me feel like a princess when we were dating, and like a queen the first few years of our marriage. He was so ambitious, and I admired that in him. But he never got over his childhood, and he refused to get any counseling to deal with it."

Jenn knew a little about her father's upbringing. She knew his family had been dirt-poor, living in a single-wide trailer set on farmland he didn't own. Her grandfather had been the barn help, mucking out the huge dairy barn and helping with milking. Her grandmother had cooked for the farmer's family and cleaned their house. In exchange, they were given the old trailer to raise their family in. It couldn't have been an easy life, but her grandparents were salt-of-the-earth people. They weren't afraid of hard work, and they'd never cared about making any more money than what they needed to survive.

Unfortunately, Jenn's dad *had* cared—very much—and was deeply ashamed of the people who raised him. By the time his own children came along, his parents had retired to a small apartment in a senior home on the outskirts of the small Iowa farm town where he was raised. Jenn and her siblings would visit them occasionally, but usually with their mother. Dad always seemed to find a reason to avoid going at the last minute.

It was sad, because his parents were kind and loving people. Grandma Bellamy would always bake something wondrous for the kids—from scratch, of course—and she'd prepare a meal fit for kings in that tiny apartment kitchen. Lexi had said once that it was their grandmother who inspired her to become a chef.

Her mother took a sip of her wine, and then another, larger drink. She set the wineglass down with a thunk against the table. "Nothing is ever enough for your father. Which is sad, because the man got everything he wanted. He wanted a family, and I gave that to him. He wanted to take over my daddy's business, and he did. He wanted to live in a nice house in the suburbs, and we did that. He wanted to be respected, and he was president of the country club year after year. And he *still* wasn't satisfied."

Lexi gave a long sigh. Unlike Jenn, she'd given up on pleasing their father a long time ago. Max had, too. "He's gotten worse as he's gotten older," Lexi said. "When I told him I was walking down the aisle alone at my wedding, he threw a fit. He threatened not to come to the wedding at all if I didn't let him give me away. Good grief, I'm a grown woman, not some state fair prize."

"I worry about him all the time," their mother said softly.

"What?" Jenn and Lexi asked the question in unison.

"He's scared, girls. He's moving into old age as ungracefully as possible, with no appreciation for the fact that all those years he's lived are *gifts*. His glass is more than half-empty—it's dry. Eventually he won't be so attractive to the young ladies he likes to hang out with. I think that's probably why he decided to marry this one." She looked at Grace again, as if wanting her to understand the family she was marrying into. But Jenn knew Max had told her all about his dad. "Have you ever seen a cat being loaded into a carrier that didn't want to be in that carrier?" Mom asked. Grace, who had a beautiful but temperamental Siamese cat, nodded with a smile. "You know how they contort themselves and grasp at anything to keep from going in there, yowling and clawing the whole time? That's Max's father facing old age. It makes me sad that he hasn't changed."

"Did something happen between you and Caylee?" Lexi leaned forward, her voice no longer sharp but concerned. Jenn picked her own glass up a few times, setting it down without drinking. She ran her fingers around the top of the glass.

"You mean other than her kicking me out of my town house?"

Lexi gasped. "*She* did that? I wondered why you moved to that little one-bedroom flat. It's practically an efficiency apartment."

Their mother waved both hands back and forth in confusion. "Wait, wait, wait. You were renting the nicest town house in your father's building—the end unit with river views. How could *she* get you kicked out?"

There was no point in keeping this particular secret from her family any longer, and it felt good to shed at least one of them. Maybe it would make up for not telling them about last night.

"She kept whispering in Dad's ear that the place was too big for me and they were losing revenue because I wasn't paying the so-called market rate. She even mentioned it to me directly at one of those stupid Sunday dinners and made me feel like I was leeching off my father. A few weeks later, Dad asked if I would mind moving to a one-bedroom apartment in his other complex so they could rent out the town house for more income. I loved the town house, but the apartment was closer to work, so I said yes."

Lexi frowned. "Didn't you get that deal at the town house because you were doing the bookkeeping for the whole building?"

"Yes—for *both* apartment buildings, but the bookkeeping wasn't that complicated, and I didn't want Dad thinking I was taking advantage." She pressed her lips together, trying to hold in her annoyance at being such a people pleaser with her father. "And surprise, surprise—a week after I moved out, Bimbette's *brother* and his family moved in. I guarantee you they are not paying 'market rate.' And Dad *still* expected me to take care of the books."

"Oh, honey, I'm so sorry," her mother squeezed her hand. "I had no idea you were pressured into making that move, or I would have said something to him."

"Mom, I'm a grown woman. I don't need you, or anyone else, to get involved in my decisions. And in the end, it *was* my decision to give up the condo. He didn't technically evict me." Although all four women knew he would have, if his wife had insisted.

"Well—" Lexi said, looking far more sympathetic than before "—no wonder you wanted to leave Des Moines. Especially after your breakup with Will."

Jenn did her best to keep a look of disgust off her face at the mention of his name. She was keeping that particular secret for good.

"And I'm glad you decided to come to Winsome Cove, baby." Her mom leaned over and kissed her cheek.

"We're all glad you're here, Jenn," Grace agreed. "Sounds like a fresh start is exactly what you need."

She gave a playful wink. "And we'll do our best not to play matchmaker or make things too lovey-dovey around you. But…there is always hope for a little romance to enter your life when you least expect it."

Jenn shook her head firmly. Last night had been wild and fun and satisfying. But it was *not* romance. It never would be.

"Not gonna happen."

Chapter Fourteen

Jenn was back in Cody's apartment on Thursday night. They'd done their best to act normal and disinterested for the first three days of the workweek, but Thursday seemed to be the breaking point for both of them.

Their glances had intensified as Thursday went on. He'd made excuses to spend time at her desk, leaning over her shoulder to look at her computer screen. Wrapping her in his spicy, woodsy cologne until it felt like her own clothes carried it. He'd pointed at the monitor, pressing against her. At one point, she almost lost control and kissed his neck, but she'd caught Nancy giving them a curious look and stopped herself.

Around three o'clock, her phone buzzed with a text. It was from Cody, who was sitting at his desk—Dinner upstairs? Aware of Nancy and now Devlin in the office, she'd quickly sent a thumbs-up emoji and gone right back to work. She struggled to keep from smiling to herself for the next few hours, her body humming in anticipation. But it wasn't just the physical companionship she was looking forward to.

Cody was funny, even though his humor tended to be on the dry side. She liked that, though. It made her pay attention to every word he said and kept her on her toes. There were some people in her life who didn't like her sarcastic side, but she made Cody laugh, and that felt like winning a little prize when it happened. They shared a lot of the same values and preferences. He liked his music a little louder than she preferred, but that was hardly a deal-breaker.

At the end of the day, it was only Devlin and the two of them in the office. Cody made a point to say good-night and head upstairs, so they wouldn't be leaving at the same time. She was nervous that Devlin might hang around after the usual office hours, but he said he was going to have dinner with his dad at the bar. She promised to close up, and she did. Locking herself in the office and hurrying upstairs to Cody's apartment.

"Okay, you've been keeping your culinary skills a secret from me, Cody O'Neil. That chicken was delicious." Jenn sat back in her chair and patted her stomach. "I might just hire you to be my personal chef."

He cleared the dishes from the table and put them in the dishwasher. "Your sister's an award-winning chef. Are you telling me you didn't get *any* of that cooking gene?"

She laughed. "It's crazy, right? I mean, I *can* cook, but I'm a 'follow the recipe to the letter' sort of cook. It feels like work to me, and I tend to stress over it. But I saw you in there—you were having fun just tossing in different spices and stuff. You reminded me of Lexi, actually."

He finished washing the cooking pan and put it in the rack. "I've just gotten into cooking over the past few years. I need to keep myself busy, and when I dive into something, I tend to go all in." He rejoined her at the table and set a refilled glass of cola in front of her. He stared at the glass for a second. "I'm sure that's not what your sister would choose to pair with lemon chicken. She'd probably serve a nice pinot grigio. Sorry."

"Cody, please don't apologize. I don't *need* a drink, and I understand why you don't keep alcohol here. How is your progress going? You said it's been almost a year?"

He nodded. "A year in December. One long-ass, difficult year."

"Are you still struggling with it?" She knew alcoholism was a disease, not a choice, but she had no idea what it might be like to deal with it.

"My sponsor assures me that I'll be struggling with it for the rest of my life. It's not something that can be 'cured.'" He made air quotes. "It can only be managed. Malcolm says it should get easier over time, but I haven't experienced that yet. I may not think about taking a drink every minute the way I used to, but it definitely crosses my mind every day."

"Well, going from hourly to daily *is* an improvement. You mentioned going to meetings. Is that a weekly thing?" She winced. "I don't mean to sound like I'm grilling you. I'm genuinely curious, but if you don't want to talk about it…"

"No, it's fine. Other than Malcolm or in a meeting, I don't have anyone else in Winsome Cove I can discuss it with. I needed this job, and I was afraid Devlin wouldn't hire me, so I decided to keep it to myself. Now that I'm here and liking it, I can't figure out a way to slide the truth into a conversation without risking losing my job for lying to him." He paused. "To answer your question, I go to a meeting in town every Wednesday at noon. Sometimes I go to another one in Falmouth on the weekend, too."

That was a serious commitment, which was a little ironic considering how anti-commitment Cody kept claiming to be. He could do it when it mattered. She realized she'd been silent too long. "Devlin doesn't strike me as the kind of guy who would fire you for that. He likes you."

"He likes me *now*," Cody pointed out. "Who knows what he'd think if the truth came out?"

"But it's hard to keep those secrets, isn't it?" It was their bond—carrying each other's secrets. "I feel like I'm on guard all the time when I'm with my family, and it's exhausting."

He nodded thoughtfully. "I don't think your family would banish you just because you had a rough time back home."

"No, but they'd look at me differently, and that feels just as bad. I don't want to be the screw-up of the family. Although I did shed one of my secrets after the dress fitting, and it wasn't too bad. I didn't like getting everyone's sympathetic looks, but I let them know about my dad and so-called stepmom evicting me from the town house I'd rented for five years."

"Why was that such a big deal to keep from them?"

"I honestly don't know. By itself, it wasn't. It was annoying, and hurtful. I had to move, but… It's not like Dad didn't offer me a different apartment."

"That sounds like you're still making excuses for him. Your dad is a landlord?"

She gave a mostly humorless laugh.

"My dad is a lot of things, but yes, he owns some condos and town houses that he rents out. That's an income investment for him. His main job is selling cars. He owns two dealerships. Took one over from my mom's family, then expanded."

She told him the story of being kicked out so that Caylee's brother could move in. The more she told the story, the easier it got. She wondered if that would work with any other secrets.

"My mom threw me a bit at dinner. She said she feels *sorry* for him. The guy cheated on her for *years*. He's one of the original reasons I'm Team Single, and she was making excuses for him. I will *never* do that for any man. Not that I'd ever give another man the chance to betray me, but if he did, divorce would be the *least* of his problems."

Cody took her hand and led her to the sofa, still covered with his daughter's collection of neon pillows. Oddly enough, one thing they'd found in common was watching the quiz show *Jeopardy* and playing along with it, so he'd suggested they watch together tonight.

"One thing I learned in anger management therapy," he started, "is that holding on to rage only hurts the person doing the holding."

She pushed some pillows aside and put another behind her back. "You sound like a fortune cookie right now."

"Maybe," he conceded. "But your mom seems to have figured it out."

"But did she *learn* anything from it? Her husband cheated and left her, and here she is, falling for a guy who owns the bar on Wharf Street. Right back into another relationship after being screwed over by my father. And Fred's a cranky old man, from what I've seen."

"Fred's okay. He's not as crusty as he comes across, and I think your mom figured that out pretty quick." He pulled her close to his side and put an arm around her, then clicked on the television in time for their show. This felt…nice. Normal. "But I heard they were battling it out pretty good the other night."

"Yeah, their on-again, off-again schtick seems to be trending to *off* lately. Mom just shrugged when I asked, but they don't seem to be talking very much right now. That's a big change from their usual nonstop arguing. But Fred's a *man*," Jenn protested. "She should be *done* with men."

"Just because you've decided to put half of the human population in a box and label us defective, that doesn't mean your mom has to agree."

She could have kept debating, but she just laughed instead. "Okay, oh wise one, I give up! I can't keep being cranky when you're being all understanding and forgiving and…*nice*. Are you *always* like this when no one's looking?"

"Not always, no," he admitted. "Why *were* you feeling so cranky?"

She waved one hand in dismissal. "I don't know. My sister's right—I've been out of sorts since I got to Winsome Cove. I'm not ready to be understanding and forgiving yet, but I'll work on it. Because you've got a point, it's not doing me any good to be mad all the time. I thought I might make it my new persona—the tough-talking bitchy old spinster that everyone leaves alone. I don't think I can keep it up, though."

Cody was rubbing her arm with his fingers, tracing lines and circles on her skin, raising goose bumps at his touch. Did this count as the *cuddling* she'd added to their list of no-nos? She hoped not, because it felt really nice.

"I definitely don't see you turning into a tough-talking old spinster, Jenn. And I don't think being on Team Single means we have to be cranky about it."

"Hey—" she turned to look up at him "—that could be my new dwarf name. Cranky!"

Cody chuckled. "That's only slightly better than Weepy. I think *Cranky* might fit me better."

"You took classes to learn how *not* to be cranky. Are you saying you flunked out?"

"No, I passed."

The room was silent, except for the television host chatting with the contestants.

"So I can dump all my trauma on you, but you're still not ready to talk about any of yours?"

Cody frowned. "I answered your questions about my alcoholism."

She didn't respond, feeling the tension tightening in his body. It's not like he owed her any trauma-dumps, whether she'd shared hers or not. This wasn't a relationship. They weren't that kind of couple. She took a deep breath and shrugged, pretending it didn't bother her. "We shouldn't miss the second half of the show. Look how close the scores are."

The atmosphere relaxed as they settled in to watch, then streamed the newest episode of a series they both liked on Netflix.

Keep things light, Jenn.
Keep things casual.

Cody woke up in bed with Jenn sound asleep close by his side. After watching TV, they'd gone into the bedroom and did what they did best—made sweet, hot love for an hour. As promised, he'd set the alarm on his phone, but they still had three hours before she needed to go. She was driving herself and wanted to make sure her car was in her driveway well before dawn. They'd both agreed to keep the relationship on the down-low, which meant no actual sleepovers. Just romps and naps. That was okay. He didn't need to wake up with her in the morning.

She breathed a soft sigh and snuggled in tight. Was she cold? He pulled up the blanket over both of them, and she fell back into a relaxed sleep.

His problem, and he was just beginning to realize it *was* a problem, was that Cody *wanted* to wake up with Jenn in the morning light. He *wanted* to share time with her during the day, without worrying about who might see them or know something. Dinner and television tonight had been a sort of revelation for him. The only other person he'd cooked for in this apartment was his daughter. He hadn't snuggled on a sofa with a woman since he was married to Lynn. He'd convinced himself he didn't need any of that relationship stuff. But he was beginning to *want* it.

Jenn had wanted to pry more from him about his drinking and his anger management, but luckily she'd let him shut her down. Sharing was *not* caring in his book. That stuff was best kept in the dark, away from people with their questions and opinions. He was shocked at himself for saying anything about what he'd learned in anger counseling. Malcolm was the only person he'd discussed that with. But there was something about this woman that made him open up whether he wanted to or not. That felt…dangerous. He smiled in the dark, remembering that Malcolm had said smart women were the dangerous ones. He moved his head to press his lips to the top of her head. Dangerous and tempting.

To his surprise, she moved at his soft touch and spoke against his skin, not moving her head. "Can't sleep? What time is it?"

"You've got a couple hours yet. I slept for a little while. I'm just lying here, enjoying the moment. Tonight was nice."

"Hmm...yes it was." She stretched against him like a cat, long and supple. "We should definitely make this a thing." She raised her head. "I mean, *not* a thing, or anything serious, but there's no reason why we can't have—"

"Booty calls?"

Her nose wrinkled. "What we have is more than that. Not so much more as to be commitment-adjacent, but... we have *something*, Cody." She rested her chin on his chest and grinned. "We don't have to define it, do we?"

"We do not. We can just take it day by day and see where it leads. Open-ended. No strings—"

"Yes, I know the rules. I helped write them, remember?" She patted his chest with her hand. "But if this is going to become a dinner and TV on the sofa sort of thing... I don't know...doesn't that feel...risky?" She might be right, but he'd really enjoyed their time on the sofa, fully dressed, watching a show. There was something comforting about it.

"I can stick to the rules if you can. And if we do that, there's no risk involved. Casual. Temporary. Either one of us can pull the plug whenever they want, and it's okay. You talked about trauma-dumping earlier, but let's make sure there's no trauma involved between us. No secrets, either." He tapped the tip of her nose with his finger. "And don't forget, we promised to remind each other *why* we're Team Single. We need to focus on that more, I think." He smiled at her, sliding his hand down her arm to capture her hand in his. "We can do this, Jenn."

She didn't agree or disagree. They just lay there together in the dark, wrapped up in each other and relaxed. Jenn finally broke the silence. "I'd still like to know more about you, Cody. As a friend. Even as a lover. I know you're divorced. I know you've had anger issues. I know you're a recovered alcoholic—"

"Recover-*ing* alcoholic," he corrected her. "There's no such thing as a recovered alcoholic. I'll always be one, just hopefully a sober one. And I told you about the meetings I go to, and my sponsor."

"You told me your sponsor's first name, that's it."

"It's called *anonymous* for a reason."

She hesitated. "I know, but…"

"No exceptions. I shouldn't have told you that much. But he's a good man, and he's been a rock for me all year. I share everything with him."

"Everything?" She pulled up enough to look down at his face. "*Everything* everything?"

Cody muttered a curse. Once again, she'd gotten him to spill more than he'd intended.

"Everything that happens, but without identifying details or tiny specifics. He knows I'm seeing a woman casually. He's not crazy about the idea, and he doesn't know who you are." It wouldn't be that hard for Malcolm to figure it out—Cody only had two female coworkers, and one of them was in her seventies.

She put her head back on his shoulder and considered what he'd said. Maybe she was done with questions...

"Is that what ended your marriage? The drinking?"

There wasn't much point in deflecting anymore. Jenn was quietly relentless once she started something.

"It wasn't *just* that," he answered, "but it was the final straw. Lynn and I got married right out of high school, and then I enlisted in the army, and we...we grew up and became different people while I was off playing soldier. She was enrolled in college so she stayed here after Ava came along. They didn't follow me to bases around the country, which made sense to me. I got back here as much as I could, but Lynnie was already moving on. She got her accounting degree and joined a startup company that became very successful, so she didn't need my income. She was basically a single mom to Ava while I was away, so she didn't need me for that, either. By the time I came home for good, I felt like I was intruding on someone else's happy family."

She patiently waited for him to tell her more, which he didn't want to do. But of course, he did it anyway. "And I was a different man in more ways than one. I deployed three times, and saw stuff...did stuff..." He hesitated. "The kind of stuff some men can't forget. I was one of those men. I couldn't sleep because of the nightmares. I scared my own daughter when I'd wake up screaming and cursing. And it wasn't just at night. Those memories were always clawing at me, crawling under my skin and making me...making me a bad person."

"You weren't a *bad* person, you were a damaged one." Jenn's voice was soft. "That wasn't your fault. Is that when you started drinking?"

He huffed a short laugh. "I started drinking hard while I was in the army. But I *perfected* it after I got out. It was my crutch…my rose-colored glasses." He'd self-medicated his pain with booze. "And when the whiskey didn't work, I got angry. All the time. No one—not even me—could blame Lynn for separating herself and our daughter from what I'd become. She did the right thing."

"I'm sorry all of that happened, Cody. But things are better with your daughter now?"

He ran his hand down her bare back. "You are just *full* of questions tonight, aren't you? But yeah, Ava and I are doing okay. I'll have her this weekend, and Lynn gave me a heads-up that Ava decided she needed pink hair. And now she's got it. And I am on notice not to give her a hard time about it."

Jenn giggled, as she slid her body on top of his. "Just like my mom? How fun! The good news is a lot of those hair colors are temporary, so try not to fret about it too much, Dad." He helped hold her in place, lying belly to belly.

"What are you doing, Jennifer Bellamy?"

"Changing the subject. You're right, I have been pestering you, but I appreciate you filling in some of the blanks for me. And now, I think we should make better use of those two hours we have left." She dropped her head and kissed him.

Malcolm had warned him not to use any relationship or sex as a replacement for alcohol. He said it was easy to find other ways to bury problems instead of facing them, but that it was just replacing one addiction with another.

Jenn sat up on top of him and moved to get things

started. As usual, his body was ready and willing. She had the ability to erase all problems from his mind.

Right or wrong, he did feel slightly addicted to the woman.

Chapter Fifteen

"I don't think I've heard you whistle before, Daddy." Ava looked up at her father in surprise. They were walking the beach near the Sassy Mermaid Motor Lodge on Sunday morning. It was something Ava had first asked to do during the summer. Now it was part of their weekend routine, even on sharply cold mornings like this, where the sun lied and laughed about it. But his daughter should be warm enough in the new clothes she'd talked him into buying yesterday at the shops in Mashpee—metallic gold hiking boots and a sparkly blue down puffer jacket. *She's growing up way too fast.*

"Dad? Why were you whistling?"

"I didn't realize I was, pumpkin. I guess I'm just happy." It was an odd sensation, and one he wasn't sure what to do with.

"What are you happy about?" Ava darted across the sand to check out a large stone that looked interesting.

"I'm happy that I'm with *you*, Ava. This weekend has been fun."

She laughed, pushing a heavy wave of pink hair off her face. He was still getting used to it, but she loved it, and that was all that mattered.

"Da-ad—" she put her hands on her hips "—you don't

like to shop, and all we did was shop yesterday. You thought it was *fun*?"

"I don't like to shop for myself, but I love shopping with my beautiful little style maven."

Her nose wrinkled. "What's a style maven?"

"It's…well, I guess it's an old-fashioned word, since you don't know it. It means someone who has good taste in fashion and style. Someone cool. Like you." She'd run back in his direction, then let out a squeal of excitement when she saw a group of seals sunning themselves on rocks up ahead. He warned her not to get close to them. They were generally shy and harmless, but he'd seen the teeth on those things.

"But Dad, I want to watch them!"

"We can do that from the overlook platform at the top of the stairs. Go on." She bolted up the steps ahead of him. Oh, to have her energy. Her joy. They'd gone through the tough times and come out the other side. All he had to do was stay sober, and he'd do that for her. He had to.

"Look!" she shouted, pointing over the rail at the seals who were now safely below. "Is that one a baby?"

A voice came from behind them. "Not quite a baby anymore, but it's definitely a youth."

It was Jenn's mother, Phyllis Bellamy, owner of the Sassy Mermaid. She was walking across the lawn toward them. Jenn was a few feet behind her. He'd seen her mom before, here and at a few business association meetings, but never to have an actual conversation with the woman. He wondered how Phyllis would feel if she knew how much Cody knew about her marriage to the serial cheater back in Iowa, and her roller-coaster relationship with Devlin's father. Typical small town—everyone was connected to each other somehow. Tiny little chains of information. Now he and Jenn were adding another complicated link to that. He gave her a quick smile over Phyllis's shoulder. How would her mother feel if she found out about *them*?

"Hi." He held his hand out. "You're Phyllis Bellamy, right? Cody O'Neil, and this is my daughter, Ava."

Ava was too transfixed with the seals to look up. Phyllis, her own hair even brighter than Ava's, took his hand and held on to it. She was dressed in a bright orange turtleneck under a dark jacket over skintight leopard-print leggings and tall black boots. Jenn was in jeans and a heavy Irish sweater that went to her hips. He knew every curve hiding under that bulky sweater.

Phyllis examined his face for a minute or two, until he started to wonder if she *did* know about him and Jenn. Then she smiled, and his breath caught at the sparkle of her blue eyes. Those were Jenn's eyes. Jenn's smile.

"Cody O'Neil," she said thoughtfully. "You work for Devlin Knight, right? Selling houses?" He nodded, and she looked back at Jenn. "You work with my daughter."

"Uh...yes, I do. Great girl...uh...woman. She's doing a great job." Jenn's brows rose in amusement.

I'm totally not having sex with your daughter, ma'am.

"I'm sure she is—my Jenn's a bright woman. And Devlin's a great boss, I'm sure. He's a good lad. My son-in-law, Sam, is his cousin, and those two are thick as thieves. You've been there for, what, a year or so now? From Boston?" And there were more of those little connection chains. "And this is your little girl?"

"Mom, ease up on the third degree," Jenn laughed,

turning to Cody. "My mother needed some help putting up Halloween decorations in the lobby, and we pulled all the Thanksgiving and Christmas boxes out of storage, too."

"Sounds like fun. I hope you don't mind us using the overlook," Cody said.

"Not at all," Phyllis said. "That's why my uncle built it. I'm glad to continue his tradition of letting everyone in town use it." She walked over near Ava. "That pup you saw was born early this summer. He's getting pretty independent now."

Ava looked up and quickly blinked. Did she know Phyllis? Then he realized she was staring at the older woman's short pink hair. Phyllis laughed.

"That's right, kid. We have the same taste in hair color."

Ava's mouth opened, but Cody caught her eye and shook his head. He didn't want her saying anything hurtful. She finally just nodded. Then she took in Phyllis's outfit and grinned. "You have a great vibe."

Phyllis let out a loud laugh and gave Ava a quick hug then released her. "I think that may be the best compliment I've ever received, Ava. Thank you!"

"And Ava," Cody interjected, "this is my coworker, Jenn."

It was odd, introducing his daughter to the woman he… What *was* he doing with Jenn? It was starting to feel like more than random hookups. They were becoming friends, yes, but something deeper was brewing.

Ava gave a quick little finger wave. "You sell houses, too?"

"No, I do office work to support the people who sell houses, like your dad."

"You have pretty hair."

"Well, thank you. So do you. That jacket is gorgeous. Where did you get it?"

With that, the shopping chatter commenced. He stood back and watched as Jenn and her mother talked all things fashion with Ava. His daughter giggled at something Phyllis said, and Jenn looked back at Cody with a smile that made *something deeper* begin to warm in his chest. It seemed the more they each agreed to be casual, the less casual their relationship felt.

The three of them leaned on the railing again, and Phyllis answered Ava's questions about the seals, and also the sharks that spent time in the waters off the coast in warmer seasons. Ava told Jenn and Phyllis about how much fun she'd had on Sam's boat a few weeks ago, and Phyllis told her that Sam's wife, Lexi, was also her daughter.

He glanced at his watch, and reminded Ava that he needed to drive her back to her mother's house. She waved him off—one of those grown-up gestures that pinched his heart a little.

"Mom and Brian went hiking up in New Hampshire. They won't be home until four o'clock." She looked at Phyllis. "Brian is Mom's boyfriend."

"I see…" Phyllis glanced at Cody, but he was no help. Ava hadn't mentioned Brian yet, and he sure hadn't asked. Phyllis leaned in toward Ava. "Do we like Brian?"

Ava thought for a minute. "He's okay. Kind of a nerd. He builds robots. He's funny. Binksy likes him." Cody bit back a smile. That was quite a bit of information, and he was relieved that she seemed okay with Brian, and with the idea of her mother dating.

"Binksy?"

Ava told Phyllis all about her beloved calico cat, and Phyllis, clearly a natural with children, listened in rapt attention. Jenn had been careful not to hang too close to either Cody or Ava. She let her mother take the lead. He imagined this was new territory for *her*, too. Meeting her lover's daughter. He winced to himself. He wasn't crazy about the term *lover*. It not only sounded outdated, but it didn't capture what he and Jenn were building together.

When he finally pried Ava away and they walked back to town, he asked what she thought about Jenn and Phyllis.

"They were nice," she answered. "Phyllis has a wild fashion sense. And Jenn guessed where you bought this jacket for me. She said she might go to that store and check it out." Then she let out a heavy sigh, as if the kid carried the weight of the world on her shoulders.

"What's wrong, Ava?"

"I'm sad that I have to change my hair."

"Why do you have to change your hair? Yesterday you told me you loved the pink."

"Dad, I like Phyllis, but I can't have the same hair color as an old lady!"

"She said *what*?" Jenn was laughing so hard she almost fell off the corner of her bed where she'd been perched. "That would have cracked my mother up! Ava seems like a really good kid."

"Thanks. Despite all my screwups, she's pretty great."

"Would you ever have another?" She wasn't sure why

she asked. It just seemed that he was such a kind and loving father.

He frowned, suddenly serious. "Not a chance. I almost ruined *her*. I can't risk putting another child through my demons."

It made her sad to think he didn't believe in himself. "Cody, you're not drinking anymore. You're getting settled. You'd be a wonderful father if you had another child."

"Jenn, that is never going to happen. I'm *done*. If having children is something you're looking for, you've got the wrong guy."

She held up her hands with a laugh. "I was not suggesting that *we* have children, trust me. There are some women who would walk across hot coals to have a baby, and I've just…never been one of them. I love kids, but if it doesn't happen for me, I'm okay with that." She realized how hypocritical that sounded and made a face. "Which means I shouldn't be pushing *you* to have another child. And honestly, I think Ava's going to keep you on your toes for years to come."

He chuckled. "You mean like calling your mom an old lady? Yeah, no kidding. But despite that comment, she liked your mom a lot. And you, too. You're a lot like her, you know."

"Like who? Ava?"

He grabbed her hand and pulled her further onto the bed, close to him. "No, Sexy. You're like your mom. Her blue eyes. Her smile. Her way with kids."

The thought made Jenn smile, even if it was a surprise to hear such an affectionate comparison with her mother.

"I do like children. I especially liked Ava. I can see

why they advanced her a year—she's very clever and mature. And I like my new dwarf name, too. Sexy, huh?"

He pulled her into his arms and rolled over so he was looking down at her with a grin. "You're a schoolteacher, so you must like children. And Sexy suits you very well."

She went still. "I *was* a teacher. Any school that does their due diligence won't be interested in hiring me." She missed being in a classroom, engaging with children. Grace had told her about some openings for substitute teachers, but she wasn't sure if that would work. It might be more painful to only be a temporary teacher. And if the news of her downfall ever reached Winsome Cove...

"You don't know that," Cody insisted. "There isn't an actual news story about it that someone could search, is there?"

"No, thank God. I wouldn't have been able to hide *that* from my family. Will emailed the photos directly to all the school board members. Once I found out, and trust me, those rumors flew like lightning, I resigned before they could fire me. It was the best solution for everyone if nothing went on record." She could still feel the burning shame and shock she'd felt when a board member reached out to tell her what they'd received. Everyone on the board had seen the pictures, men and women.

Still looking down at her, Cody gently brushed hair from her face, his eyes warm with affection. With *deep* affection. Tenderness. Caring. She lost her train of thought for a moment, wanting to linger there in that coffee-colored gaze.

It had been her idea for Cody to come to her house tonight instead of the apartment. She wanted him to see her home, however temporary it was. But she did *not* want her neighbors to see him there, so she'd insisted that he park his car around the corner, where he'd dropped her off before. Cody had jokingly asked if she wanted him to sneak through the neighbors' backyards to get to her place, but she thought that might be riskier than walking down the sidewalk after dark. Too many neighbors had motion-sensitive spotlights and cameras. It would be disastrous if anyone called the police on him while he was trying to get to her place.

He'd waited until nine o'clock to come over, and they'd gone straight upstairs to the bedroom. It had been a long time since Thursday, and they were both hungry for each other. Then she'd made a run downstairs for water and snacks. Cheese, grapes, prosciutto and crackers was the best she could manage, and they'd made a picnic of it on the bed.

"So he emailed them instead of posting them on social media?"

Her body tensed, and she shook her head back and forth on the bed. "I don't want to talk—"

"Hey, I told you about my drinking. And my divorce." He sensed her tension, and stopped teasing. "I won't force you to talk, Jenn." He chewed his lower lip. "But I gotta tell you, as much as I didn't want to share my stories with you, saying some of that out loud helped. I think secrets carry a lot more weight than they should. If you and I are the only ones who know them, we can at least unburden ourselves to each other. We're each other's safe haven."

What he said made sense. It *had* been hard not to be able to talk about what happened in Des Moines.

"Okay, okay," she sighed. "But I swear, if I'm *Sexy*, then you're *Vexy*, because you're vexing me right now."

He chuckled. "Fair enough. Vexy works. What happened?"

"It was all my fault," she said. "I was the one who texted those stupid pictures to him. It was supposed to be a joke—a racy lingerie selfie to tease him while he was away on a business trip. We were engaged, so it wasn't like he hadn't seen me like that. He texted me back to send him something even more risque, so I took off my bra and took a selfie in a…in a goofy pin-up pose." She shuddered, and Cody rolled onto his side and pulled her close.

"Months went by and I never thought about those pictures again. It was just one silly night. Then I found out he'd cheated on me with his sister's best friend. They were an item back in high school or something. Whatever. Will gave me a big song and dance about how sorry he was, and he really expected me to forgive him. After knowing I'd watched my dad doing the same nonsense for years. I broke off the engagement and told his parents why. Maybe I shouldn't have gone that far, but they were nice people who kept pressing me for an explanation." She snuggled into Cody's embrace, soaking up his heat. "I guess they really let Will have it. The very next day, Will sent those pictures to the school board. And just like that, my sweet little life in Des Moine was over."

Cody was right. She felt lighter after saying all of that out loud. It didn't change the horror of what happened, but holding it all inside took so much effort. After a brief silence, he kissed her lips softly.

"You should tell your family. Will was a douche. None of that was your fault."

"Oh, come on," she scoffed. "I'm the one who picked

yet another jerk as a boyfriend, after marrying and divorcing one straight out of college. After being the *daughter* of one. And then sending him those pictures—so stupid."

"Stop it. You're beating yourself up more than anyone else would ever think of doing. You have a trusting heart. That doesn't make you a bad person, or a stupid one." He stared down with that warm smile again, and suddenly Jenn realized she could easily fall for this man. And he didn't seem to be a jerk at all. The only problem? He wanted nothing to do with anything that looked like a real relationship. Just her luck.

"And if he only emailed them," Cody said thoughtfully, "which was *really* a dirtbag move, and there wasn't a news story, then they might not show up in a background check for a teaching job. Don't give up your dream, Jenn. Don't let him win."

Chapter Sixteen

"**A**re you *whistling*?" Nancy turned toward his desk with a big smile. "I have never heard you whistle before, Cody."

He grimaced. He needed to start paying attention to when and where he let his happiness show. It apparently freaked other people out.

"You're not always in the office, Nancy. I'm sure it's not the first time." He lightly tossed a folder on top of a small stack on his desk, and got up to grab another property from the file cabinet.

"Oh, I'm pretty sure it is," Nancy said. "You've got a little pep in your step, too." She sat back with a wide grin. "Oh, somebody's getting lucky, isn't he?"

"Who's getting what?" Jenn walked in the front door with their lunch orders. Cody prayed Nancy wouldn't answer, but that was too much to hope for. The woman lived for stuff like this.

"Our boy Cody seems to have found a lady friend."

Jenn stopped abruptly, staring wide-eyed at him. He gave a quick shake of his head to let her know he hadn't started this awkward conversation.

"Wh-what makes you think that?" she asked.

"He was *whistling* just now," Nancy replied. "You

know, the way *happy* people do? It was very un-Cody-like. And look at that face of his, all soft and smiley." Cody had been smiling at Jenn. He couldn't help it.

"Oh, I don't know." Jenn was regaining her composure as she handed out the lunch bags. "People can be happy about more than just getting lucky. Cody just listed that big place in Sandwich, right? And he had a closing yesterday." She set his lunch on his desk and winked. "That commission was enough to make *anyone* happy enough to whistle."

That was no lie. His savings account, funds set aside for a house of his own, was finally looking big enough for him to start looking. Lately, though, he'd been, too busy spending time at Jenn's place, or having her stay at his. Nancy turned back to her desk, and her lunch, without saying any more. Jenn sat at the reception desk, but kept sending him sly glances.

Nancy was right—he *was* getting lucky. Lucky to have found someone like Jenn. The past few weeks had been fun, spending every moment they could together. And it wasn't just about sex anymore, if it ever had been. They actually *liked* being with each other. Laughing in one of their kitchens as he did his best to get her to loosen up about cooking. Snuggling up close on one of their sofas to watch zombie shows. Jenn insisted she liked them, but she covered her face during the more graphic scenes. She cried over sappy commercials. And giggled every time a certain commercial came on about keeping dog food in the refrigerator.

He and Jenn had also started spending time outside of their homes. Not for date nights or anything, but for "friendly" adventures like hiking the trails that were everywhere on Cape Cod, or exploring beaches together.

And he'd invited her to go into Boston with him next weekend. It was far enough away from Winsome Cove that they shouldn't have to worry about the gossip grapevine. She hadn't seen much of Boston proper, and it would be fun to show him his city.

Jenn had even joined Ava and him on another shopping trip to Mashpee, where she and Ava had oohed and aahed over clothes, shoes, and jewelry together. The unexpected shopping trip had been Ava's idea. She'd been in the office with him one Saturday morning, waiting for him to make a few calls to calm down a seller and buyer who were both panicking over a bank delay. Jenn had stopped in to get documents together for a Monday morning closing for Devlin, and she and Ava started to chat about Ava's puffer jacket again. That was when Ava had suggested that he take her and Jenn back to Mashpee so she could show Ava where she bought the jacket. And, of course, as long as Ava was near a store, she would shop, too.

It had been one of Cody's best days in a long time. Jenn knew how to talk Ava's language, and Ava had warmed to her immediately. It was like having two little girls, the way they giggled and ran ahead of him every time they saw a shop they wanted to check out. He became the caricature of the token man on a shopping trip, carrying their bags and waiting on a bench outside while they shopped. But he'd been able to see Jenn in a different light, away from the office and away from it always being just the two of them. The three of them had lunch together before heading back to Winsome Cove, and he'd spent most of it watching Jenn and Ava talk a mile a minute with each other. It had been the kind of day he'd like to put on repeat.

Nancy left the office shortly after lunch, leaving him and Jenn free to talk.

"You have Ava this weekend, right?" she asked. "What are your plans?"

"I told her I'd take her out to P-town, and maybe take a whale-watching cruise if the weather cooperates." He turned in his chair. "Want to join us?"

A guarded expression crossed her face. "I don't think that would be a good idea. I don't want Ava to get confused about what we're doing. There's no sense letting her and me get too close when..."

He remembered their rules. Oddly enough, he hadn't thought about those rules in a while. Casual. Temporary. No commitment. No expectations. Blah, blah, blah. For the first time since they'd met, he found himself resenting the agreement they'd made. But Jenn had been adamant, and he had no idea what she might say if he suggested tossing them out. One thing he *did* know? He wasn't ready to lose her from his life. So he nodded and played along.

"You're right, sorry. Ava's my number one priority, and she doesn't need to get attached when we're just..." He couldn't bring himself to say the word, but Jenn could say it with no problem at all.

"Temporary."

Jenn knew it was what he wanted to hear. As much as his invitation had surprised—and tempted—her, they needed to stick to their agreement. And they needed to keep their…whatever it was…quiet from everyone else. She didn't want to deal with her family's gleeful speculation, because then she wouldn't be the only one disappointed when it came to an end. And it would. Cody had made that very clear.

It was a little confusing, the way he'd been suggesting more outdoor, and borderline public, activities together. But she had to remember that this man was *not* a forever man. No man was.

She was still mulling over that fact early Sunday afternoon. She'd had brunch at her sister's restaurant with her mom. It had been a nice meal, but Mom was unusually quiet. And Fred Knight was quiet, too, sitting in a nearby booth with Devlin and Carm. It was weird to see the two of them in the same room and not hear them throwing insults and challenges at each other.

Everyone else in the restaurant noticed, too, casting suspicious looks at the two of them, as if they thought it might be a prank by Fred and Phyllis. But, judging from her mother's frosty composure, it was no prank.

"Mom, do you want to talk about it?"

"About what, dear?" She batted innocent, if very long, eyelashes at Jenn. When Jenn just stared right back, her mother's shoulders fell in surrender. "No, I don't want to talk about it. That fool of a man had me thinking things were…serious. But I guess they're not."

"You've been together for two years, Mom. That seems pretty serious. What happened?"

Her mother's mouth twitched in annoyance. "It's not like I *needed* things to go to the next level. I was *fine* with us keeping it casual." Jenn kept herself from wincing at that damn word. *Casual.* Mom folded her linen napkin and slapped it down on the table. "But then he made me think he *was* going to do something. He kept teasing and hinting that he'd found something special for me, and that I was going to be surprised, and he couldn't wait to show me. I was dumb enough to think it might be a ring."

"An *engagement* ring?"

"Like I said, it was dumb." Her voice dropped. "But when he handed me that little box one night after the bar was closed up, I got all…misty-eyed. Like I was young again, you know? Like…someone *loved* me. Like Cinderella." Her mother sniffled, and Jenn's heart broke for her. Mom had been so fierce since coming to Winsome Cove, and now she looked broken.

"So it wasn't a ring?"

Mom laughed so loudly that people turned to look, including Fred. But her laughter was bitter.

"Oh, it was a ring, all right. It was a *key* ring!"

"No way…" Jenn breathed.

"A *key* ring, in a velvet box. He bought it because it had a mermaid on it, like the motel. A *key* ring!" She was animated now, puffed up in indignation and the center of attention for the entire place. "I threw it right back at him and it hit him square in the chest. Damn fool."

Fred had heard enough. He jumped to his feet and pointed a finger at her mother. "That thing was gold-plated, and that mermaid had pink hair and real crystals in her tail. Your name was engraved on the back! I paid a bundle for it, and you threw it at me like it was from some dime store. How could a key ring insult you so badly that you can't even *talk* to me anymore?"

Poor Fred. He really did look distraught. He had no idea what he'd done. Devlin stood and patted him on the shoulder, but Fred shrugged him off angrily and stomped away, heading to the bar next door, muttering about ungrateful women.

"Mom, do you think he intentionally made you think it was going to be an engagement ring?"

Her mother stared down at the table, cheeks red with anger and hurt, but she eventually shook her head. "No. He wouldn't play a trick like that. But…he gave it so much buildup and I not only thought it was going to be a ring, but I *wanted* it to be one. It's been two years. I love the man, and I'm sure he loves me, but…is he ever going to do anything about it?"

It was a good question, and one Jenn had been asking herself lately. She comforted her mom the best she could. She hoped she and Fred could figure things out. As much as she'd worried about all their saltiness together, they made a weirdly cute couple.

She'd just waved goodbye to Mom and headed to her car when her phone chirped with an incoming text message. It was from Cody: Can you come to the apartment? Urgent.

What could possibly be urgent? Then she remembered he had Ava with him. Instead of texting, she called his number, and he answered instantly.

"Hey," he said, almost breathless, "Can you drive over real quick? Ava needs you."

Her throat caught at those words. "What do you mean, she needs me? What's wrong?" She thought about Fred's screwup with her mom. "This isn't just some ploy to get me—"

"Damn it, Jenn, she wants her mom, but I can't reach

Lynn because she's off hiking another stupid mountain with Brian. You're the next best thing."

"The next best thing to her *mother*?" She had no idea what he was talking about.

"It's a…a *female* thing. She's locked herself in her room and won't talk to me." He sounded completely adrift.

"O-o-o-h." She had an idea what it might be. "I'm actually just leaving 200 Wharf. I'll be right there." She made a quick stop in the office restroom before going up to the apartment.

Cody looked shell-shocked when he opened the door, and he scooped her into his arms for a quick embrace. "Thank God you're here. She's in there crying, and we can't get in touch with her mom, and Lord knows *I* don't know how to help her."

She patted his chest. "I've got this, Daddy. Take a breath and have a seat."

She tapped on Ava's door lightly.

"Go away, Dad!" Ava almost screamed the words. "I don't *want* you here!" Jenn glanced back at poor Cody, pale-faced on the sofa.

"Ava? It's me, Jenn. Can I come in?"

There was a beat of silence, then the door was unlocked. Ava's tearstained face looked past Jenn. "He can't come in."

"It's just me, honey." She stepped into the bedroom and Ava quickly locked the door. "What's going on that you can't talk to your dad about?"

"I'm…bleeding." Ava sniffled. "Down there."

Jenn sat on the bed next to the girl, putting her arms

around her and letting her cry against her chest for a minute.

"Is this the first time that this has happened?" Ava nodded against her. "Do you know *why* it's happening?"

"I guess so. I saw a video and Mom talked to me, but…" Ava looked up, almost hyperventilating in panic. "She's not answering and I don't know what to do and now my pants are stained and I can't tell Dad." She threw herself against Jenn again, and Jenn held her close. That first rush of hormones was truly raging right now. Jenn started to rock back and forth with Ava, hoping the motion would calm her, and eventually it did. Ava was hiccup-crying instead of sobbing.

"Ava, this is a really important moment in your life, and in *every* woman's life. There's nothing to be ashamed of, because it's completely natural."

"Mom said this was going to happen every month forever, and I don't want to do that. I don't want to."

"It's not quite forever, even though it might feel like that sometimes. But yes, this will happen every month for a very long time. And you'll be prepared for it after this, which makes it a lot easier to deal with. And honey, your dad might not have experienced this himself, because he's a man, but you can always talk to him. He loves you."

Ava sat up, gaining a little more control over her emotions. She stared flatly at Jenn.

"He laughed at me."

Jenn gave a little gasp. "He *what*?"

"He *laughed* and asked me what I sat in."

"What?" Jenn still didn't understand…*oh*. He saw, and didn't know.

"I didn't know it had happened," Ava sniffed. "He saw a spot on my pants and asked me what I sat in. He was laughing about it. It was *so* embarrassing, Jenn."

She cringed in sympathy with the girl. "Again, he's a man, and men don't know much about this stuff. It probably never occurred to him that you were starting your period, but I promise he knows what it is and what it means. And I'll make sure he *never* laughs about it again." She said that emphatically enough that Ava smiled a little. "How do you feel, other than mad and embarrassed?"

"Okay, I guess. My stomach hurts a little."

"Dull like a tummy ache or sharp like a muscle cramp?"

"Sharp."

Jenn nodded, sending a quick text to Cody with instructions to heat a damp towel in the microwave and put it in a Ziplock bag. She explained to Ava that her father was going to make a heating pad to make her cramps feel better. "Do you have another pair of pants and panties you can change into?"

Ava nodded. "But won't I—?"

"I grabbed a few pads from the office bathroom on the way up, and I'll show you how to use them so you won't bleed through anything else. And we'll treat and wash these pants as soon as you get them off. Ava, millions of girls around the world are dealing with becoming young women, just like you are. It's an exciting time, and you should be proud. *Never* ashamed. Okay?"

"I don't feel proud, but...okay."

Ava was curled up on the sofa with Cody's homemade hot pack on her stomach when her mother called her. Jenn was in the kitchen, making grilled cheese and tomato sandwiches—comfort food for a stressful day. She'd negotiated a truce between father and daughter, making Cody apologize and convincing Ava to accept it.

Ava was talking to her mother, crying again, but just a little. She explained that "Daddy's friend" had saved the day. Ava handed the phone to Cody shortly after that, and he left Ava watching a movie and walked into the kitchen. Jenn could tell he was trying to explain who "Daddy's friend" was and why his ex-wife hadn't heard about her before now. *Awkward.* Even more awkward was the moment he handed the phone to Jenn. She waved her hands to reject it, but he didn't blink. She finally grabbed the phone, giving him a withering glare.

"H-hello?"

The woman's voice was tense, but not angry. "I hear you're the woman who helped my daughter get through a bad time today."

"I'm Jenn, and I was glad to help. Ava's a special girl."

"I didn't know you'd spent enough time with her to know that. I didn't know anything about you at all." Jenn didn't respond. She wasn't going to apologize over communication that should have happened between Cody and Lynn. She heard an exasperated sigh. "I'm sorry, that's not your fault. I'm just mad at myself for not being there for Ava. Sounds like she was pretty upset."

"It didn't help that her father accidentally laughed about it."

Cody narrowed his eyes and mouthed the words "Thanks a lot" to her. He finished grilling the sandwiches while she stepped away and filled Lynn in on what had happened, from an adult woman's point of view. By the time Jenn handed the phone back to Cody, she and Lynn had exchanged numbers and promised to keep each other informed if anything was going on with Ava that the other should know.

"I'm glad you found yourself a nice, normal woman to date," Lynn said to Cody when he took the phone back.

"A nice *normal* woman? As opposed to what?" He'd stayed in the kitchen as Jenn took sandwiches to Ava in the living room.

"As opposed to some woman you picked up in a bar somewhere."

"Come on, Lynn," he snapped, "I've been sober for months."

There was a slight pause before she responded. "You're right. It's just that I spent a lot of time after we split up worrying about what sort of woman you'd bring into our daughter's life. And I think I might actually like this one."

He looked at Jenn, who was giggling with Ava now, and toasting something by clicking their hot cocoa mugs together. "Yeah, I think I might like her, too. But it's nothing serious."

That last sentence had come out without thought, as if he was reminding himself of the deal. A deal he'd like to rip up if he could. Because he hated the thought of *not* having Jenn in his life. Maybe he'd test the waters with her next weekend, when they were in Boston.

Maybe they could redefine this thing they had together. Maybe she'd stay.

Chapter Seventeen

Jenn felt a sense of exhilaration as she walked through a crowded Quincy Market in the center of Boston. This city had a frenetic energy that she'd never felt in Des Moines. It was an assault of noise, colorful tourist shops and tempting foods. And she had Cody at her side through it all. He protected her as much as he could from being jostled as they purchased ridiculously expensive lobster rolls and a small box of cannoli from the food court vendors to take home for dessert later.

It had been a great day, strolling through shops and watching street performers, not worrying about who saw them together. No explanations needed.

It felt like they were a real couple. It had felt that way since the beginning of November, and now Thanksgiving was almost upon them. Being a couple was the one thing they both claimed *not* to want. She'd told him it was never going to happen for her. No way she was *ever* going to date again. He'd said the same.

And here they were, laughing and eating together, sipping from their cups of pricey cappuccino, like some old married couple. It was nice. It was also painful. Because she hadn't seen any indication Cody might be having any doubts about their elaborate rules. It was their mutual disgust at relationships that had brought them together in the first place. So how was she going to tell him she'd changed her mind?

Even more worrisome, what if it was a mistake to change her mind? What if she'd been right all along to think she wasn't cut out for being with anyone long-term? Just because Cody didn't seem to be a jerk like the other men she'd dated, that didn't mean he was good for her. He had his issues. And he still claimed he hated romance. She watched him munching on his messy lob-ster roll and smiled. Maybe she should follow his lead and try to enjoy the moments they had, instead of wish-ing for something different.

After all, things had been going so well lately. She'd even taken on a few days as a substitute teacher at the elementary school, and she'd *loved* it. Cody had been her biggest cheerleader, and he'd convinced Devlin to flex her schedule so she could continue to teach occasionally.

They were lucky enough to grab one of the café tables in the atrium in the middle of the building and settled in to eat and people-watch together. Cody nodded toward a couple walking by, sharing a single ice cream cone, and he made a face.

"That's one of those lovey-dovey things I'll never un-derstand," he said. "Sharing food. It's gross. How is that romantic?" He brightened. "You know, you and I vowed to remind each other why relationships were dumb, and we haven't done it very often. This is the perfect oppor-tunity to find all those things that drive us crazy about couples."

"Really? Because it seems you *constantly* mention all the reasons and rules."

Oops. Didn't mean to say that out loud...

His brows lowered. "I don't think I talk about our rules any more than you do. They're important, right?"

They were clearly important to *him*. "You're right, sorry. Forget I said that."

She was in a mood. She'd been moody the past few weeks, bouncing from happy to angry in a heartbeat. She was blaming it on lack of sleep. They ate in silence for a while before he spoke again, sounding cautious. "Jenn, do you *want* to revisit the rules we set? I mean, when we said *temporary*, that could mean the rules, too. Or we can keep everything the way it is." That last sentence was spoken quickly and emphatically.

Was this a test, or did he really want to reconsider everything they'd agreed to?

"Um...it doesn't hurt to talk about it," she finally said. "At the time we originally made our agreement, we both had one-track minds."

He nodded, wiping away a smear of sauce at the corner of his mouth. "Yup. Sex." They both laughed, and his sounded as uncomfortable as hers felt. "I don't think we expected to last more than one or two more times together," he continued. "We didn't think we'd start...hanging out like this. I *never* imagined you meeting Ava."

"Or talking to your ex?"

His laugh was more genuine now. "*Definitely* not that. As much as we said 'no relationship,' I think we have to admit we've at least built a friendship."

Could that be enough for her? Maybe it would become *more* if they just took it slow. Friendship could be the first small step. "I agree. We're friends. *Good* friends, I hope."

She saw the mischief in his eyes and knew what it

meant. Whenever he was uncomfortable with a conversation, he tried to joke his way out of it. It was an annoying defense mechanism he'd learned long before she came along.

"We're good friends. With *great* benefits." She sighed inwardly, hating that term but not wanting to dampen his good humor. He didn't seem to notice she wasn't laughing along. "You know," he added, "we can replace a lot of those rules by just saying that we're keeping things... open-ended."

"What do you mean?"

"Let's stop pretending we're not in *some* sort of relationship, but our relationship doesn't need a label. We'll just take it day by day. If it lasts a while, it lasts a while. If it doesn't, that's okay, too. If we don't pressure each other for anything, all's good. When one of us decides the *benefits* part is over, hopefully we can still be friends. If that happens next month or next year, we can still have fun in the moment."

"In the moment..." She considered what that might be like. "Does that include going public? I'm getting tired of sneaking around all the time. We're not doing anything to be ashamed of."

"I don't see why not. I still don't want to label this... whatever we have. You're not my girlfriend. We're not dating or anything like that." It wasn't meant to be hurtful, but it stung just the same. "I don't want anyone picturing cupids and wedding bells in our future."

"Of course not," she agreed, knowing it was what he needed to hear. She leaned forward. "Except for Max and Grace's wedding bells. Do you want to be my plusone at the wedding?"

He swallowed hard, clearly hesitant. It was a risk to ask, but she couldn't imagine going with anyone else.

"How soon do you need to know?"

"Soon. The wedding's next month. Sorry to spring the invitation on you, but… I don't want to go by myself when everyone else in the world is paired up. It could be our first foray into public as a not-couple."

Things felt heavy and out of balance between them again. Stupid rules. Casual. Temporary. And now…open-ended. And *maybe* public. But *not* serious. *Not* romantic. Every time they tried to simplify things, it got more complicated. She took a breath and gave him a bright smile. She'd give him a way out if he needed one.

"You know what? Don't worry about it. I'll order the pork chops for you for the reception, and if you don't show up, I'll take them home for myself."

He didn't look convinced of her latest change of mood. She *had* been a bit erratic today. Up and down. On edge. *Hormones?* She tried to calculate if that time of month was approaching, but she couldn't remember her last period. She must have had one since moving here, but for some reason she couldn't put a date on it.

Two young men almost bumped their table, walking so close together that they looked like one person. They mumbled an apology and kept walking while sharing an order of fried clams, each reaching into the same little red-and-white clam box.

"See, there's someone sharing food again." Cody turned, then made a face. "It's so unsanitary. What could possibly make sharing germs romantic? Why can't people just eat their own food?"

Distracted, she agreed. "Very unsanitary."

"But if you think about it," Cody said, "romance is germy in general. Holding hands? Why do that? Where have those hands been?"

Jenn smiled and tried to play along. "That's true. And don't forget kissing—talk about a germ exchange, right?"

He looked at her in surprise. "I hadn't thought about it that way, but yeah. But I do like kissing. Kissing *you*, especially."

Whoops. She'd been too busy calculating dates in her head to pay attention. "Well, yes, but *we* kiss as part of making love, in private. We don't do any silly love pecks in public."

"Good point. Speaking of that, look at those two up on the balcony." She looked up and saw a man and woman in a tight embrace up against the stone wall. Their hands were everywhere, lips locked together. Cody snorted. "Get a room, right?"

"Right. No need to be a spectacle."

He looked at her and frowned. "Is something wrong, Sexy?"

She shook off her other thoughts and laughed. "And that's another one to watch out for—nicknames! My brother-in-law calls Lexi 'Pookie' sometimes and it makes me crazy."

"But…*we* have nicknames. Dwarf names. Whatever you want to call them."

"Yes, but they're just for fun. We don't get all gooey with them."

Cody agreed. "True enough. So let's make sure we don't fall into that romance trap, okay? We're taking a risk if we start being in public in Winsome Cove. Everyone's going to assume we're a couple. So none of the smoochie-coo stuff for us. No sharing food—" he started counting off on his fingers "—no holding hands, no public displays of affection of *any* kind, especially kissing. No using gooey nicknames."

Jenn pressed her lips together and hid her annoyance.

Just what they needed—*more* rules.

"Let me get this straight." Malcolm raised one brow as he sipped his coffee. "You're going to a *wedding* with Jenn. As a couple. But you're *not* a couple, because you have rules to prevent that. But you're spending almost every night together, and you're going to a *wedding* as her *date*, even though you're not dating?" He sat back in his chair at Jerry's Java and started to laugh, slow and deep. "Man, do you have *any* clue what you're doing with this woman? Any clue at all?"

Cody wanted to defend himself, but there was no defense when the guy was absolutely right. "Zero clue. Every time I think I'm going to make it clearer, I make it worse."

Malcolm was still chuckling, but there was concern in his eyes. "This right here—" he gestured in Cody's direction "—is exactly why we tell people to avoid relationships in the first year or more of sobriety. I told you before, relationships are messy. And messy is not a good place for an alcoholic to be. I'm laughing, but this could go bad in a dozen different ways."

"I know. I keep trying to do what I think she wants from me, and that's also what I wanted to start with, but the more we say the word 'casual' to each other, the more *not* casual it feels. I really care about her, Malcolm. She's…different from any woman I've known. Well, you've met her."

Jenn and her mother had walked into the coffee shop last week, the day before Thanksgiving. Cody had made quick introductions, not saying *how* he knew Malcolm, of course. It was hardly unusual for a real estate agent to have coffee with an attorney, even if it *was* an immigration attorney. But he'd mentioned Malcolm's name to Jenn a while ago, and he could see in her eyes that she'd remembered. They'd chatted about Thanksgiving for a few minutes and parted ways. Jenn had spent the holiday with her family, and Cody had spent it with Malcolm and his wife, Margie. The couple had hosted several people from the support group in their home. It wasn't the same as being with family, but it was good to not be alone.

"I only met her for a minute, but yes, she seemed nice. Pretty, too. And look—none of my concerns are about Jenn. I'm not against you two being together if you think that's what you both want. I'm just saying you both need to stop complicating things. You two are *messy*."

"How am I supposed to tell her that I want to break all the rules we keep agreeing to? I asked her if she wanted to set them aside a couple weeks ago, and she didn't say yes. And then we came up with all the PDA rules on *top* of that. I keep trying to dig out of the restrictions, and we keep ending up with *more*."

"Can I make a suggestion?" Malcolm asked.

"Please."

"Why don't the two of you sit down and actually talk to each other? You're both intelligent people. Just *talk* about how you feel."

"Every time I try that, we—"

"From what I've heard, every time you try that, you say what you *think* she wants to hear. Try telling her the *truth*."

"You're probably right." Cody stared into his coffee cup. "I'll do that after the wedding this weekend." Before Malcolm could object, he talked over him. "Her brother's wedding is a big deal for Jenn, so I'll be following the rules all the way. I don't want to spoil anything for her or her family."

Malcolm was silent, then he shrugged.

"I hope you know what you're doing."

Chapter Eighteen

Jenn stared at her reflection in the bathroom mirror and blinked away tears. Max and Grace's wedding was days away. Jenn was going with Cody. Their first opportunity to go fully public about…whatever it was they were doing. Team Single had turned into Team Maybe over the past few weeks. Jenn had known for a while that, whether she wanted to or not, she was falling in love with the man. But that was still against the rules, wasn't it? Did the rules even apply anymore? Well, she was pretty sure one big one did.

Even if they went public as…dating, being together, having a relationship of some sort—Cody had made it very clear that he did not expect anything long-term. Not even with her. He'd told her once that monogamy was unrealistic. He didn't want another marriage. He didn't want another family. He didn't want a commitment of any kind. She'd agreed wholeheartedly when he said it. It was easy to laugh and say that love was for losers. So why did she find it so hard to imagine her life without Cody in it? And why was she convinced that a life without him was coming much sooner than she'd ever guessed?

She'd thought they had time to figure things out. Maybe he'd fall eventually, too. After all, they had agreed to leave their relationship open-ended. No time frames were imposed. They were together until one of them said they weren't. And *she* had no intention of ever saying they were through. It was a nice thought, but life had other plans. She roughly wiped tears from her cheeks with both hands, then looked down at the bathroom counter.

There were four pregnancy test sticks sitting there. From three different manufacturers. And they all verified—either with the word, symbol, or a color—that Jenn was, indeed, pregnant. Which was impossible, right?

She was on the pill, for heaven's sake. It may not be one hundred percent effective, but what were the odds that she'd be one of those four-percenters that got pregnant anyway? Someone had to be, of course, or the manufacturer wouldn't warn about it. But why *her*? Why *now*? Just when she'd agreed with Cody that, no matter what happened, their relationship would never result in a family.

That tiny word *Pregnant* on one of the test sticks might as well have been a flashing strobe light, forcing her to blink and look away. Whether they wanted a child or not, one was on the way. She sat on the edge of the tub, suddenly lightheaded at the thought.

Her hand moved to her flat stomach. She couldn't be more than a month or two along. She'd had that urinary infection before leaving Iowa, and she'd been on antibiotics for two weeks. At the time, she hadn't worried about the risk of antibiotics affecting the viability of her birth control pills. Clearly, that was a mistake.

She still had options. She could choose *not* to have the

child. That way, Cody would still be in her life. But she couldn't make that decision—*any* decision—alone. Her eyes closed. She was going to have to tell Cody. They'd just agreed over Thanksgiving weekend that the secrets that brought them together were too much of a burden. They'd said they'd never keep secrets from each other. So very mature. And Cody hadn't hesitated to share his true feelings about children.

I already have a child. I don't see any more in my future. If that's something you need, I'm the wrong guy.

At the time, she'd responded the way she thought Cody expected. Respectful of his choice. Mature. Understanding. And why shouldn't she be? She hadn't been lying when she told him she wasn't sure if *she* wanted children, either. She adored children, of course. She loved teaching. She adored Ava. She'd told herself that getting back to teaching and being in Ava's life would be enough.

It had never bothered her before that she didn't feel that overwhelming desire to give birth the way that some women did. Her fingers moved in a light circle on her belly before standing. Jenn had a hunch she might start to feel differently about all that once she wrapped her head around the fact that she was pregnant.

Another thing Jenn hadn't anticipated was how difficult it was going to be to see Cody at the office the next day and not just blurt out the news. But that wouldn't be fair to him, and it was guaranteed to blow up their workday, which wouldn't be fair to anyone else. Devlin was bringing in new clients that day to sign a purchase offer.

Besides, she'd decided to wait until after the wedding to tell Cody. She had no idea how he'd react, and she didn't want to spoil anyone's fun. More selfishly, if it was going to be their last weekend together, she wanted it to be a happy one. The decision had made sense at the time, but now that he was walking into the office, she had her doubts.

Jenn had chosen her favorite Irish sweater to wear over slim black jeans. It wasn't as if she had any baby bump to hide, but the big, heavy sweater still felt like armor. As soon as Cody came down the back staircase, she'd had to bite her lip to keep from saying anything. She didn't even turn around until she heard his warm "Good morning" behind her. She made sure she was smiling when she did.

"Hi, Cody." No one else was in the office, and he leaned over to kiss her softly. Their lips had barely touched when he raised his head and frowned.

"What's wrong?"

I'm pregnant.

No, this wasn't the time.

"Nothing. I just didn't sleep well last night." She forced a quick laugh. "My sister's *fra diavolo* pasta sauce talked to me until the sun came up."

Cody kissed her forehead and straightened, his hand resting on her shoulder. "Oh, I'm sorry. I wish I'd been there to hold you."

She'd told him a story about having a girls' night with her sister, that might end with Lexi staying over. Just a little fib so that he wouldn't stop by. She wouldn't have been able to take those tests with him right outside the door. She patted his hand and tried to sound playful.

"And then *you* wouldn't have had a good night's sleep. I missed you, but it was better this way." Nancy came in the office, raising her eyebrow at Cody's hand on Jenn's shoulder.

"Well, I see we're no longer playing make-believe that you two aren't dating."

Cody left his hand where it was. "Not dating, exactly."

The words, which she'd agreed wholeheartedly with just a week ago, now felt like razor cuts on her heart. She hadn't even realized she'd been lying at the time, even to herself. That whole "let's not define this thing we have" conversation had sounded so progressive and wise. But she'd hoped in her heart that it *would* end up with a definition. Just not necessarily the one it was going to have now...*parents.*

"Cody and I are just taking things day to day." She forced some lightness into her voice. "Nothing all that serious. It won't affect anything here at work."

Nancy made a scoffing sound as she sat at her desk. "Puh-leeze. You two have had the hots for each other from day one, so it's *already* affected things here." Her thick accent made the last word come out as *hee-yah.* "But not in a bad way. It's not like you're screwing on the desks or anything, or...did you?" She looked over at them and must have sensed Jenn's tension. She waved her hand with a laugh, gold bangles jingling. "Oh, come on, I'm kidding. I know you wouldn't do that. It's been fun to watch you try to hide it, though, even on the mornings when you tiptoed down the stairs from his apartment and pretended you'd been in the office kitchen."

Jenn gasped. She really thought they'd been more careful than that.

"Don't look so surprised," Nancy continued. "You think that just because I'm old I didn't have my fun back in the day? If you need any tips on how to sneak around, I'm the one to ask, trust me. And if you think you can *fool* me, guess again, 'cuz I've done it all."

"It's just casual," Cody said, making Jenn physically recoil. He felt her twitch and looked down at her. "You okay?"

Big smile, Jenn. "I'm fine, just tired, like I said." She turned back to Nancy. "He's right, we're…just casual."

Were babies considered casual?

Nancy's eyes narrowed as she looked between the two of them. "Keep telling yourselves that, kids. But if you want my opinion—and I'm sure you don't—I say go for it. Quit being scaredy-cats."

Cody patted Jenn's back and went to his desk. "It's not about being scared, Nan. Just practical. We're friends. We like being together. And we've agreed that neither of us wants anything permanent. So don't go making googly eyes at us, okay?"

Jenn swallowed hard, knowing babies were about as permanent as it got. She met Nancy's gaze, and watched it soften in sympathy. The older woman couldn't possibly know about the baby, but she could tell that this relationship was far from casual for Jenn.

"No googly eyes. Casual. Temporary. Got it." Nancy turned away and started typing. "Good luck with that."

Cody frowned as Jenn moved around his kitchen, making Swiss cheese omelets for dinner. He'd offered to cook, since she'd said her stomach was off all night, but she'd brushed him off. It felt like she'd been doing that all day. Not making eye contact, sighing at her desk, and tensing just a little whenever he touched her. Was she angry? Or preoccupied with something? Maybe the approaching wedding was making her anxious.

He called out to her. "I think I saw Devlin put a bottle of chardonnay in the office fridge if you want me to go look. I don't mind." Devlin occasionally toasted a good sale. "I'm guessing white wine goes with eggs? You know, like egg whites?"

"Probably…" She didn't get the joke. Instead her eyebrows gathered together in worry. "But I'm not drinking tonight. Taking it easy on my tummy."

She patted her stomach and smiled, but the smile didn't reach her eyes. Her hand lingered there for a moment before she turned and plated the omelets, filled with cheese and crumbled sausage. His portion covered his plate, while hers was much smaller. Was she more ill than she was letting on?

"Hey, do you think you should see a doctor?"

She was just sitting down, and her fork slid off her plate and clattered onto the table.

"Wh-why would you say that?" she blurted, eyes wide as she settled in her chair. Her face was pale. Cody started to worry for real.

"You said you didn't sleep last night because you didn't feel well. You made omelets because you wanted comfort food. And now you're turning down a glass of wine."

"I'm okay, Cody. It's just—"

"Is the wedding stuff getting to you? Because it's finally here and after this weekend you'll be done."

She gave him a more genuine smile, and her shoulders eased. "Yes, that's it. It's going to be great, but I'll be glad when it's over. All the activities are wearing me out. I can't imagine how exhausted Grace must be."

They started to eat in silence, then Cody shook his head. "The whole wedding industry is such a trap. All that money for a couple hours of your life, to celebrate something that—odds are—is not going to last."

Jenn set her water glass down hard on the table, her mood quickly shifting. "Could we...could we just *not* with all the negative stuff this week? We've both been burned in the past, but I refuse to assume the same thing will happen to my brother. Max and Grace are really happy together, and they're *good* for each other, and little Tyler adores them. Let's not wish a cloud over them on their wedding weekend, okay?"

Cody sat back in surprise. "I never said I wanted anything bad to happen to them. I just don't get the need for couples to have all the pomp and circumstance. I like what *we* have. Respect. Affection. And no expectations weighing us down." He thought about her request. Max Bellamy *was* her brother, after all. "You're right, though—I shouldn't rain on their parade. Sorry. I promise to keep my opinions to myself, okay?"

She stared at him hard enough to make him squirm in his chair. He had no idea why she was acting so edgy today. Then she took a breath and blew it out slowly through puckered lips.

"Yes, let's just enjoy what we have, while we have it."

They finished their meal, and he moved the conversation to safe topics like the weather and the spectacular waterfront mansion that Devlin had just listed. They watched some television together, then went to bed, where Jenn snuggled deep into his arms and fell fast asleep. He didn't mind the nights when that happened. They didn't need to make love every time they were together. Besides, morning lovemaking was great. In fact, he found himself enjoying nights like this more and more, with her arm draped over his chest and her head on his shoulder.

He and Jenn were in a good place, where they had no need to prove anything to each other. He'd never thought a relationship could be like this—relaxed, friendly, with no pressure to "perform" a certain way. They had no claim on each other's forever. They were having fun in the here and now, and that was good. Live in the moment. It was smart. Practical. Mature. Totally free. No chains. It was exactly what he'd wanted.

A long sigh escaped him.

Liar.

Cody rested his cheek on top of her head and closed his eyes, taking in her sweet scent and holding her close. Here in the silence, in the darkness, with her sleeping peacefully in his arms, he could admit the truth.

He was in love with Jennifer Bellamy. He loved every inch of her, every essence of her. Her laughter. Her tears. Her soft breaths right now as she slept. He loved her trust. How she embraced Ava and had immediately partnered with Lynn. Hell, he loved how she ran the office. He loved watching her calm anxious clients and explain things to them—not as children, but communicating in a way he knew she'd learned as a teacher.

He loved watching her with actual children, too. The way she'd blossomed after taking those few substitute teacher days at the elementary school. That took a lot of courage, and she'd stepped up. He knew she'd end up teaching again—there was no doubt in his mind. And he loved that for her.

Cody also loved the way he and Jenn had agreed on their approach to their relationship. Both of them had good reasons for not wanting anything long-term. For not believing in romance and happily-forever-afters. They'd had fun mocking everyone else's romantic nonsense. Agreeing that it wasn't for them.

Until he broke the number one rule they'd set.

He fell in love.

Cody wanted forever with this woman. They'd left things open-ended, so…maybe they *could* just go on like this forever. Except they'd also agreed that either one of them could walk away at any time, and the thought of Jenn walking away made his chest go tight with fear. Should he tell her how he felt, or keep it to himself and blindly hope she stayed for good? He frowned in the darkness. That was a huge gamble, and he didn't want to gamble with Jenn.

Agreeing to be in a relationship didn't have to mean having a big wedding and all the flowers and hoopla. It didn't have to mean a wedding at all—they could just… agree to be together from now on, without a piece of paper between them. She and Ava genuinely liked each other, so no worries there.

More important, Jenn understood that he was finished having children, and she'd supported that. She'd been clear about not feeling a burning need to have her own child. Especially if she went back to teaching—she said she'd have plenty of children to worry about. She said being with Ava was enough for her. That was important, because, in his experience, most women wanted babies of their own. And—in love or not—he didn't think he'd ever be ready to face that kind of responsibility again. It had been hard enough to feel himself falling in love and not go into a tailspin. Not reach for a drink. Not feel like he was losing control. Thinking of starting a new family? That didn't feel safe at all. Which was okay, because he and Jenn were on the same page—no babies.

So maybe they *were* ready to talk about making a commitment to each other. Maybe she wouldn't mind that he'd fallen in love with her. Maybe she'd come to love him in return. To trust him with her forever. He turned his head and kissed her hair and she sighed in her sleep. The thought of her in his arms for the rest of his life made him happy. *She* made him happy. They could do this.

Just the two of them together forever.

Chapter Nineteen

Jenn scowled at the full-length mirror and tugged on the hem of the top she'd planned on wearing to the rehearsal dinner. Her mother had picked it out while they were shopping in Boston, and she had to admit the shade of dark blue picked up the color of her eyes nicely. And it complemented the shimmering ice blue of the short, sequined skirt Mom had also chosen for her. Her mother insisted it was time for Jenn to "get some pizzazz." She probably just wanted someone else to be in sequins because that was what she'd chosen for *herself*, buying a bright pink sequined dress.

Grace—perhaps becoming a little sensitive about overdoing the Christmas wedding theme—had declared the Thursday evening rehearsal and the private dinner at 200 Wharf afterward to be Christmas-free. No green or red anywhere. And this outfit fit the bill.

Jenn's only concern when she bought the top was that it would give off too many *Elsa* vibes, making her look like a winter snow queen instead of a bridesmaid. She tugged at the hem of the top again, then pulled at the side seams. Her *current* concern was that it was hugging her chest a little too tightly...to the point where she looked like Marilyn Monroe, with her chest very much in the spotlight.

It didn't make sense. She'd tried it on in the shop a month ago and it hadn't fit this snugly. The neckline hadn't seemed low or revealing. But tonight, her chest was definitely the first thing anyone was going to see. Front and center.

Hello, world, look at Jenn's plump, pregnant boobies!

She muttered a curse and went to her closet. There had to be a solution hanging in there. Lexi made fun of her cardigan collection—part of her schoolteacher uniform—but that might be the only thing that would camouflage these spectacular new breasts of hers. She'd lucked out on not getting morning sickness—yet—but her body was definitely changing. She hadn't gained an ounce, but her curves were somehow fuller. Rounder. She had been hoping she was just imagining it, but the blue top confirmed she was not.

Maybe that was why Cody had looked at her so funny that morning, after they'd had easy morning sex and snuggled together as the sun rose. He'd insisted on making breakfast, because he still believed all of her distraction yesterday was left over from Lexi's spicy pasta sauce. As if the award-winning chef would ever make a dish that would upset anyone's stomach. She was relieved he'd fallen for her little white lie, though. It kept him from pressing harder to see what was bothering her. She wanted to wait until after the wedding to tell him they were going to have a baby. A baby he'd made very clear he did not want.

Didn't want a baby. Didn't want a commitment. Didn't want anything permanent. Didn't want a "label" on what they were doing. Didn't want to fall for what he called *romantic nonsense.* To be fair, she'd called it that, too. Until she fell in love with him. But that was a dilemma for next week. She took a deep breath. This weekend was all about Max and Grace.

She spotted a white angora cardigan that was shorter and dressier than her usual work sweater. The soft wool was loosely knit in a lacy pattern. It would send her outfit even further in the winter princess direction, but it was soft and loose enough to disguise how tight the blue top was underneath.

The rehearsal at the historic white clapboard church in town went smoothly, and Jenn's sweater solution had worked—she didn't feel like her chest was a distraction. They had to have rehearsal on Thursday night because the church had a Friday night wedding on their calendar. Max had joked that he thought everyone could remember their places for forty-eight hours.

The ceremony would be very traditional, and six-year-old Tyler was going to play a solo on the piano. Jenn was surprised to learn about that, but she'd forgotten that Tyler, like his late mother, was a near prodigy on the keyboard. It was one of the things that had brought Max and Grace together, as she'd been Tyler's piano teacher after they moved in next door. Tyler played the song at rehearsal—"My Funny Valentine"—and there wasn't a dry eye in the wedding party. When he finished, Grace sniffed, then laughed and warned everyone to plan ahead and have tissues ready during the actual ceremony on Saturday.

Tyler was also going to walk Grace down the aisle.

Her father was recovering from a recently broken hip, and insisted he didn't want to hobble down the aisle with a cane. Her brother, Aiden, had volunteered, but once Tyler said *he* wanted to do it, Grace and Max had agreed immediately.

After the rehearsal, they all went to the restaurant, where Lexi had a large table set up along the back wall. Cody was waiting there when they arrived. He'd been invited to the rehearsal itself but had protested that he wasn't part of the wedding party. Grace had already promised that there would be a chair for him at the head table at the reception, as Jenn's plus-one. Maya's husband, Leon, would have a seat there, too. As Grace put it, "It seems so silly to make couples sit apart."

Fred joined them at dinner, too, kissing her mother tenderly before sitting next to her. Apparently, they were back *on* again. He'd apologized—many times—for the key ring debacle, and Mom had agreed to give him one more chance.

Jenn suspected Cody had skipped the church rehearsal because he wanted to spend as little time as possible next to what he deemed the *wedding industry*. As if romance might be contagious. But she had to smile when she saw him stand and pull out the chair next to him tonight. She hoped he was right about it being contagious, because that meant there was a chance he'd catch the love bug from her.

Dinner was filled with laughter and stories about Max and Grace and the other couples there. Stories about how each couple met, first dates, first fights, funniest dates, and so on. She and Cody kept telling people they weren't necessarily a couple, or at least... *Cody* had been saying that over and over the past couple of weeks, just as he had with Nancy. *Nothing serious.* But he didn't seem to object when they were treated as an actual couple tonight.

They couldn't tell anyone the truth about their first meeting, of course. That story was too full of the secrets they were still keeping for each other. Everyone assumed they'd met at the office, and Cody and Jenn let that story stand. A lot of their funniest times had been at the expense of all the lovey-dovey things they had mutually abhorred. Without a word between them, their eyes met and they agreed it was probably best not to share those stories two nights before her brother's wedding. Instead, Cody had everyone laughing with his story of walking downstairs and scaring Jenn in the office the night of the bridal shower. He conveniently skipped the sex-on-a-desk part of the evening.

Jenn followed by telling how they'd discovered they were both runners, often joining each other for at least part of their morning runs. And how she fell right in front of him on an evening run, forcing her to have a bandaged knee during the dress fittings. Like Cody, she skipped the hot sex part. But her mother had an odd smile as Jenn spoke, so much so that Jenn finally turned to her and said *"What?"*

"Oh, nothing," Mom answered with an exaggerated fluttery wave of her hand. "It's just that you're telling this story as if no one knows that. The two of you jog right past your sister's house and the Sassy Mermaid. Sometimes you even cross the motel parking lot to get to the beach together. Do you think you're invisible?"

Jenn and Cody looked at each other as the table laughed. There was a spark of humor in his dark eyes, and of something else, too. She knew what his desire looked like, but this was more than that. This was from someplace deeper in him. The intensity of it made her heart skip a beat.

Sam leaned forward to look down the table at them. "Exactly, Phyllis! Lexi and I set our clocks by you two running by. And all those weeks you kept telling everyone that you were finished with love and romance. You had to have known how ironic you were being, right?"

"We're just friends," Cody said firmly, sitting back in his chair and breaking the heat between them. "Anything more than that is a label of *your* choosing, not ours. Right, Jenn?"

She didn't answer right away, reeling from the change in atmosphere. For just a moment there, she could have sworn she saw something that looked like *forever* behind his eyes. The way they softened and darkened and swept over her face as if trying to memorize every inch of her. She'd almost convinced herself it was love. But that was just wishful thinking. Or desperation, created by the child she was carrying. What he'd said—*just friends*—felt like a bucket of ice water had been thrown on her.

He'd made his feelings clear from the start. He wasn't going to allow himself to be serious with anyone. Not even her. Not even after she told him about the baby. She had to face the fact that it might just be her and the baby together. With Cody a secondary character, at most, in their lives.

Someone at the table made a joking comment about them not fooling anyone, and the conversation swirled on happily without them. Cody went back to his dessert as if nothing had happened. But something *had* happened.

Jenn had just faced the reality that, no matter how hard she wished it, Cody's feelings about relationships were unlikely to change. Which meant she needed to decide how to move forward. Alone, if necessary.

Cody felt the air between him and Jenn shift and grow sharply chilled, but he had no idea why. He'd said what he knew she wanted to hear. What they'd agreed on. No strings attached. Sure, he was actually in love with her, but he wasn't going to spring that on her at dinner. Especially at a dinner that was centered on her brother and future sister-in-law. That would be a jackass move.

If he was going to shock her with his confession, it would be in private, where they had a chance to talk it out and figure out their next moves. But in public, he needed to pretend to be committed to the deal they'd made—just a casual, open-ended relationship that could be ended by either of them at any time. No harm, no foul. It was what he and Jenn had agreed on all along, so he'd keep up the act until they could figure things out. Which didn't have to happen tonight.

As the evening broke up, everyone made their plans for Saturday. What time to be at the church—before noon. Where to meet for photos after the ceremony—at the Sassy Mermaid overlook. How long they'd spend on photos before going to the country club for the reception—thirty minutes tops.

Max and Grace were getting lucky with the weather. It was supposed to be cool, but clear and sunny, with light winds. He smiled, standing back to let the wedding party buzz with their plans. He was just an observer here. Jenn's plus-one. He'd felt a little weird when he heard he'd be joining her at the head table at the reception, but Grace had insisted. Her best friend and maid of honor's husband wasn't a groomsman, but he was joining his wife at the table, so Cody wouldn't be the only one.

He and Jenn walked to his car together. The plan was for him to stay at her house tonight, then leave after breakfast so she could go to work, then do all of her night-before-the-wedding duties with Grace on Friday. He'd see her at the church Saturday morning, then join her at the reception.

They'd dance together for the first time. Well, the first time in public. Maybe that would be a good time to tell her he loved her—right in the middle of a great song, surrounded by happy friends and family. He could whisper it in her ear and see how she reacted. Maybe she'd whisper her love back to him and they'd spend the night dancing and saying *I love you*s to each other.

"You've gotten awful quiet." Jenn's voice cut through his fantasy. There was still a chilly edge to it. She was angry about something. About him?

He kept his response light. "I'm just thinking about how much fun it will be twirling you around on the dance floor this weekend." He opened the passenger door for her. She got into the car without saying a word. *So much for lightness.*

Not sure what was happening, and not wanting to rock the boat any further, he made the short drive to her place in silence. They waved to Max and Grace across the driveway and walked into the house. Once inside, she started walking toward the kitchen, but he took her hand and turned her around.

"What's going on?" he asked, searching her face for

clues. She wasn't giving anything away. Her eyes were guarded, and her lips pressed tightly together as if she was struggling to hold words back. "I can tell you're upset, Jenn. What is it?"

Deep furrows appeared on her forehead, then vanished again. She looked up at him with that artificial smile she used when she wasn't in the mood to smile. He knew what her next words were going to be, and he shook his head sharply before she could lie to him.

"Don't tell me you're *fine*. I know you better than that, and you're clearly annoyed. I'm assuming it's with me, but for the life of me, I don't know why."

Her smile faded in defeat. "I just...we don't *always* have to tell people how casual we are, Cody. Sometimes it feels like you're saying it just to goad people into arguing with you. Like you need to prove it all the time." She was warming up to sharing her feelings, and her hands waved angrily. "Like you're bragging about how much you don't want anything more than friendship with me."

He heard her words but couldn't make sense of them, so he fell back to his usual defense in uncertain situations, even though it hadn't worked earlier. He tried to lighten things up again, giving her a wink.

"Well, I want more than friendship when we're in bed together."

That was a bad move. Her eyes narrowed on him. "And that's it, right? Friendship with a side of sex."

The edge in her voice told him this was no time to kid around. She sounded...hurt. But *why*?

"Isn't that what we agreed we wanted?" He reached to hold her, but she shrugged out of his grip, folding her arms to warn him off from trying again. His hands fell.

"Okay, I'm confused. You and I agreed that we didn't want to put any labels on what we have."

"Yes, but it was something we agreed to between *us*. We don't have to tell the whole universe how very special we are. Has it ever occurred to you that our arrangement might not be as *evolved* as we like to think it is?"

Cody replayed the evening in his mind, trying to figure out what had ticked her off so badly, because he was starting to get a little ticked off himself. "Tonight I said that we aren't putting labels on what we have. And that's true. Do you want us to pretend to be something else when we're in public? Put on an act? Lay on the public displays of affection? Be all kissy and handsy with each other? Confess our undying love whenever people are looking?"

Please say yes...

He knew what *he* wanted to do, but this seemed like a bad time to blurt out that he loved her. If she gave him any hint, though—

"Oh, sure. God forbid I force you to be kissy, Cody."

That was clearly sarcasm, but was it the angry kind or the I-forgive-you kind? Hoping it was the latter, he went for a joke again.

"Hey, that could be my dwarf name—Kissy." He stepped toward her, but she flinched away again. The move stung. "Okay, what the hell is going on with you? How can you be angry just because I clarified our relationship tonight? I didn't say anything you didn't already know. I didn't say I hated you, or that I was using you in any way. I said we were *friends*. Isn't affection a good thing?"

"You said we were *just* friends. It sounded like there wasn't a chance for anything more for us."

"Do you *want* something more?"

She started to answer, then stopped. She was staring straight ahead, at his chest instead of his face. When she spoke, it looked like she was talking straight to his heart.

"Whether we want it or not, we *have* something more."

Was she talking in riddles on purpose? He put his finger under her chin and gently lifted it until their eyes met.

"Tell me what that means."

She closed her eyes, breathing deeply. Then she opened them again, staring up at him in...fear? Hope? Anger?

"I'm pregnant, Cody. We're going to have a baby."

Chapter Twenty

In her dreams last night, in what little sleep she'd had, Jenn had pictured this moment. She'd dreamed about telling Cody he was going to be a father again. In that dream, he wept for joy and swung her around in the air to celebrate the news. He told her he couldn't wait to have a family with her. He told her they'd get married. He talked about how happy Ava would be to be a big sister. How happy *he* was. How much he loved her. Yes, it had only been a dream, but it felt so true that she really had hopes this conversation would play out just like that.

She'd planned on waiting, yes—but it was too big a secret to keep. He'd noticed how distracted she was. And then, like a fool, he'd tried to tease her out of it, as if becoming parents was some big joke. But he didn't *know* they were going to be parents. So she had to tell him.

Jenn watched a dozen or more emotions cross his face as he stood frozen in front of her. Most were gone before she could name them, but she recognized shock and fear in the mix. At no time did he reach for her with joy in those deep-set eyes. He didn't declare his love for her. There was no swinging. No celebration. No mention of family. No mention of anything. Just stunned silence.

After what seemed like an hour, but was probably just a minute or two, he cleared his throat and tried to speak.

"You…you're…pregnant." He wasn't questioning it, at least. Just rolling the fact around on his tongue. "But… you said you didn't want…"

She shook her head, growing more tense by the moment. "No, I never said I didn't want a child. I said I'd never felt the overwhelming desire to give birth that some women feel."

"What's the difference? You said you were fine with not having children." It was his turn to have an angry edge to his voice now. She felt defensiveness rising, but she tried to tell herself that the man was in shock. Then his eyes hardened. "I definitely told you I did not want this, and you agreed. We said no kids."

Her temper could only be contained for so long, and the hormones flooding through her body right now weren't helping. Still, she tried to say her next words as slowly and carefully as possible. "We said a lot of things, Cody. We said *casual*. We said *temporary*. We said *open-ended*. And *flexible*. And *subject to change*." She put one hand on her flat stomach, feeling the crunch of the sequins beneath her fingers. He followed the motion with his eyes, looking baffled.

"But *no kids* was something we both agreed on."

"Actually, *you* said no kids and I didn't argue with you."

"What I said was that I wasn't the man for you if you wanted children. I made that clear. And it's true—I'm not."

He took a step backward, as if parenthood was something he could avoid by keeping a safe distance. He looked terrified, but she was past caring. Self-control be damned. Still holding her stomach, she shook her free hand in front of his face, her finger close enough for his eyes to go wide in alarm.

"We can argue about semantics all night long, but none of that changes the fact that I *am* pregnant. With *your* child. And it doesn't matter if *you* want it, or if *I* want it. I am pregnant."

Silence hung heavily in the room again.

"*Do* you want it?"

She had no idea what he wanted her to say. What answer he expected. And in that moment, she realized she didn't *care* what he expected of her.

It wasn't that she didn't *want* him at her side, but she was suddenly no longer interested in just agreeing with the man to convince him of that. She'd spent too much time worrying about the words she said around Cody for fear of losing him, and not enough time focusing on sharing how she *felt* about him. On telling the *truth*. To everyone.

It was strange to feel such an overwhelming epiphany in the middle of her living room, but it was as if she could read the words of her mind written on the walls around her. All the times she'd blamed other people or her choice of people for failed relationships. How angry she'd been that people wanted her to change. But new-found knowledge washed over her now like a baptism and gave her a sense of calm unlike anything she'd felt before. *She* was the one who always tried to change herself, whether a man asked her to or not. That was on *her*.

She'd even done it with her own family—held back news she thought might upset them, or might make her look bad. But that had been *her* choice, not theirs. And she wasn't going to do it anymore. She was freeing herself from the burden of making everyone else happy. Her chin rose, and she dropped both hands to her sides. Not only had she found inner peace with this revelation, but she'd found, without a doubt, the answer to Cody's question.

"I am keeping our baby."

His mouth opened, but he didn't answer. His face was pale, glistening with a sheen of sweat. She may have discovered exactly what *she* wanted, but those answers clearly hadn't come to Cody. To be fair, she'd just blindsided him with some pretty shocking news. He stared up at the ceiling for a moment, then scrubbed both hands up and down his face in agitation. She knew he was really upset when he used both hands like that. And she'd never seen him leave those hands over his face and groan the way he was doing now, taking long deep breaths like a drowning man.

"Cody, are…are you okay?"

He dragged his hands down off his face and stared at her.

"Were *you* okay when you got the news?" He paused. "How *did* you get the news? Are you sure?"

There was no accusation in his tone, just a tumble of questions about things that didn't matter right now.

"I haven't seen a doctor yet, but four different pregnancy tests say yes."

He scowled at the floor.

"You know how I felt about having any more kids…"

"Like I said," She spread her hands and shrugged, "Your *feelings* about it don't change anything. You're going to have a second child, whether you want to or not. And you really need to stop acting like this is something I did to you on purpose. Sometimes birth control fails."

He let out a breath so long that she thought he might disappear right in front of her, with nothing left to hold him upright.

"How am I going to tell Ava? I just got us back on track this year and now there's going to be a baby that will take attention away from her." It was a weak excuse on his part.

"Ava has never struck me as a child who needs constant attention. And she loves her new baby cousin." Lynn's sister had just had a baby in October. Ava had told story after story a few weeks ago about little Bradley and how cute he was and how much she liked to hold him.

But Jenn's words didn't reach Cody. He'd withdrawn in a way she'd never seen before. He seemed smaller. And very, very distant. Without moving a muscle, it felt as if he'd already left. And not just left the room—left *her.* When he finally looked up, his eyes were shuttered and...cold.

"I told you I didn't want a child." He bit out the words, just shy of snarling at her. She stepped back instinctively. "You know *why* I said that, Jenn? Because I *meant* it. Because I can't handle another child. Because I'm not a natural at fatherhood." His voice rose with every sentence. "It takes time and energy that I'm supposed to be devoting to my sobriety. I wasn't sure I should spare energy for a relationship, but you were just... I couldn't help wanting you. But now you think I'm capable of starting another family? Well, I'm not." He stepped backward again, holding his hands in front of him. "I'm *not.* I'm not ready for any of this. I can't do it." His eyes were shining with unshed tears, making Jenn's heart catch, because they weren't tears of joy. "I can't do this. I can't…" He turned away and reached for the door.

"Cody… I love you."

He needed to know that. His head dropped as if she'd just said the worst thing possible. His shoulders were rounded in defeat. He didn't look back, yanking the door open.

"I hate to tell you this, Jenn, but you picked the wrong guy again."

And he left. Jenn stood motionless in the middle of the living room, her hand back on her stomach, as if to shield their child from what had just happened. She listened to the angry roar of his car going down the street. Going away.

You picked the wrong guy again…

Cody avoided the office on Friday, telling Devlin he was out prospecting for new listings. In reality, he was just driving around aimlessly, lost in thought after a sleepless night. There was no way that he was ready to see Jenn. He didn't know if he'd ever be ready. He'd have to change jobs again. His thoughts were coming in erratic sequence now, leaping from one fear to another. He literally hadn't slept at all last night, and he knew he was too tired and distracted to be driving, but…he had to keep moving.

She told you she loved you.

That couldn't have been true. She'd been desperate. After all, she'd never said it until the minute he'd turned away. He wasn't proud of that move. Only a jerk would leave her standing alone after what she'd told him. But then…that was what he'd always been. A jerk. He'd blown every relationship he'd ever had, and he was continuing his losing streak with Jenn. It just verified what he'd known all along—he was a loser.

A loser who's about to be a dad again…

He couldn't even let himself think about that. He pulled off the main highway and meandered through the winding side roads of Cape Cod, up and down and back and forth. The narrow roads required his attention, and that was good. He needed to focus on anything other than becoming a father. He'd make a mess of that, for sure.

You make a mess of everything.

There was no denying that. He'd joined the military because he was a screwup of a kid whose father told him repeatedly that he'd never amount to anything. His carefully pressed army uniform and mirror-polished shoes made him feel like he'd proved his father wrong. He *was* something. He was a soldier, eager to go to battle.

Except "battle" wasn't like it seemed in video games. It was real. It was confusing, because it might start at any moment. Gunfire could erupt in the middle of handing out candy to little kids. Laughter one second, people running in panic the next. He was on alert the whole time he was in the Middle East. Head on a swivel. Trust no one. Trust nothing—not even the things you saw with your own damn eyes.

Was that a simple goat cart? Or was it a bomb on wheels? Was that old man a "friendly" or was he radioing their coordinates to the enemy? Was that *really* an infant wrapped in those cloths or was it something far more sinister? He'd heard the stories. He eventually learned not to trust his own mind.

Some guys could come home and leave that behind, but he wasn't one of them. He didn't think he'd slept more than a couple hours a night for his first year at home. Lynn tried to understand, but she wanted him to *talk* about it, and that was the last thing he'd wanted to do. So he'd started drinking. And drinking helped.

It didn't help your temper...

Maybe not, but it dulled the pain. Let him sleep. And it was something to do. Going to the bar was better than sitting on the sofa at home, listening to baby Ava cry, fighting to make sense of his jumbled thoughts. Booze quieted those thoughts. At first, it had seemed like alcohol was the answer to everything. With more sleep, he could function as an adult. Get a job.

And all the pretending involved in being in sales was good for him, too. He'd learned that a good salesman was a good actor. And acting like someone else made him feel better, at least while he was doing it. He could come home and playact being a good dad, too, when in reality he had no idea what he was doing. He adored his daughter, of course, but she terrified him. Ava had always had a way, even as a toddler, of looking at him and... seeing him. The real him. She had to know that he was a pretender. So he drank more to hide his fear that she'd reject the real him.

He must have sat too long at a stop sign, because a horn blew behind him. He hadn't even noticed there was a car there. He gave a quick wave of apology and crossed the intersection. He eventually got all the way out to Provincetown and parked his car in the lot near

MacMillan Pier. He walked into town for another coffee, ignoring the Irish pub he'd had to walk past. When he got back to the car, he sat there and just stared out the windshield. It was a cold day, but the sun was bright and warmed the interior. It lit up the colorful small buildings along the pier. The coffee—he'd asked for a triple shot of espresso—was strong enough to make him grimace, but that was okay.

That was all he was running on today. Caffeine and fear.

A baby. Another baby. The problem with children was that they didn't have a fake bone in their little bodies. They took the world as they saw it. And they saw a lot.

Ava loves unconditionally.

Sure, all little kids do that. But…should they? Did Cody *deserve* the gentle touch of tiny Ava's fingers on his head on the mornings he'd been hung over? She'd smooth his hair and lay on the bed with him, telling him she hoped his bad headache went away. That was what he and Lynn said when he was recovering from a night of binge drinking. *Daddy has a bad headache.* Never *Daddy is a weakling.* Never *Daddy drank up the mortgage money again.*

But even if they'd told Ava the truth, she still would have crawled in bed with him and told him it was okay. Because kids loved unconditionally, even when it didn't make sense. He should be grateful for that—it was Ava's love that had kept him going. That pushed him to be better.

But none of that had been easy. How many times had he promised her and Lynn that he'd be a better man, and then—a few days, weeks or months later—he'd fail them. Over and over.

You've been sober for almost a year.

Sobriety was the hardest thing he'd ever done in his life, and it would never be "finished." As Malcolm liked to say, you didn't graduate from the program—you were in it for life. There were days when that thought seemed overwhelming. He'd been doing better, but this was one of those days. This was the worst of those days in months.

You should call Malcolm right now. Reach out. Tell someone you need help.

That made perfect sense. But he wasn't going to do it. He was sure that he had to get through this on his own. Jenn had never known him when he was drinking. She had no idea what she might have to deal with if he lapsed for the millionth time and started drinking again. She didn't know the highs and lows of life with a drunk. The fun parties that could turn into a brawl with no warning. Someone would say something that didn't sit right, and Cody would be ready to rumble. Lynn had dragged him out of more than one holiday party, apologizing to their friends for his behavior. But Jenn didn't know.

She'd never seen the hangovers, the headaches, the throwing up, the promises that he'd never drink again. Usually followed with him insisting that the *hair of the dog* was the best cure. More alcohol always fixed his problems. And destroyed his marriage. And disappointed his daughter. But those things didn't hurt so much when he drank.

The problem with being sober was it meant *feeling* everything.

He reached up to touch his face, surprised that his cheeks were soaked with tears.

You're a coward.

Yup.

You're weak.

That, too.

A drink would help.

He wiped his face dry with his hands and shouted a string of curse words at the top of his lungs while pounding the steering wheel. He would always be fighting this demon, and Jenn had never once met the devil inside him. He didn't want her to, because he *loved* her, damn it. What terrified him was that he couldn't promise her, or himself, or their unborn child, that he could save her from seeing him as a drunk. That was why *forever* was such an impossible concept for him.

Nothing was forever in his life.

It never had been.

Chapter Twenty-One

Jenn was relieved Cody was out of the office on Friday. She'd had no idea what to expect from him after last night, and they didn't need to bring that drama to work. She didn't believe for a minute that he was out looking at properties like Devlin said, though. He was avoiding her. Which could make working here a problem, especially if he wanted nothing to do with their baby. She hated to even think that could happen, but after he'd walked out on her and driven off last night, with no contact today, it was feeling like more of a possibility.

She went through the motions at work, answering calls and delivering messages. Nancy had come into the office that morning, but after an hour or so, she said she had to meet someone and left. That was another relief, because the older woman kept asking if Jenn was okay and staring at her in concern. Jenn took a call from one of Cody's clients, and she'd called his phone from the office line. He hadn't answered, so she'd left the client's information on his voice mail without saying another word.

The ball was in his court now. She'd told him about the baby. She'd told him she loved him. He had to decide what to do with that information.

"Oh, Nancy was right." Jenn looked up in surprise

when her mother and sister walked in. Lexi tipped her head to the side as she examined Jenn closely. "You look like sh—"

"She looks *tired*." Mom was quick to intervene. "Don't make her feel worse. Rough night, honey?"

You have no idea.

"Something like that, yeah. What are you two up to…" She took in a sharp breath. "Oh, you're off to pick up the dresses, right?"

"I think Lexi can handle that by herself, can't you, dear?" Mom looked at Lexi, who clearly hadn't expected the suggestion.

"I thought we agreed the two of us were going to drive up and get them?"

Their mother nodded in Jenn's direction, her expression so full of understanding that Jenn had to blink back tears. How could she possibly know?

"I'm going to spend some time with Jenn today. Nancy said she could watch the office…there she is now."

Nancy came in and gave a quick finger wave to Jenn. "I've got the office, girl. You've got the wedding coming up tomorrow and I have a feeling you could use some mom-time."

Lexi looked between the women and her eyes went wide in sudden comprehension and compassion. "Yeah, sure. There's no need for two people to go. They're just dresses. I'll lay them out in the back of the SUV and it'll be fine." She nudged Phyllis. "Give her the sharks and seals talk, Mom. That was a good one." Lexi spoke to Jenn. "Our mother is a pretty smart cookie. I'll see you guys later."

* * *

The wind had calmed and the sun was bright, so Jenn and her mother walked out to the overlook at the Sassy Mermaid and sat in the Adirondack chairs. They each had warm jackets on, and a mug of hot cocoa in their hands that her mother had picked up for them at the coffee shop in town. Jenn knew Mom had something to say, but she had no idea what it would be. Mom might know that Jenn was upset, but there was no way she could know about Jenn and Cody's—well, it wasn't quite an argument, but it was heavy—conversation last night. Her mother didn't know any of the secrets Jenn was holding, and it was time for that to change.

She'd realized last night that she was done trying to be what other people expected. What other people wanted, or at least, what she *thought* other people wanted. She'd been twisting herself into knots for the past few years, trying to be what others wanted her to be. Good old, reliable Jennifer. She'd let her dad push her out of the town house. She'd let her fiancé push her out of her job. Out of Iowa. She'd let Cody think she was on board with their vow to be anti-commitment…even after she'd fallen completely in love with him.

She wasn't going to tie herself in knots anymore. Not for anyone. She brushed moisture from her face, surprised to feel her own tears. She'd cried so much this week that there shouldn't be any moisture left in her.

"Mom, I need to tell you—"

"That you're pregnant?" Her mom chuckled at the shock on Jenn's face. "How far along are you?"

"H-how did you know? I just found out myself!"

Her mother ran her hand through her bright pink hair,

pushing it off her face with a wide grin. "My breasts and hips started changing within the first six weeks whenever I was pregnant. I thought I was seeing things last week, but one look at you in that blue top last night and I knew." She grew serious. "Does Cody know?"

Jenn sipped her cocoa, gathering her emotions together enough to be able to speak. "I told him last night."

"And how did that go?"

"Not great, Mom."

Her mother nodded in silence. They sat and stared out over the gently rolling ocean waves. One of the seals that were perpetually on the rocks below let out a bellow, prompting Jenn to turn to her mother.

"What is the sharks and seals talk Lexi mentioned?"

She was deflecting from talking about Cody and her mom knew it. And she went along.

"Lexi was in a spot like you—not pregnant, but trying to decide if falling in love was worth the risk. She and I were watching the seals pushing off the rocks and into the water. It was shark season, so there was a huge risk involved. But they did it anyway. They had meals to catch. They had babies to feed. Babies to teach. They had no choice but to dive into that water and take the chance." She hesitated. "I didn't always do a great job of teaching *my* babies."

"What? Mom, you were a rock star. You were always there for us, driving us all over for sports and things. Chaperoning everything from grade school field trips to proms. We were the *cool house* where the kids wanted to hang out."

Her mother raised a brow high. "I think that had more to do with the swimming pool than with me."

"Oh, come on. You baked a million cookies for everyone. You made sure we had a safe place…that everyone had a safe place. You and that gingham apron of yours!"

Mom smiled with a faraway look. "That was my grandmother's apron. She made it herself."

"I remember. You told us all about it. You were the perfect suburban mom. We loved you then and we love you now." She couldn't stand the idea that her mother might not know that.

"Thank you, honey. But I didn't teach you girls that there was more to life than being in the kitchen or running country club events. The example I set for you was of a lonely woman who was hiding her unhappiness behind aprons and fundraisers. I was putting on a good front to the world, and to you kids, but everyone knew the stories of your father's unfaithfulness. *You* knew. I kept pedaling as fast as I could to keep up that so-called perfect image." She gave Jenn a soft smile. "You got that urge from me, and I'm sorry."

Jenn blinked as she started to understand. She'd been doing the same thing—pedaling as fast as she could to appear perfect. Hiding her true self to make everyone else happy. Whether they asked her to or not.

"Mom…" She didn't know what to say.

"I'm not suggesting you need to follow my current example, either." Her mother pretended to fluff her short hair. "Don't go cutting that beautiful hair off and dying it pink!" They both laughed, easing some tension before she continued. "I've been waiting for you to figure it out for yourself—that you don't have to be such a people pleaser all the time."

"I think I'm finally getting that. I've been hiding so

many silly things from you. I didn't want you to be disappointed in me. I didn't want you to know—"

"Didn't want me to know you lost your teaching job over some private photos that were shared with the school board?"

Jenn's mouth dropped open in disbelief. "You *knew*?"

She got a *well, duh* look in return. "Jennifer, I still have friends in Des Moines. People hear things. People share things. I knew about it before you arrived in Winsome Cove."

"Why didn't you say anything?"

Mom shrugged, taking a sip of her cocoa. "I was hoping you'd tell me on your own. And when you didn't, I decided not to push it. I can't imagine how hard that must have been. But it's over."

"It's not over, Mom. Those pictures are out there now. I'll probably never get a full-time teaching job again." There was something in the finality of how her mom spoke that made her curious, though. "What aren't you telling me?"

"Jenn, what Will did is called 'revenge porn' and it's against the law in Iowa. Luckily he only emailed it to specific people instead of blasting it out on social media. Of course, we can't control what happened after it was emailed, and there are no absolute guarantees once something's on the internet, but my divorce attorney paid Will a little visit and explained what could happen to him if he didn't put a lid on things. Immediately. It might be a misdemeanor, but the fines can be substantial, not to mention possible jail time. Will deleted the photos in front of the lawyer, who then quietly mailed letters to the school board, letting them know that it would be very wise of them all to delete those images, too."

Jenn winced, hating to think of anyone looking at those photos, even if just to delete them. But there was nothing she could do about that. If the photos were really gone, she might be able to safely apply for the third grade opening she'd heard about at Winsome Cove Elementary.

"I don't know what to say, Mom. Thank you isn't nearly enough…"

Her mother reached over and took Jenn's hand, squeezing tight. "Just like those momma seals swim out into dangerous, shark-invested waters to feed their pups, we human mommas will fight Godzilla himself to protect our babies. You'll see."

"Oh, Mom, what am I going to do?" Jenn blinked back more tears. "Cody made it very clear that he doesn't want any more children. He doesn't want this baby. He doesn't want a commitment of any sort, to anyone. He walked out on me last night."

"What? That doesn't sound like Cody."

"Oh, it's very much like Cody. I broke the rules that we agreed to. No labels. No romance. No commitments. No forevers."

"Why on earth would you agree to those things?" Her mom shook her head. "Oh, because you wanted him to be happy? Because you thought he might change his mind if you waited long enough? I'm so sorry, Jenn."

"The sad thing is, I honestly agreed with those promises when we made them. I didn't want any sort of serious relationship after what happened in Des Moines. Cody and I bonded over making fun of everyone falling in love. We called ourselves Team Single."

"Wow. Okay. Does he know that you're in love with him? Does he know he's in love with you?" Jenn looked up in surprise, and her mother continued. "Baby girl, it's so obvious to anyone who pays any attention at all. You two love each other. Now you're going to have a child together." She squeezed Jenn's hand tightly. "You're going to be a family."

She closed her eyes tightly, willing the tears to stop. "I don't think so, Mom. One of the things he was very firm about was never falling in love, and *definitely* never having more children. He kept saying he couldn't do it last night, and then he left. Even after I told him I loved him. He just...walked away."

"You *do* know about Cody's...um...drinking issue, right?"

"Yes, but how do *you* know?" That was one of his big secrets, and she'd never told a soul.

Her mother waived her hand in dismissal. "*Everyone* knows. Well, not everyone, but all the people it matters to, like Devlin, who told Sam, who told Lexi, who told me. But Cody has stopped drinking, right?"

Jenn knew Cody would be shocked to discover his secret wasn't a secret at all. And yet, she'd never seen Devlin act as if he knew anything. No one had treated Cody differently.

"He's been sober for a year this month." She didn't know a lot about the step program he was in, but she knew that a year was a big deal. She was proud of him.

"That's wonderful news. But what he's battling isn't ever going to just go away, you know. He'll always be in this fight, and if you love him, you'll be in it, too. And in big moments like this—like falling in love or finding out he's going to be a dad—well, even *good* stress is stress. When he told you he couldn't do this, he might have been saying he didn't think he could do this *and* stay sober."

Jenn slumped back in her chair. She was ashamed that she hadn't thought of that. She'd never pushed to know much about Cody's alcoholism fight. He was winning it, and that was all she'd needed to know. She'd met Malcolm, and thought he was a great coach for Cody. After all, Cody had stayed sober. But that didn't mean he'd be sober forever.

Because forever was a very long time.

It was late by the time Cody got back to Winsome Cove. He was sober. But…barely.

He'd spent hours that day alternating between pacing up and down the pier in Provincetown and sitting in his car. Anything to stay away from the multiple bars open in town. It was December, so a lot of businesses in P-town, just like in Winsome Cove, were closed up for the winter. But there were still bars. There were always bars. In fact, there was one on nearly every block of the winding Commercial Street. So he'd stayed out of town. But the town stayed right there, in his rearview mirror in the parking lot.

He knew a couple of the places well. There was an Irish pub that served a near-perfect Guinness. There was a seafood place with a bar in the back that always had a nice variety of imported whiskeys. There was the townie place on the corner with pool tables set up.

He stayed away from all of them. But they were on his mind. They were stabbing his brain, to be more exact. All the way back to Winsome Cove.

He could have called Malcolm. Who was he kidding? He *should* have called Malcolm. He could call him right now. He parked his car and looked down Wharf Street. Jenn's sister's restaurant was busy, as usual on a Friday night. And the Salty Knight Pub was right next door. Fred had always quietly served him nonalcoholic versions of whatever the other guys were drinking. His throat went dry as he got out of his vehicle.

You should go straight up to the apartment.
You should call Malcolm.
You should call Jenn.

Instead, he walked down the hill to the Salty Knight.

Chapter Twenty-Two

Fred looked up in surprise when Cody walked in. It was a Friday night, so the bar had some action, but there was no one Cody knew well. That was a relief. Jenn's mother usually worked the bar on weekends, running drinks to Lexi's restaurant, which was connected by a hallway. But with the big wedding tomorrow, she and Lexi had probably taken the night off, or had at least gone home early.

Cody headed straight for the bar, taking a stool at the far end, near the back wall. Fred headed his way with a ginger ale, but Cody shook his head.

"Give me a Crown Royal. Neat."

Fred froze for a moment.

"You sure that's what you want to do?"

Cody's temper was boiling just below his skin.

"Did I stutter?"

Fred studied him, then shrugged. "Nope, you didn't. Crown Royal neat coming right up."

When the glass hit the worn bar in front of Cody, he inhaled the scent of what had always brought him such comfort. He stared at the amber liquid, glowing golden in the dim lights of the bar. He didn't touch it. Not yet. Maybe sitting here and smelling it would be enough to calm his rattled nerves.

Fred left him alone, walking back to the front of the bar and staring at his phone. That was a good thing, because Cody was in no mood for company. But he also didn't want to be alone in his apartment. Energy twitched inside him like wires were short-circuiting in his chest. He needed to get his head sorted, but he had no idea how to do that. One second he was furious with Jenn, and the next second he felt a flood of shame for even thinking that. The only thing she'd done was make him want the one thing he didn't believe in—*forever.*

Either he'd been wrong all these years, thinking love was for fools, or... Oh, hell, he'd been wrong about a lot of things. Falling in love with Jenn had proven that. And now she was going to have his baby, and he'd turned his back on her. He was such a freaking loser. He didn't deserve to have someone like her in his life. The thoughts just kept spinning on repeat in his head. He heard the door to the bar open and close, but didn't bother looking up. He was too busy sinking into despair. First, he'd made the mistake of falling in love. Then he'd walked out on the best thing he'd ever had.

"Hey, Dad—give us a couple Molsons, will ya'?" Devlin Knight slid onto the bar stool next to Cody. Someone else sat on the other side of Devlin—Sam Knight. Another familiar figure moved behind Cody and squeezed between him and the wall, leaning against the bar.

"I'll take a ginger ale." Malcolm looked at Cody. "Make it two."

Cody wasn't sure what was happening. Where had these guys come from at eleven o'clock at night? How the hell did his sponsor know he was sitting in a bar staring at a glass of whiskey? They'd made it very clear they were there because of him. And he didn't like it one bit.

"Guys, I'm in no mood. You don't want to do this… whatever it is you think you're doing."

"Who, *us*?" Devlin put his hand on his chest in exaggerated innocence. "Me and my cousin are just grabbing some ice cold Canadian beer. And Malcolm here, well, looks like he's thirsty, too. Right, Malcolm?"

"That's right." Malcolm thanked Fred for the ginger ales and took a drink from one. He slid the second glass close to Cody. Just an inch or so beyond the whiskey.

Cody had been careful not to let his boss know about his alcoholism. He needed his job. Especially with a baby coming. He blinked. Apparently his brain had decided to accept the fact that he was going to be a father again.

That whiskey was still sitting right there in front of him, calling his name.

"And what we're doing is…" Devlin started. "Well, we don't want you doing *that*." He nodded to the whiskey.

Malcolm answered before Cody could, his voice deep and steady. "Don't worry, boys. That whiskey hasn't been disturbed yet. This is a test."

"A test?" Devlin repeated.

"Yup." Malcolm took another drink of his ginger ale, savoring it and smacking his lips like it was a twelve-year-old scotch. "I've seen it before. Call it a strength test, or a stress test. I definitely don't recommend it, but sometimes an alcoholic will put themselves in front of booze to see how long they can last. Or *if* they can last. And some of them don't last at all. But Cody here has been winning so far."

Damn. His sponsor, from the *anonymous* program

they were a part of, had just blurted out to Cody's boss that he was an alcoholic. He probably shouldn't be surprised. Trust was for suckers. He scowled at Malcolm.

"Why don't you tell the whole town I'm an alcoholic, Malcolm? So much for trust and following program rules about staying anonymous, eh?"

Malcolm held up his hands with a short laugh. "Man, *they* called *me* and asked for my help."

Cody turned to Devlin and Sam. "How did you...?" Then he closed his eyes as he came to the only logical conclusion. "Jenn told you. That's just perfect."

Devlin put his hand on Cody's shoulder. "Jenn never said a word. I know I seem like just some laid-back lobsterman-slash-real estate guy, but I would never hire a full-time employee without checking their background. I've known at least part of your story from the day I hired you."

Cody had been careful to provide a good friend's name as a reference. Another agent who'd worked in the office. Todd was a guy Cody had gone drinking with on many occasions. He promised to give a glowing recommendation if Devlin called. Devlin patted his shoulder again and reached for his own beer.

"It's very easy to track where any real estate agent has worked. I talked to your former boss. I also talked to some guy who said you punched him in the face." Devlin leaned toward his cousin, his voice a heavy stage whisper. "That's generally not a smart move."

Sam pretended to consider the comment thoughtfully, then shrugged. "Unless the guy deserved it."

"Fair point. After talking to the guy for five minutes, I wanted to punch him, too."

Cody's nerves were about at their end. Instead of reaching for the whiskey, though, he needed to clarify what Devlin was saying. Cody had been tiptoeing around since he got to Winsome Cove, trying to hide a past he wasn't proud of. Keeping secrets. But if Devlin had known the truth *before* he hired Cody—

"Why would you offer me the job if you knew?"

"I liked you from the start." Devlin smiled. "You reminded me a lot of a very good friend of Sam's and mine—our best friend since childhood. He wasn't lucky enough to make it home from his second deployment. When I saw you were a veteran, it put some of the other stuff in perspective."

"Being a veteran doesn't excuse what I did."

"No, it doesn't," Devlin agreed. "But you kept talking about making a fresh start, and I thought you seemed like a guy who really needed one." He looked at the glass of whiskey. "No matter what happens tonight, I don't regret that decision."

For the first time since walking out on Jenn, Cody felt a wave of tension leave his body. He was almost light-headed from the release of it.

"I worked so hard to keep it a secret. And you knew all along. Everyone did."

"No," Devlin said firmly. "Not everyone. It wasn't my story to tell."

"But…your father knew. He's always given me non-alcoholic drinks."

Fred had worked his way close enough to hear the conversation, while pretending not to be listening. Until now.

"Kid," he said "I saw the panic in your eyes that first time you stopped in with the guys and they all ordered drinks. I've been behind this bar from the time it was legal for me to pour booze, and that's a long damn time. I know a guy in trouble when I see one. But it was none of my business…" Cody couldn't believe it, but Fred Knight seemed to be *blushing*. "Until tonight. I made it my business tonight."

"You called Devlin."

"No, I texted my Philly-girl and told her you were here, sittin' within sniffin' distance of some expensive whiskey. She's the one who got the ball rolling."

It took Cody a minute to realize Fred was talking about Phyllis Bellamy. Jenn's mom. And Jenn had met Malcolm.

"So Jenn knows I'm here. In a bar."

Fred's expression was only a little bit guilty.

"Probably. Phyllis said she'd call in the cavalry, and these guys showed up. I assume Malcolm's not here as your attorney."

Malcolm didn't answer right away. This was putting *him* on the spot, too, if people didn't know he was in the program. But he finally chuckled. "I would be, if he needed one. But tonight I'm here as his sponsor. Fred, you and I have talked more than once about me being available if you ever got worried about a customer who might need help. And not just the legal kind."

"Jenn called you." Cody didn't have to ask.

"She texted Devlin my number." Malcolm nodded. "She's worried."

"Not worried enough to come to the bar." He sounded petulant. Childish.

"And what was she supposed to do here? Beg you not to drink? Snatch that glass away from you and order you out of the bar?" Malcolm shook his head. "That would have just made you want it even more. Instead, she called me."

"And did she tell you her big news?" He wanted to be angry, but the question didn't have the edge he'd intended. The rage had left him at the same time the secrets did. It was time to face the fact that Jenn hadn't ever done one damn thing wrong. The only reason he'd been angry was because her pregnancy—*their* pregnancy—scared the hell out of him. His anger with her was the ultimate case of shooting the messenger.

"What big news?" Fred wasn't pretending to be listening anymore. He was at the bar in front of Cody.

"Never mind. We had a stupid argument last night, and it…sent me spiraling." He reached out and could almost feel his friends holding their breath. But it was the ginger ale he wanted. As soon as he picked up the glass, Fred quickly slid the whiskey away. Cody mumbled a quick thanks. "The argument was my fault, and then I walked out on her. I've got some really big bridges to mend."

"Well, I think we *all* have some experience at that, my friend," Sam said. They laughed, and Cody smiled for the first time in a day.

He took a drink of the ginger ale, then stared down at the bar as conversation moved around him. Sam was saying something about big, bold gestures.

Jenn hadn't shared his secrets. He wasn't about to share news of her pregnancy, not without her being there. Because it wasn't her news or his news. It was *their* news. *They* were going to be a family. He sat back, suddenly weak at the thought.

This wasn't about him or her anymore. It hadn't been for a while, if he was honest with himself. If she meant what she'd said last night—that she loved him—then they'd both broken *all* their stupid rules. They loved each other. It was the biggest commitment a person could make. And it didn't scare him at all anymore.

He'd been flailing around for the past twenty-four hours, trying to keep from admitting one simple truth. There was nothing *casual* about what they had. There never had been. And there sure wasn't anything *temporary*. They were together because they loved and believed in each other. He'd told her last night that he couldn't do this. Couldn't do parenthood again. Couldn't do *forever* with her. But that was a lie.

He didn't want anything else in this life other than to spend forever with Jennifer Bellamy.

To build a family with her.

To marry her.

Chapter Twenty-Three

Jenn stood in front of the mirror of the church's library, which converted to a dressing room for weddings. This was Max and Grace's wedding day. Jenn needed to focus *all* of her energy toward them and the joyous celebration of their love. She could not, even for a minute, spend energy worrying about Cody, worrying about the baby, worrying about her future.

At least she knew Cody was okay. Fred had called her mother around midnight and told her that things had "gone well" at the Salty Knight, and that Cody had gone home without touching the whiskey he'd ordered. Mom had called Jenn to let her know.

What exactly did "okay" mean, though? For Cody. For their future? She had no idea. But he was safe and sober, and for the moment, that was all that mattered. She'd sent him a text in the early morning hours, telling him she'd understand if he didn't come to the wedding. That it might be best if he didn't. They could talk next week, but she didn't want to be arguing with him on the happiest day of her brother's life. They'd all been careful to keep the situation away from Max and Grace, at Jenn's insistence. Cody never responded.

"You two girls look so beautiful." Her mother put

her hands on Jenn's shoulder, looking between her and her sister in the corner, slipping on her shoes. "I know you both had some doubts about this Christmas wedding theme, but everything looks stunning, including these dresses." Her eyes shimmered with unshed tears. "I'm so proud of you both. I'm so happy to have all my children here in Winsome Cove." She squeezed Jenn's shoulder. "And everything's going to be fine with Cody. I just know it in my heart."

Jenn shook her head sharply. "I'm not going to worry about that today. In fact, I told Cody it would be better if he didn't come." She talked over her mother's objection. "I don't want to cause any drama at this wedding. I don't want our issues taking attention away from Max and Grace in the slightest. Cody and I will talk *after* today, and we'll…make whatever decisions we make."

"But—" Lexi walked over and looked into the mirror's reflection with Jenn and their mother. "You *want* that decision to be him being happy to be a daddy again. With you."

Emotion rose inside of her, and she blinked a few times to regain control. "Don't, Lex. I don't want to think about that. I'm just…putting it all in a box and closing it up for today, okay?" She turned and looked at them directly. "Let's go give Max and Grace a legendary wedding day they'll never forget. And don't you dare give me any pitying looks or anything. I'm all about joy today. I'm not making room for anything else."

Cody wasn't at the church ceremony. She'd told him *not* to come, but she still had to fight to hold on to her smile when she got to the altar and looked out over the sanctuary as Grace came down the aisle. It was little Tyler who escorted her, while Grace's father stood near the altar.

Jenn's father wasn't even there. An ice storm in the Midwest—and last-minute planning on his part—prevented him from arriving in time. Max didn't seem to be very upset by the news that there would be no father of the groom present. Their relationship with their father was complicated, and probably always would be.

It wasn't a huge wedding, so it only took a sweeping glance to know Cody wasn't there. She felt her chin start to quiver, but she took a breath and focused on Grace's smile as she approached Max. Jenn now knew what the term "radiant bride" meant, because Grace was absolutely glowing with love and happiness.

The wedding itself was brief and…perfect. As they spoke their vows, Max's voice cracked with emotion, and Tyler, close by his side, reached out to hold his hand. There was an almost silent *aww* that went through the pews, and more than one quiet sniffle as tissues came out. They all broke into applause and happy laughter as the minister pronounced them husband and wife, and Max bent Grace low and kissed her long and hard before standing her up again.

They didn't spend long at the motel for pictures because, despite the bright blue sky, it was December on Cape Cod, and it was cold. But they posed for both serious and silly photos on the overlook deck and in front of the colorful and newly updated Sassy Mermaid Motor Lodge sign. In what was sure to be a favorite shot, the Bellamys posed together—Max, Lexi, Jenn and Phyllis. The ocean breeze had the women's hair blowing across their laughing faces, and when the photographer turned the camera so they could see it, they saw nothing but the joy they'd each found in Winsome Cove.

When they arrived at the country club, Grace and Max had decided against an elaborate entrance for the wedding party. The emcee, who was also the DJ, announced their names and they all walked in together, arm in arm, with Max and Grace following. Lively music kicked off and the dance floor filled. Since it was an afternoon reception, Max and Grace wanted the fun to start right away, and they'd take a break for dinner later. The wedding party went to the head table. Some were checking place cards, but Jenn didn't need to.

Cody was standing there, holding out a chair for her.

At first, she was filled with anger. She'd managed to *not* think about the man for the past hour or so. At least… not think of him *much*. She'd thrown herself into the celebration and was actually enjoying being with her family and laughing together. It wasn't hard to be happy as long as she wasn't thinking about the way he'd walked away from her and their unborn child.

I can't do this…

Not only had he walked away, but he'd come so close to drinking again. She'd pushed him to that. *No.* That was a choice he made. She wasn't going to take responsibility for other people's actions anymore. But she *was* going to protect her brother and new sister-in-law on their wedding day. Her chin lifted, and she met his gaze head-on, her smile still firmly in place, talking through her teeth.

"We're not doing this here, Cody."

"Whatever you say, Lambchop. But won't it be weird if we leave the reception?"

"Lambchop?"

"Yeah, that doesn't sound like a dwarf name, does it, Buttercup? Let's see, I think our most recent dwarf names were Sexy and Vexy, right?" His slanted smile made her pulse jump. What was he up to? Whatever it was, it had prodded a small seed of hope to grow inside of her.

Behind her, the wedding party, including Max and Grace, were headed for the dance floor with the rest of the guests. Her mother and Fred were in the center, of course, Mom's hands up in the air as she shimmied against Fred's side. Her mother-of-the-groom dress was dark gold, covered with sequins and crystals. It was skin-tight, naturally. And low cut. And slit up to her hip on one side. Her hair was spiked in front, with just a light spray of golden glitter over the pink. Once Grace had told Phyllis she didn't need to tamp down her style for the wedding, Mom had taken it to heart.

It was odd her mother wasn't hovering nearby, with Cody showing up like this. Neither was Lexi—she was at the bar with Sam. Devlin and Carm were dancing. No one seemed surprised. Jenn felt Cody's fingers intertwining with hers. She stared down at those fingers, and her eyes followed as he lifted her hand to his lips and kissed her fingertips. He grinned through his kiss.

"Want to find a quiet corner, Honeybear?"

Before she could answer, her brain too busy trying to figure out what was going on, he tugged her toward the large stone fireplace. It was electric, but the flickering flames on the screen were real enough to feel cozy. Along the way, he spotted a tray of hors d'oeuvres and grabbed a large stuffed mushroom with his free hand.

He popped it into his mouth, bit off one half, then held the other half up for her to take from his fingers. She took it, still confused.

Was he…was he sharing food with her?

And holding her hand?

And calling her nicknames?

Before she could speak, he swooped in for a kiss, humming to himself as he did it.

"Oh yum, I love the taste of that mushroom on your lips, Cutie Pie. You make it taste like candy."

Her jaw dropped, and she began to understand…she hoped. She tried to keep a straight face, but couldn't. Her mouth twitched into a smile.

"Okay, Vexy, you are breaking *all* the rules right now. Nicknames, holding hands, sharing food, acting all romantic…"

"Don't forget the big mushy public display of affection."

He put his hands under her arms, raised her up above his head, then let her body slide down his until their lips met. Someone behind them—was that her *sister*?—let out a whoop and yelled, "Go get her, Cody!"

Jenn's arms went tight around his neck as he let her feet hit the floor. He didn't show any signs of wanting to let her go.

"I think it's time you and I threw away *all* the rules, Bubbles."

Her laughter broke free at last. "These nicknames are killing me! What other rules did you have in mind for us to break?"

"Let's start with the one about staying casual. That rule really sucks. And let's dump the one about no commitments. I want *all* the commitment I can get from you. And definitely screw being temporary."

Her laughter faded as his words sank in.

"Cody, this is too much. What's happening?"

He grew serious, pulling her closer to the fireplace and farther from any other people.

"Tell the truth," he said, "were you crossing your fingers when you agreed to all those rules?"

Her first thought was to wonder what answer he wanted to hear, and then she remembered she wasn't doing that anymore. He'd asked for, and deserved, the truth.

"I wasn't at first. But…yeah, after a while I was going along to go along."

"Wanna hear something funny?" he asked, taking her hands in his. "So was I."

"What…?"

"I've known I was in love with you for a while now, Jenn. But that was against all the stupid rules we agreed to, even though we were both lying to each other."

A gentle warmth worked its way down her spine, radiating through her body as if carried by every vein, pouring into every cell. Cody loved her. That was what he'd just said, right? He *loved* her. Her lips went dry, and she ran her tongue along them before she spoke.

"Are you saying you want to break the rule about never falling in love?"

"I think that horse has left the barn, don't you? If you were serious about what you said the other night—"

"I was. I was very serious. I'm in love with you, Cody." A slow, sweet song was playing now. They needed to get back to the wedding reception before they became a distraction, although the only people interested in them seemed to be her family at the moment. But first...

"What about the agreement to not have children?"

He raised his hands and cupped her face, leaning close.

"Again—horse, barn."

"I know it's too late to change it, but are you sure—"

"Jenn, the thought of having another baby scares the hell out of me." He gave her a quick kiss on her forehead. "But the thought of having a baby *with you* makes me want to burst with joy. *Nervous* joy, but still—" he swiped a tear from her cheek with his thumb "—let's build a family together, Weepy."

She started to laugh for real now, from a joy that ran deep and felt strong. Safe. She kissed him, and the kiss lasted long enough that the song ended. With a start she realized she heard applause. For them.

She pulled away and turned, covering her face with her hands. This was exactly what she didn't want to happen. But it was Max and Grace who were front and center, and Grace was wiping moisture from her cheek. Still, Jenn cringed.

"I'm so sorry for—"

"For *what*?" Grace laughed. "Falling in love in Winsome Cove? Haven't you heard—that's kind of a thing with your family. Come dance with us, you two!"

Jenn started toward the dance floor, but Cody held her back. He gave Max and Grace a pleading look. "Give us one more song, okay?"

Max waved them away as a lost cause, and the music started again.

"Cody, we can't become the main event. It's rude. And…tacky."

He knew she was right, but that wasn't his priority at the moment. This conversation had gone even better than he'd hoped, and certainly better than he'd feared. But there was one more thing Cody needed to make clear.

"I need to apologize for Thursday night. And for making you worry last night. I panicked, Jenn. I felt things spinning out of control, and…well, it's hard to describe. I handled it badly." He kissed her softly. "You deserved better, and I'll try to *be* better."

She stared up into his eyes, and he felt himself drowning in hers. Lost in the warm blue depths of this woman he loved. The woman who, by some miracle, loved him back.

"Please," she said softly, "promise me you won't ever walk away again."

The way he hesitated clearly scared her, and he felt her body go tight, almost pulling back from him. If they were going to be honest with each other, it should start right now.

He held her close, folding his arms around her and rubbing her back.

"I don't want to lie to you, and I'd be lying if I said I could promise something like that. The truth is, I don't know. I'll always be an alcoholic. I'll always be dealing with memories of my time in the military. Things overwhelm me sometimes." She was very still in his arms. "But I can damn sure promise you this—I'll always come back. You and I are *it* for me. If I'm struggling, I'll tell you. If I freak out and walk away, I'll come back. And I'll ask for help. I promise I'll ask for help."

Her body finally relaxed against his, and he kissed the top of her hair. She spoke against his jacket, so softly that he barely heard her.

"When you weren't at the church today, I thought we were over."

He winced, hating the thought that he'd hurt her so much.

"I'm sorry. I know you'd told me to stay away, but there was no way I could do that. I was going to be there, but then I heard about a Saturday morning meeting in Chatham. Malcolm insisted I do a meeting a day for a few weeks to get myself back on track."

She pulled back far enough to look into his eyes.

"But you didn't actually…?"

"Drink? No. But I came *way* too close. If you hadn't called in the troops, I'm not sure what would have happened." He put his hands on her shoulders and turned her around to face the dance floor, pushing her gently in that direction. "By the way, did you know Devlin already knew all my big, dark secrets? I was sweating that stuff for nothing!"

She reached back and took his hand in hers. "I'm not surprised. Turns out Mom knew all of mine, too. She even guessed this one." She patted her stomach with her free hand. An odd quiver of emotion went through Cody at the thought of her carrying his baby.

Joy. Pride. Love.

"Does anyone else know? Do you want to tell them today?"

"No!" She shook her finger at him playfully. "We aren't going to do anything more to distract from my brother's big day. Besides, I haven't even seen a doctor yet. Let's make sure we have all the facts first before we share this secret—our *last* secret. And there's one person who needs to know before anyone else."

"Ava." Cody was still anxious about that, but he had a feeling his daughter would be happy about a new baby. She liked Jenn, and they'd have time to get to know each other even better during the pregnancy. But...where? "We have a lot to think about. Like where to live, and—"

A sultry Tina Turner song began to play just as they reached the dance floor. The classic song started slow, but would turn upbeat quickly. Jenn spun and pulled him in, her arms wound around his neck. She pressed her body against his. His hands dropped to her hips and held her close as they moved together.

What was it that he'd been worried about again? God, he loved this woman.

Jenn went up on her tiptoes to speak in his ear. "All those things can be decided another time. Today is a day to celebrate love. Dance with me."

The brass section in the song started playing, and Jen stepped back far enough to move with the music. He took her hand and spun her around, making the dark green dress swirl and flare at her ankles. Her bright smile wrapped him in love.

If anyone had told him two years ago that he'd be here today—sober, dancing, expecting another child, in love, laughing with friends—he would have bet them a million dollars that it would never happen.

But it *did* happen. With this amazing woman who

loved him right back, exactly as he was. She'd known his secrets literally from day one, and he'd known hers. And love still came for them, binding them together. Creating a family. And a future.

Their very own happily-ever-after.

He was going to make sure of that.

Epilogue

June 16

Phyllis scooped her granddaughter, Amanda, into her arms as she tried to run by, and she swung her up over her head in the bright sunshine. Her brightly flowered wedding gown wrapped around her legs, but that didn't stop her. She'd chosen to wear glittering pink Western boots, which were a lot more stable on the motel lawn than stiletto heels. Amanda's belly laugh made Phyllis laugh right back at her.

"Hey, don't get any ideas there, Cinderella." Fred's arm slid around her waist. "You conned me into getting married, but we ain't having no babies that we can't hand right back to their parents."

She laughed and set Amanda down to run to her approaching parents, Sam and Lexi. Sam caught his daughter and tucked her under his arm like a football, running ahead with the girl squealing in delight.

"Isn't that the best thing about grandbabies, Freddie? All of the fun and none of the work." She slapped her hand on his chest, right over his suit jacket pocket. For all his grumbling about wearing a suit to their wedding, he'd relented at the last minute, as long as he didn't have to wear a tie. "And I didn't con you into anything, you old geezer. *You're* the one who proposed, remember?"

It had been a Valentine's Day surprise. She'd gone to work at the restaurant for the big night, delivering drinks from Fred's bar to Lexi'srestaurant. He'd been as cranky as usual, if not more so from his nerves. The restaurant finally began to empty, until it was only her three children and their spouses, along with Fred's son, Devlin, and his date, Shelly, from the interior design shop.

Yes, that had been a surprise—everyone was so sure Devlin would end up with his lifelong pal, Carm, whose family owned the fish market on Wharf Street. But it turned out the two really *were* just friends. Carm was dating a bright, sassy woman she'd met in Boston last fall, and they seemed to be getting serious. In fact, they'd both come to the wedding today, and were standing near the overlook deck by the ocean. The deck had been transformed into an altar, complete with a floral arch, where Fred and Phyllis had said their vows an hour ago. Now it was set up as an open bar, with the DJ and a temporary dance floor next to it. Fred was walking to the bar now, laughing with one of his buddies.

On that Valentine's night at the restaurant, it had been just family. Phyllis had no idea they were all there for her and Fred. No idea that she'd turn around and find that man on one knee, holding up a blue velvet box with a sparkling platinum and diamond ring. No idea that she'd begin planning a June wedding here on the lawn of the Sassy Mermaid Motor Lodge.

Her and Fred's relationship had finally settled down after a bumpy year. The more serious they'd become with each other, the more he tried to run from it. After he gave her that ridiculous key ring last fall, she'd told him they were through. No more booty calls at her motel apartment. No more "friendly" cocktail-mixing competitions at the Salty Knight. If he couldn't figure out why she was tired of waiting for him to get serious, then he would have to figure out how to be alone again.

Within a few weeks, he'd come back to her and apologized. He'd been conflicted about falling in love again after losing his beloved first wife—Devlin's mother—to cancer years earlier. And he'd fretted about his age, convinced he was too old and stubborn to start over. He didn't want Phyllis to be stuck with an old man she might have to take care of as he aged. And he really *had* thought she'd love that silly key ring with the sparkly mermaid. And she *did*, once they'd talked things out and decided to give their relationship another try.

And then he gave her a *real* ring. She looked down at her hand, where the ring sparkled in a rainbow of color in the bright sun.

She'd had her doubts at first, too. Fred was nothing like her first husband—a serial cheater terrified of his own mortality. But from the first day she and Fred exchanged insults when she'd helped Lexi get the restaurant started, the man had worked his way into her heart. It had happened one argument at a time, until there was nothing to fight over except how much they loved each other.

And damn, the man was good in bed. And on the sofa. And on the overlook deck one moonless August night.

She was a lucky woman in so many ways.

"Mom, you definitely lucked out on the weather," Lexi walked up, talking as if she knew Phyllis's thoughts. "What a gorgeous day. And what a beautiful bride you are." Lexi kissed her cheek. "You are an absolute inspiration. The poster child for it's never too late to find love."

"Thanks, sweetheart. I was just following the examples you and your siblings set for me. It's been a wild ride for all of us, hasn't it? But Winsome Cove set us on the right paths."

Lexi nodded in agreement, her arm resting around Phyllis's shoulders as they looked out at the blue waters of the Atlantic, then back to the motel lawn, where guests mingled. Most of Winsome Cove was here. "I thought you were *crazy* when you said you wanted to stay in this place after we saw this old motel."

The Sassy Mermaid had been pretty run-down when she'd inherited it from an uncle she barely remembered. Lexi, Max and Jenn had pushed her hard to sell it, cash out and retire. But that didn't feel like it was what her life needed. *Winsome Cove* felt like what she needed. So she'd settled in to fix the old place up, embracing the mid-century feel and creating a now-popular destination for vacationers on Cape Cod. And in the process, she'd found friends—and a husband—in the little town.

First, Lexi had found Sam, the troubled marina owner too consumed with guilt and grief to be able to see the joy he deserved. Lexi, fiery and strong-willed, had pushed him to seek the help he'd needed. It hadn't been easy, but once his walls came down, they'd found true happiness together. And they'd brought little Amanda into the world—a girl who made everyone's face light up.

And speaking of lighting up her life, her other grandchild, Tyler, was on the swing set near the pool, swinging as high as his kicking legs could get him. Almost seven now, he was showing a hint of the young man he was going to be—kind, sensitive and musically talented. He had the same sly humor, and stubbornness, of his father, Max. But his stepmother, Grace, was softening Tyler's edges the same way she'd tamed his swordsmith father. Grace and Max were sitting on the top of a picnic table near the swings, keeping an eye on Tyler as they talked with Cody and Jenn.

Jenn was sitting on the picnic table bench with Cody, her legs extended on the bench, leaning her back against his chest with one hand resting on her substantial baby bump. She was due any week now, and the Bellamy clan would have another little girl. They'd already gained one in Cody's daughter, Ava. She was twelve and would tell anyone who'd listen that she was going to classes to become a certified babysitter so that she could watch the baby when she arrived. Ava was chasing after little Amanda now, while Sam and Lexi joined the others at the picnic table.

Cody lowered his head and whispered something to Jenn, making her smile. His arm reached around her until his hand rested over hers, on her rounded stomach. He'd been sober nearly eighteen months now, and his sobriety seemed much more stable these days. It was as if being sober was becoming more natural for him than drinking, and less of an effort to maintain. He and Jenn had bought Grace's house in March. Then they'd surprised everyone by quietly going to a justice of the peace one Friday in April and getting married. Ava had been their only guest. They announced it to the family that weekend while everyone was at their place for dinner. Of all the rules they'd made with each other, they'd kept the one about not wanting a big wedding.

Sam and Lexi joined the others at the table, and someone must have cracked a joke, because all three couples burst into loud laughter. They were all so close now—friends as well as family. And her children had picked such fabulous partners. Each couple was perfectly balanced. More important, each couple was *happy*. And settled.

And now, so was Phyllis. She'd moved into Fred's cozy ranch house on the edge of Winsome Cove shortly after he'd proposed. The house sat on a large corner lot, with a swimming pool and an enclosed porch that caught the morning sun and overlooked a fenced yard full of flowering shrubs. It was one of Phyllis's favorite spots to sit with her coffee.

Sure, she missed waking up to the ocean, but the apartment at the motel was just too small for her and Fred full-time. And Fred had accurately pointed out that, eventually, that long flight of stairs to get there would become too much for them. The ranch made so much more sense, and the apartment was quickly becoming a moneymaker as a vacation rental above the motel lobby.

"Hey, wife." Fred's voice was low and rough behind her. She turned and he handed her a flute of champagne. "Drink up. We've still got a case of that bubbly nonsense on ice. I told you we ordered too much."

She put a soft kiss on his cheek, and his eyes softened. He kissed her back, but on the lips. If anyone listened to them without knowing them, they'd think Fred was just…awful. He was cranky, opinionated, and sarcastic. But she'd found the *real* Fred under all that bluster, and *that* Fred was a treasure—sweet, sexy, protective and generous.

Devlin joined them, hand in hand with Shelly. Those two were getting more and more serious, and Phyllis wouldn't be surprised to see an engagement ring on Shelly's hand before long. It was a match made in real estate heaven—a man who sells houses and a woman who decorates them.

"Congratulations again," Devlin said, clapping his dad on the back. "We weren't always sure if you two would make it to the finish line without killing each other, but you did it. It's been a great day."

Shelly nodded in agreement. "And Phyllis, your dress is incredible. It's so *you*, especially with the boots. I love it."

The dress had been a happy accident—she'd seen the bolt of hand-painted satin in a bridal store and loved the bold colors and the giant flowers. It had been ordered for a custom gown that was then canceled when the engagement ended. No one wanted a wedding dress made of fabric from a canceled wedding, and people supposedly started whispering that the fabric was "cursed."

Luckily, Phyllis had too much Midwestern common sense to believe in something like cursed fabric, so she'd managed to negotiate a good price. A seamstress in Chatham made the sheath dress with a high side slit, and covered it with a sheer gossamer outer layer that muted the flowers just enough for them to look more bridal. The soft outer fabric moved like a feather in the ocean breeze.

She'd had fun creating her eclectic style in Winsome Cove—one that would have made her ex-husband pass out from embarrassment. Back in Iowa, she'd always been in stylish, but conservative, clothing. Expensive suits that she was often complimented on, but she'd chafed at looking like every other suburban country club soccer mom.

But today, she felt…beautiful. Maybe it was the love in Fred's eyes that made her feel that way. Or seeing the children she'd raised having children of their own and being so happy doing it.

It didn't matter that she was a nearly seventy-year-old bride. In fact, she was proud of that. She thought about it for a moment, not listening to Devlin and Fred talk. That was the sensation she'd been having a hard time defining today. She was not just happy. Not just lucky. Not just loved.

She was *proud*. Proud that she'd raised such resilient and talented children. Proud that she'd helped—at least a little—as they found their life partners. Proud of their families. Getting this far in life was a privilege for anyone, and she'd done it.

Her intention had never been to bring her whole family to Cape Cod with her, but one by one they'd followed. And Winsome Cove had given each of them their happily-ever-after. Maybe she and Fred didn't have as long of an *ever after* to look forward to as their children did, but they'd make the most of every single minute they had.

Fred reached over and took her hand as he and Devlin talked about a property on the coast that Devlin was thinking of buying for himself. As Devlin described the house, Fred glanced at Phyllis and gave her a quick grin and a wink. His eyes held nothing but love.

Yes, Phyllis Bellamy Knight was exactly where she was supposed to be.

In Winsome Cove.

And in love.

* * * * *

Get up to 4 Free Books!

We'll send you 2 free books from each series you try PLUS a free Mystery Gift.

FREE Value Over **$25**

Both the **Harlequin® Special Edition** and **Harlequin® Heartwarming™** series feature compelling novels filled with stories of love and strength where the bonds of friendship, family and community unite.

YES! Please send me 2 FREE novels from the Harlequin Special Edition or Harlequin Heartwarming series and my FREE Gift (gift is worth about $10 retail). After receiving them, if I don't wish to receive any more books, I can return the shipping statement marked "cancel." If I don't cancel, I will receive 6 brand-new Harlequin Special Edition books every month and be billed just $6.39 each in the U.S. or $7.19 each in Canada, or 4 brand-new Harlequin Heartwarming Larger-Print books every month and be billed just $7.19 each in the U.S. or $7.99 each in Canada, a savings of 20% off the cover price. It's quite a bargain! Shipping and handling is just 50¢ per book in the U.S. and $1.25 per book in Canada.* I understand that accepting the 2 free books and gift places me under no obligation to buy anything. I can always return a shipment and cancel at any time by calling the number below. The free books and gift are mine to keep no matter what I decide.

Choose one: ☐ **Harlequin Special Edition** (235/335 BPA G36Y) ☐ **Harlequin Heartwarming Larger-Print** (161/361 BPA G36Y) ☐ **Or Try Both!** (235/335 & 161/361 BPA G36Z)

Name (please print)

Address   Apt. #

City   State/Province   Zip/Postal Code

Email: Please check this box ☐ if you would like to receive newsletters and promotional emails from Harlequin Enterprises ULC and its affiliates. You can unsubscribe anytime.

Mail to the **Harlequin Reader Service:**
IN U.S.A.: P.O. Box 1341, Buffalo, NY 14240-8531
IN CANADA: P.O. Box 603, Fort Erie, Ontario L2A 5X3

Want to explore our other series or interested in ebooks? Visit www.ReaderService.com or call 1-800-873-8635.

*Terms and prices subject to change without notice. Prices do not include sales taxes, which will be charged (if applicable) based on your state or country of residence. Canadian residents will be charged applicable taxes. Offer not valid in Quebec. This offer is limited to one order per household. Books received may not be as shown. Not valid for current subscribers to the Harlequin Special Edition or Harlequin Heartwarming series. All orders subject to approval. Credit or debit balances in a customer's account(s) may be offset by any other outstanding balance owed by or to the customer. Please allow 4 to 6 weeks for delivery. Offer available while quantities last.

Your Privacy—Your information is being collected by Harlequin Enterprises ULC, operating as Harlequin Reader Service. For a complete summary of the information we collect, how we use this information and to whom it is disclosed, please visit our privacy notice located at https://corporate.harlequin.com/privacy-notice. Notice to California Residents – Under California law, you have specific rights to control and access your data. For more information on these rights and how to exercise them, visit https://corporate.harlequin.com/california-privacy. For additional information for residents of other U.S. states that provide their residents with certain rights with respect to personal data, visit https://corporate.harlequin.com/other-state-residents-privacy-rights/.

HSEHW25